Praise for *Nappily Ever After* and Trisha R. Thomas

"Thomas's debut novel places her among today's most promising and entertaining new authors." —*Library Journal*

"Thomas delivers up a powerful, funny, and sensitive novel. She is, without a doubt, a talented newcomer to the fiction scene." —*Black Issues Book Review*

"A fresh and funny novel from a talented newcomer." —*Honey* magazine

"From the moment I started reading *Nappily Ever After*, I couldn't put it down! Trisha Thomas gives us a stellar first novel that gives new depth to the age-old relationship that we sistahs have with our hair. This is a jazzy, hip must-read!"
—Debrena Jackson Gandy, author of *All the Joy You Can Stand*

"Trisha Thomas's debut novel is a fusion of humor, a fast-paced plot, and characters we care about. Venus Johnston's journey is a familiar and compelling one that will have satisfied readers craving an encore from Trisha Thomas." —Patricia Elam, author of *Breathing Room*

You've got to get up every morning
with a smile on your face and show the world
all the love in your heart

Then people gonna treat you better
You're gonna find. Yes you will
That you're beautiful as you feel

—CAROLE KING, "BEAUTIFUL," 1971

Nappily ever after

TRISHA R. THOMAS

THREE RIVERS PRESS
NEW YORK

Published by Three Rivers Press, New York, New York.
Member of the Crown Publishing Group

Random House, Inc. New York, Toronto, London, Sydney, Auckland
www.randomhouse.com

THREE RIVERS PRESS and the Tugboat design are
registered trademarks of Random House, Inc.

Originallly published in hardcover by Crown Publishers in 2000.

"Beautiful," words and music by Carole King.
©1971 COLGEMS-EMI MUSIC INC. All Rights Reserved. International Copyright Secured.
Used By Permission.

"I Heard It through the Grapevine," words and music by Norman J. Whitfield and Barrett Strong
©1966 (Renewed 1994) JOBETE MUSIC CO. INC. All Rights Controlled and Administered by
EMI BLACKWOOD MUSIC INC. on behalf of STONE AGATE MUSIC.
(A Division of JOBETE MUSIC CO., INC.)
All Rights Reserved. International Copyright Secured. Used by Permission.

Printed in the United States of America

DESIGN BY LENNY HENDERSON

Library of Congress Cataloging-in-Publication Data
Thomas, Trisha, 1964–
Nappily ever after / Trisha Thomas.—1st ed.
1. Afro-American women—Fiction. I. Title.
PS3570.H5917 N37 2000
813'.6—dc21   00–0029440
ISBN 0-609-80898-2
10 9 8 7 6 5 4 3 2
First Paperback Edition

To the group that made it look easy:
Ayesha, Jennifer, Scott, Rachel,
Trisha, Lenny, and Susan.

Acknowledgments

If I could be seen right now, I'd be screaming "yes" from the top of the Space Needle with my head thrown back and my arms extended in the air, for I am grateful for every day there is breath in my body. Life. What would it be without pain, trial, error, and love experienced and lost? To those who have experienced it with me, I am grateful.

Rena Logan, you've shown me that I could do anything I put my mind to. Thank you for giving me the tools to do so. When I wanted to be a fashion designer, you bought me a sewing machine; when I wanted to be a photographer, you bought me a camera. When I wanted to fly, you said, soar high in your imagination. And it is there that I find my stories, it is there that I hold you near even when you are so far away. I've been blessed with two parents who saw light in all of their children's eyes.

To my husband, Cameron Thomas, the melody in my heart, and the song in my mind: Thank you for showing me life has infinite possibilities and encouraging me to take them on. Your belief in me is my motivation, and your love is my guide.

Tiffany, my dear, thank you for all the sandwiches, keeping me fed when I could not pull myself away from the computer. Quinlan, thank you for the many cups of hot tea brought in by your tiny seven-year-old hands (and without spilling a drop). Mommy loves you both and appreciates your patience. We can bake cookies now.

Without you, my dear sister, Karen Logan, it would have been a lonely road. You are my best friend, bless you for always knowing when to call with ego massages and gentle pushes of encouragement.

Lillian L., your words of advice ignited my determination, changed my path, and delivered a new destination.

Marie D. Brown, I love you. You have an uncanny ability to know just when to call, always there to save the day. Thank you for being a sustaining line in this tightrope business. Your belief in me brought this book to life.

To my editor, Jennifer Hunt—I knew you were going to be the high note on what was a beautiful song, yet needed your ability of fine-tuning. Ayesha Pande, thank you for opening the door and inviting me in. Rachel Kahan, I feel lucky to have you in my corner. Dr. Dwayne Logan, your entire life is an inspiration, a story all its own. Vernon Logan, now it's your turn; get out your pen. Cynthia Hollis, thank you for sifting through the pages even after they blew away. Your critique was invaluable.

Thank you to:

Dave and Anna for giving me a second home. To Ora for showing me that persistence gives great rewards.

To my Manassas family and friends, you know who you are, thank you for your support. To the Bull Run Library gang, how could I forget you all? Thanks for having every book worth reading.

Nappily ever after

CLINT TOOK A DEEP BREATH. HIS MIND WAS RACING WITH THOUGHTS OF his soon-to-be bride, the woman he'd spend the rest of his life with. He let a sheepish grin rise on his face when he pictured hers, overcome with emotion when she pulled the silver ribbon and opened the box to the book of love poems that said all that he could not.

That was one of the things he adored about her. The simplest acts of kindness brought joy to her—toast and coffee on a morning tray, an unexpected lunch date that neither one of them really had time for. He thought about the time he'd borrowed the out-of-production Angela Bofill album from a friend and made a tape, placing it in her cassette player so that "I'm on Your Side" would be the first thing she heard when she started the car. He had watched her as she tried to ward off the impending tears. He was proud to have that kind of power over her. To know so easily how to make her fall in love with him again and again was like being the richest man in the world. She didn't need master plans with attached instructions. Like Clint, all she wanted was to be loved unconditionally and, on occasion, to be shown how much.

He looked out on the audience that was gathering to witness their unity, sisters wearing brights and pastels on their various tints of dark satin skin, brothers walking around clean and polished like a brigade of Farrakhan soldiers, everybody trying to outdo everybody else. Even the babies were wrapped up like dolls in the toy store, wearing their little bonnets and pink ruffles. And him, standing in the sweltering humidity, dressed in black tails, glossy black patent leather shoes, and a grin-and-bear-it smile, making him feel like the lone black male model in the pages of the Sears catalog.

Clint shook the hands of relatives he didn't know by sight, repeating the same thing over and over because he didn't have much else to say except "thanks for coming" and "good to see you all." Kissing aunts who still called him Baby Blue, a nickname that reminded him of the shame he used to feel for being one of the darkest little boys on Ames Street. His just reward was that now his smooth midnight skin was deemed one of his best qualities; seductive, smoldering, even the word *elegant* had been used to describe him. He didn't like to harp on the flattery he'd received from women over the years, but it quieted the fires that would still erupt every now and then in his mind, the childhood memories of feeling inferior because of the blackness of his skin.

Clint shifted slightly. His lean tall body stood erect like the rest of the props, the pew, the arch with the fresh flowers. As he looked across the makeshift ballroom, he scanned the neatly aligned white chairs where his aunts sat patting the moisture from their plump necks with handkerchiefs that probably had four generations of owners before them. Fans were being whipped out and waved back and forth, actually increasing the perspiration they were fretting over. The electric fans set up in the tent were blowing the same warm air that everyone was trying to escape from outside. Near the entrance Kurt and Eddie were hovering around waiting for more guests. Marcell and Clint's brother, Cedric, had just seated three guests on the bride's side and were ready to take on new escort duties. It's comical, Clint thought, while watching them tussle over who would show the decent-looking ladies to their seats, then watching them spread like wildfire when a bad gene walked in, braids too thick, skirt too tight over an ass too wide.

Kurt was the only one being an equal-opportunity player. Swinging his long arm through theirs, striding them down the aisle in assembly fashion. Clint wished they'd all act with a little more sense and maturity. They were supposed to be his representation, his dutiful guards, posted to serve and protect. These were the ones who helped get him through a grueling bout of medical school. They'd be friends for life, no doubt, like comrades of war. They'd survived while many others had not.

Kurt waved at Clint to get his attention. Now what, Clint thought. Kurt threw his eyes in a jerky movement to the right of him. Clint's eyes widened when he saw *her* walk in. She showed up.

He couldn't believe it. Her chiffon dress skimmed every curve of her body, stopping at the point where her legs began. She looked his way. Clint gave her a nod of acknowledgment. He knew he could do no more than that. All questioning eyes were upon him. *What's she doing here?* The whispers were floating through the air. Or was it his imagination?

Clint didn't know what to expect when he'd personally dropped off the invitation in her mailbox. He didn't dare take a chance on the U.S. Postal Service. He wanted to know it had been delivered. If she didn't show up, he'd know it was intentional and not an oversight. But *she* had taken the high road and walked in here polished, radiating happiness.

"How ya holdin' up, man?" Cedric inquired, already knowing the answer.

"I'm all right." Speaking was painful for Clint. His tongue was glued to the roof of his mouth.

"You see who showed up?" Cedric let out a small laugh and slapped his baby brother on the back. "You look like you could use a drink."

Clint could feel the shirt underneath his tuxedo jacket stick to the spot where his brother's hand landed. It clung to his perspiring skin.

"Nah, man, just water."

"That's all I'm offering, my brotha. You can barely stand now. Don't worry, man. I'll make sure no catfights go down." His older brother walked away the same way he'd come, smiling and kissing babies like a politician. Cedric hadn't worn a suit since his own wedding ten years ago and was taking advantage of his day in the sun as the best man.

He returned with the same affable expression, carrying a large crystal goblet of water. "Here you go, man."

Clint took the ice-cold water and drank, sipping slowly to loosen up the parched edges of his mouth. He felt like a dying man, and this was his last drink of water . . . as a single guy. He had to admit to himself he was scared. After this day, there would be no more choices. No more contemplating, struggling for the right answer. No one should ever have to make the choice between two women. Especially when both were everything you could ever want in this lifetime. But it was done. He had chosen.

Clint shook himself a little to stay in the here and now. He took a few more quick breaths, but he was still in the smooth arms of the past. The music started playing a nondescript tune. The last available seats had been filled with more pastel hats, suits and ties. Clint tried to focus, refocus. He lost sight of *her*. He couldn't tell where she was sitting, if she was still there. Maybe she had changed her mind. Told herself, "after all he'd put her through, he didn't deserve *her* blessing."

But when he caught sight of her standing, the coral splash of color, the right amount of spice on her tangy light brown skin, greeting Cedric with a hug, for that moment it was Clint, there, in her arms. In his mind, he hugged her back. He could smell the airy sweet perfume she always wore, feel her lips pressed against his cheek.

The sound of the loud organ gearing up threw Clint back into reality. He eyed the full expecting faces sitting in rows, all waiting for the show, the unity of man and woman till death do they part. The pounding of the three chords reverberated through his feet and rose up in his chest. This was it. If he didn't stop this thing now, there would be no turning back.

In the Beginning There Was Venus

THIS WOULD BE THE LAST TIME I needed to set foot in this hotbox. I stared up at the yellowed water spot on the ceiling while my hair was being washed. The water sprayed and landed on the fresh foundation I'd put on knowing it would be melted away with the mist and heat from all the blow-dryers set at maximum wattage. Tina was standing over me wearing her pink smock with the initials "TE" monogrammed in black letters on the front. As always, her chest was inches away from suffocating me. Over the many years I'd been Tina's customer, I could tell those monsters had gotten bigger, grazing my face with every change in her position. She squeezed the last drop of water she could out of my hair, pulling my skin back until my eyes hurt. She wrapped the towel neatly around my head, making me wonder how Erykah Badu could carry around such weight on her trim little body. I made my way to Tina's station, grabbing the latest issues of *Vibe* and *Source* on the way. This was my ritual, getting in the know right here in her chair every other Saturday morning.

"This is it, Venus. Once I make this cut there's no turning back, girl." Tina's voice rose above the noise of hair dryers and gossip.

"Just cut it off," I said firmly, turning my attention back to the article on the hottest new R&B girl groups. The picture of the trios and four-somes all looked strangely alike with their cocoa brown skin, plastered hair, and pouty lips. What was taking Tina so long? I just wanted it to be over with. Raising my eyes to the mirror, I caught a glimpse of Tina as she combed through the wet slickness. Let her say good-bye, I thought. Tina will miss it more than I will.

This was my ball and chain, aka my hair and about 360 relaxers. What was the sense of going through the ritual, the wash, the conditioner, and combing it out ever so gently so as not to raise the grain? I counted back to the age of four, the tender age of my introduction to the lye. Aver-aging out to fifty bucks a pop, it could've been a nice little padding for my retirement fund, to the sum of eighteen thousand dollars, not including interest. I didn't even add in all the moisturizing shampoos, conditioners, gels, hair creams, appliances, and in-between-wash-and-blow-drys. The way I figured it, I had pretty much paid for that new Beamer Tina was driving while I still had the keys to the beat-up Hyundai that was parked out front. The truly amazing thing was that I never could afford all the upkeep, but like a drug addict who needed a fix, I always found a way.

I'd look to my checking account balance first, my Visa limit second, and the calendar last to see when the next payday was, and if I could wait that long. The endless cycle put strains on my life and relationships. I knew the cycle could only be broken by me. I was responsible. I couldn't blame my mother who introduced me to the salon chair. She didn't know it would become a life sentence.

Like most African-American mothers I knew, mine was consumed by the presentation of her children. Black children had to be cleaner, neater, and sit up straighter at all times. It was an ever-present source of anxiety for my mother to prove that my brother and I were just as good, just as smart, just as well groomed as any white child. When we'd moved away from the inner city of Los Angeles to the little tree-lined community named Los Feliz, translated, *The Fortunate*, we were one of a handful of black families that claimed this area as home. Home, a place where you could be comfortable, loved unconditionally, and among people with the same traditions, likes, and dislikes.

I watched the little white children on my block as they played outside, hair uncombed, no shoes on their feet, traces of everything they'd eaten still smeared on their faces, completely happy and oblivious to any possible defects in their appearance. Nothing was wrong with them, they were in fact ideal, children in the image of their creator, angels with blue eyes and blond hair, just as they'd seen in the storybooks they'd opened and read. I, on the other hand, did not feel perfect, not until my hair was as straight as my next-door neighbor's, Tiffany Larson, a little redheaded girl with pink freckled skin whom I deemed my best friend.

We were equal partners as long as my hair shined and glistened in the sun, too. And every month or so, when my hair became more difficult for my mother to smooth and flatten into two pigtails securely fastened with the fancy elastic colored balls, I'd lose my footing. I didn't want to come out and play hopscotch, or jacks, or any of the games I'd been taught by my friends. I was suddenly content to watch reruns of *Bewitched* and *Gilligan's Island*. And if I was really desperate, I'd sit through *Hazel* and listen to her whiny voice give out whimsical advice to the family she took care of.

By Saturday, after a full week of hiding, I was anxious to accompany my mother to the beauty salon. I'd sit patiently in the hard vinyl folding chairs lined against the wall, chewing on Hot Tamales candies as I waited my turn. When the stylist finally motioned me over, I'd jump into the big brown leather cushion, sitting up straight and tall so that the seat could be swirled around and around to the appropriate height.

Once the miracle product was rinsed out of my hair, the spongy texture, referred by most as just plain old "nappy," was replaced with straight glossy roots and I'd feel an immediate sense of relief. Almost like a light being flicked on, my confidence would rise. I could jump rope all the way through the alphabet, or swipe all ten jacks up within one bounce of the ball. I was restored, revitalized, ready to enter the world. My mother would beam at me proudly; her little girl was back, beautiful as ever, sweet with the smell of bergamot and spray sheen.

When my mother was a child in the 1940s in rural Muskogee, they could only afford one way to straighten hair, and that was the cast-iron comb into the fire. She swore I would never have to suffer the sizzling heat and the raw smell of my own flesh when the comb slipped too close to the nape of my neck as it straightened every strand of the hair. She was upgrading me, giving her little girl the best.

In the early 1920s, the black elite straightened their hair with sodium hydroxide in its purest form. The Harlem Cotton Club dancers were the first real testament to the miraculous results of chemically straightened hair. They could dance and sweat all night on stage and never worry that their hair would spring back to the wiry frizz they had left behind. Once the word of the miracle product got out, there was no stopping its rapid spread. Anybody with two dollars to spare could get their own jar of straightening cream. And even some who didn't have it to spare would forfeit the milk and bread their babies needed to thrive just to be seen in the latest coif.

From one generation to the next, the status of a black woman was defined by the straightness of her hair, with the exception to the Afrocentric '70s, when for a brief period the trend was the nappier, the better. By that time, Los Feliz had become inhabited by more blacks and Hispanics. The influx supplied me with a new batch of friends who didn't approve of my basic need to sit with Tiffany Larson at lunch.

"What are you hanging out with her for?"

"She's my friend," I replied, cautiously.

"She's white," Kelly Barns whispered in my ear, as if it were a secret. Kelly Barns was a fair-skinned black girl not much darker than Tiffany Larson herself.

"I know that. She's still my friend." I kept my place at the lunch table with my white friend almost through the end of sixth grade, until the judgmental eyes cast upon me became unbearable, almost like weights pressing down on my shoulders. It seemed the separation between the colors and race was drawn with chalk everywhere I went, in the classroom, the bathroom, and even the playground. I was the scab who crossed the picket line every day at lunchtime. When I finally stepped back over the line, it was like I had never been on the other side at all. Tiffany Larson and I passed each other in the halls of middle school, high school, and beyond without so much as a word to each other. The days of making mud pies, playing house with our Barbie dolls, and eating ice cream on the porch were over like they had never happened; our friendship disappeared.

With new best friends, Cynthia, Karen, and Evelyn, I listened to the Emotions, "Best of My Love," all day, every day, until we all got the words right, singing at the top of our lungs. I had no need for hopscotch or any other activity that didn't revolve around boys. We spent our time reading the backs of album covers, voting on who was cuter, Michael or Jermaine. We wanted to have Afros, too, like the Jacksons. But with all our hair chemically straightened down to the roots, it was impossible.

So we'd braid each other's hair into skinny braids, wet them, and then let them dry, hoping the frizz and wave combined could be teased into a six-inch-high bush. Someone would always have a sunken hole in the top or middle of their Afro where the hair would lie down after a while, from a gust of wind or the sheer weight pulling down what wasn't meant to be.

Our experiments were cut short when we caught a real look at ourselves in a Polaroid snapshot of the four of us, taken by Evelyn's visiting aunt, posing, hands on hips, wearing too-tight Angel Flights, thinking we were hot. It was a shocking betrayal to see ourselves standing there looking nothing like the pictures we'd seen of Angela Davis or the perfect round Afro of the fictional woman painted on black velvet canvas that hung on nearly every apartment wall.

My mother was relieved when I came to my senses. Natural Afros died a gradual but sure death when the "Jheri curl" became available. Even the rebels, male and female alike, were in line to get the chemical treatment, marketed as the next best thing. If you weren't born with the "good hair," you could always get a Jheri curl.

But as I sat in Tina's chair, twenty years later thinking back to all the hairstyle trials and errors, the dreams of having curly hair like Irene Cara or Lonetta McKee in the movie *Sparkle*, I came to only one conclusion: *I was fed up*. The "look" that would allow me to be accepted and privileged to walk amongst the blue-eyed angels and achieve the American dream was all a lie. Tiffany Larson never cared if my hair was straight and shiny. It was all a fairy tale invented for little girls by some evil hairdresser to keep us coming back every week so that she could continue to pay for her nice buggy while we stayed on foot.

"Just cut it off," I repeated. "I want it gone."

"Not even long enough to curl. Venus, you are going to regret this and then you gon' blame me." Tina stood next to me breathing Juicy Fruit gum into my face.

"Oh, I know that's right." Carmen, the hairstylist from the next station chimed in. Her own hair was worn in large twisted braids that met at the top of her head. She was in the process of sealing the deal with another young victim. Carmen slid the white ooze down every strand of the little girl's dark hair. She couldn't have been more than seven or eight. *Say good-bye to your freedom, baby.*

"Tina, I don't have all day. Just cut it off." I tried to give her my no-nonsense face. Our eyes met in the reflection of the mirror. She stood with my silky mane wrapped around her hand in one tight ball. In the other hand she held her plier scissors, the ones used for synthetic hair.

"Please don't make me do it. Maybe you should think about it some more. Are you having problems with Clint again? That's what it is. You guys aren't gettin' along—"

"Tina. I'm not going to tell you again." She finally realized I was serious. With one large squeeze of her hand, strands fell down my face, ears, and down my back and landed on the pale pink acrylic floor. Most of it remained in Tina's hand. She stood holding the brunette ball wrapped around her hand as if she'd just been an unwilling participant in a native scalping. The silence was deafening.

To her it was the act of a traitor, a turncoat. I had done the unmentionable, unthinkable. Still, I knew I was rushing to freedom. The open door of life was calling me. I continued to run toward my freedom. My voice broke through open air. "Use the clippers, 'cause I don't want nothing I have to deal with."

The other stylists had all stopped in midstroke to catch a glimpse of the unruly customer, the client from hell. Of course, I wouldn't be invited to any more of the hair shows or barbecues. I would be shunned, no longer a team player.

Tina moved slowly, plugging in her white-and-black clippers with the shiny razor edge. She attached the largest safety grid and peeked at me for response. I shook my head "no." She pulled them all out so that I could choose for myself. I picked them all up one at a time, fingering them, studying them. Which one was going to do the honors?

"This one is fine."

"Girl, that's only a quarter of an inch. You are going to look like some little boy."

"It'll grow in. I want to start as low as possible, so I don't have to cut it again for a while."

"You have lost your mind. That's it, you have lost your mind."

"Uh-huh. You know that's right." Carmen spoke again, not bothering to look up. Her dark hands were working at bullet speed, smoothing out each and every visible crinkle in the little girl's now-shoulder-length hair.

"Here goes nothing." The buzzing in my ear sounded like angels, little brown angels with coal black hair and glossy brown eyes who looked like me, singing, calling me to the freedom I knew I deserved and craved. It sounded like my name had been called at the Sunday night raffle. The sound couldn't even match Clint screaming my name at the height of *his ecstasy*.

"How's that?" Tina's voice had taken a surrendering tone. She spoke softly. "More off the sides?"

I turned side to side. "Do you have a handheld mirror?" She spun the plush black leather around so I could get the perfect rear view. "It's fine. It's perfect." Relief in the form of laughter poured out of me. Tina and Carmen looked at each other, thinking how unfortunate it was that I had lost my mind. They gave the "she'll be back" look to each other.

I would miss Tina, too. She was more than a hairdresser. She was my therapist who asked all the right questions to keep me talking so I wouldn't notice I'd been in her salon for three solid hours and sometimes four if Mrs. Burdell wanted extensions put in. When I stepped out of the salon, the cool air hit my scalp and parts of my body responded to the stimuli. Maybe this was the beginning of something freaky. I could deal with a little excitement in my life. Since Clint's exit I was stuck at the peak of my sex drive with no way to get down.

"Whoa, watch it now, young lady." An older gent swung around me. Instead of watching where I was going, I'd been catching glimpses of myself in every storefront window and bumped smack into him.

"Oh, excuse me." I regained my balance and couldn't help taking another quick look as soon as I safely passed him by. The only thing really noticeable was the determination that framed my high cheek-bones and pointed chin and the slim neck underneath. Nothing special was going on. I didn't really have a new standard of beauty to judge myself with. All I knew was that I no longer looked like the women on the black hair-care product boxes. This new creature I was staring at was in a whole new segment of the market. That's the term we used at Don-nely Kramer Advertising, where I'd been working for the last four years. Everybody falls into a segment or group. When that group is discovered and identified, the attack is planned. It felt good to know I was no longer in a category that could be so easily marked, or could I? Maybe I had become the most simple to define.

As I rounded the corner I faced a group of young black men coming toward me. I braced myself for the usual rumblings and accompanying remarks. But when they walked past me, without a sign, no grunting or teeth sucking, or "how ya doin'," I was suddenly deflated. I had become invisible. I can't say I was completely surprised—disappointed, yes, sur-prised, no.

When I'd finally reached my destination of the coffee shop, I checked the reflection in the door window. I could see more defining features this time. The perfectly arched brows over my china doll eyes that made me look like my hair was pulled too tight. The tapered nose and full lips. I wanted to make sure I was who I thought I was, *mis thang*, with a newfound freedom. When I opened the door, the strong smell of coffee and cigarettes rushed at me.

"Can I get a caffè latte, skim milk only, please?"

"Sure, $3.25." The young girl held out her pale white hand over the counter. The black and blue ink marks of a cross and dagger tattooed on the stark background of her translucent wrist held my attention for a few seconds too long. I was summing up who this girl was, what she did at night when she left this part of her life. What she must have been thinking the night she prodded her own skin until it bled. I dug in my purse for the quarter. This was part of my new freedom, to buy an over-priced coffee and not feel like I was being ripped off. I was determined not to care that I could've gone straight home and mixed some hot milk and coffee in my blender and come out with the same thing.

I sat at a table in the corner of the small space. I stared out the win-dow and watched everyone walking by. It was the middle of November and it was beautiful outside. The leaves struck their pose of bright yel-lows, orange, burgundy, and dark browns. The street held many of the leaves in the crevices of its edge, but most of them still hung tightly on the branches even with the wind threatening to pull them away. There was nothing like the fall season in Washington, DC. After spending time in different states, including Florida, California, Texas, and a little time in Colorado, the DC area was by far the best place I'd lived. It's a fact there are a lot of negatives, such as the crime and a bad mayor here and there. What states didn't have their faults?

I had accepted a job as a contract coordinator, thankful for the move out of Los Angeles where people were getting hostile with the wave of unemployment from all the aerodefense companies shutting down. Los Angeles had become a serious battleground with carjackings and drive-by shootings. My personal relationships were being affected, too. It seemed everyone I knew was either losing their house or job or both, and I wasn't running the Do-Drop Inn. I lost a lot of good friends by saying no.

Of all the things I'd heard and seen on the news about DC, the traffic, the murders, and high cost of living, the most important of them all was the three-to-one ratio of women to men. Now that was scary. Who wants to live in a place where there are more women than men? That reduced odds even below the nation's average, which was already at an all-time low. With all these good brothers coming out of the closet, it was reduced even further.

I met Clint shortly after I moved to DC. He was just starting his internship at Howard University Medical School. I remembered every detail of the day we met. I was doing my routine grocery shopping and I ran right into him. Literally! My car bumped his leg when I was backing out of the Shoppers Club parking lot. I felt the thud and jumped out of my car without putting the car in park. It started rolling forward. I panicked, jumped back in, and accidentally stepped on the gas instead of the brake, almost backing over him again. He was down on the ground holding on to his ankle. I was certain that I hadn't hit his ankle or anything lower than his thigh. I asked him if he needed the paramedics. He moaned and rocked like he had a broken bone. When he opened his eyes to look at me, he straightened up real quick. A sweet apologetic smile appeared on his face, but I was the one who felt guilty. To make it up to him, I offered to buy lunch. Sparks flew immediately. He was twenty-five and I was thirty at the time. The age difference was the furthest thing from my mind. He carried himself with grace and charisma when it counted. He was a man with a future, a gorgeous dark chocolate body, and a smile that should have been in Colgate commercials.

After our first date, we moved in together. Not right after, but two weeks tops, we were cohabiting. My house was first choice, of course. I had just purchased it with my entire savings, as well as a chunk of my parents', while his place was the back of an elderly white couple's home just outside of Washington, DC, in Alexandria. We lived in shacked-up bliss, sharing hopes, plans, and dreams. But that had all changed in the past year when I had run out of patience.

I pulled up to my three-bedroom Tudor-style castle and pushed the automatic garage door; it rose slowly and the light popped on. With each inch of its rising I could see more and more of the white Jetta parked on the far right side. The license plate came into view, BABY-DOC. I laid my head on the steering wheel. The last thing I needed right now was to deal with him.

I walked in and threw my keys on the kitchen counter. He was comfortably positioned in my teal leather sofa in front of the TV, surfing the channels with the remote.

He looked up and did a double take. "V, what the hell did you do? Your hair!"

Whose Head
Is It,
Anyway?

ONCE CLINT STOPPED CRYING LIKE a baby, he looked at me, really looked at me, and told me it was flattering. His hand went up to touch my head, and I blocked it like Bruce Lee. This was no longer his domain. That understanding was made two weeks ago when he walked all over the ultimatum that had been set before him. The conversation played in my head like we'd had it yesterday. It was the evening of my thirty-fourth birthday and I was feeling used up and old. It didn't help that he had shown up late, and by the time he walked through the door I was ready for battle.

"Why do you want to get married now?" he had whined. "We've

been together four years and all of a sudden it's now or never. Are you pregnant?"

"No, I'm not pregnant, but I would like to be. I would like to start a family and be on my way to adulthood, but I'm too busy here playing house with you."

That day, I'd put my foot down. I was tired of his excuses. First it was, "wait till I finish medical school," then it was, "just let me pass the boards," and after passing the boards it became, "V, let me get on my feet." The way I saw it, he was never going to get on his feet as long as I was carrying him around like a small child.

Clint now stood in front of me with his shirt buttoned only halfway. I tried not to let the solid rippled mass distract me. "When did you decide to cut off all your hair?" he asked, slowly recovering from his shock.

I opened the bottled water sitting on the counter and took a swig. "Not that it's any of your business, but it's something I wanted to do for some time." I took another swig. "It had nothing to do with you."

"Damn, V. That's kind of whack, ain't it? You know you did it because you were mad at me. Did I hurt you that bad? You were trying to get back at me by cutting off all your hair. You know how many women would pay to have the hair you had? And then you go and cut it all off."

"Excuse me. This is my head. If I wanted to do something to hurt you, I would've thrown that damned dog out the window, the one you forgot to take with you. That belongs to you. My hair or lack of, does not."

"Sandy was your birthday present, remember?" Clint bent over and stroked the cocker spaniel's shiny tan mane.

How could I forget, nothing personal, but Sandy was supposed to be a solitaire diamond in a small gold box. When he'd walked in carrying the large white cardboard box with holes punched in the top and a big pink bow, I became furious.

"Baby, I'm sorry. Let's squash all this fighting."

"We're not fighting. People in relationships fight. We no longer have a relationship."

"V, you need to snap out of it. Why does everything have to happen when you click your heels? Don't I have any say?"

"You said all you needed to say when you walked out of here," I reminded him.

"What was I supposed to do? Damn, you told me to get out."

"I didn't tell you to get out. That was a choice you made. Now I'm telling you to get out." I opened the front door. "I'll need the garage door opener back, please." I held out my hand with the badly chipped Butter Frost polish. He wrestled the key chain remote off the rest of his collection.

"Thank you."

"I need to get my car out," he grumbled while following me to the front door. "How am I supposed to get my car out?"

"You should have thought about that before you stuck it where it didn't belong."

I slammed the door in his face and pressed the remote button to lift the garage up. I hugged Sandy and scratched behind her long brown ears. She licked my chin. I planted a kiss on the top of her soft warm head. "We'll get through this, girl."

One
More
Chance

"Hey, V, call me when you get in, please."

The last message of three played while I kicked off my shoes and let Sandy jump on my knees, leaving tiny snag marks in my pants. The telephone rang and I picked it up quickly.

"Hello."

"It's me, V. You weren't going to call me, were you?" Clint spoke low, making a rush of heat pour into my ear.

"I just got home from work. I didn't have a chance. You called me first." I held Sandy close for strength.

"I wanted to see if you calmed down any from the last time I saw you."

"I was calm then and I'm calm now. Nothing has changed."

"Can we get together, hook up for dinner and a movie or something?"

"I know what your 'or something' is and I'm not falling for it."

"V, you know I'm not about that. I finally got a day off rotation. I've been working nonstop for two solid weeks."

"I have plans."

"You have plans tomorrow?" he asked in a disbelieving tone.

"Yep."

"What about Saturday?"

"Busy."

"Sunday?" His voice rose a little out of his cool shell.

"I'm busy all weekend." I accidentally squeezed a little too hard, making Sandy bark in her small raspy voice while squirming out of my grasp.

"Yeah, all right V. I'll check you out later." He hung up the phone before I could say good-bye. I grabbed a nearby pillow and punched it hard before making it my new best friend. I could use a good romping session, but I wasn't giving in. I had to stand my ground, for myself as well as all the sisters out there, black, brown, yellow, and white. If he wants to play in my yard, he's going to have to come correct. There would be no more fertility dances without the ceremony.

"Clint, what's up, man?"

Eddie Roy spoke too loud, trying to make up for his lack of stature. Some of the other interns had named him Tatoo. "What are you doing with your two days of freedom?" he hollered through the phone.

"Just kickin' it, E-man. What's up?"

"Kurt and Scott wanted to head out to H-Town. It's ladies' night, so you know what that means."

It didn't mean anything, but Clint was listening.

"You want to go check it out, man?" Eddie's excitement was coming through loud and clear.

"Hey, why not?" Clint looked around his furnished studio, decorated in the tweed era. "I'm not looking very prosperous over here. What time you coming through?"

"Kurt's driving. We'll pick you up around ten."

"Cool. I'll see you then. Oh, you know, I'm over here in Clifford Hall. I don't know if I told Kurt or not." His voice faded off in babble as he gave sketchy details of why he was no longer living with Venus. "So I'll see you at ten." Clint hung up the phone, feeling half embarrassed. It wasn't cool to be kicked out of a lady's pad. It was a sign that a man wasn't handling his business. No matter what you had accomplished in this world, a woman could always make you look weak.

He gave calling Venus one more stab. The last thing he wanted to do tonight was go hang out in a club. All this fighting was so petty. It was driving him crazy. Why couldn't she see how ridiculous she was acting? He'd give her one more chance not to send him out there howling with the wolves. He dialed her number.

Clint wore his lucky jacket, the midnight blue one, with a black turtle-neck and black slacks that were creased so hard he could cut someone if he bumped into them. He had to admit it felt good getting out with the fellas, especially after having no luck reaching Venus. The music was so loud he could feel it vibrating up from the floor and through his legs. It was early. The dance floor wasn't crowded. The view was still easy, not that he was looking. Long brown legs with pumps were in every space of the room. Some thin, some thick, and some a little lumpy and bumpy, but hey, all divas need love. There were a few short skirts walking around that caught his eye. The first young lady he noticed staring at him was wearing a knit sky-blue dress that showed a lot of body. Her curves were serious. She watched him as she turned her glass up to drink whatever she was nursing. She straightened her back, allowing her chest to stick out even more, stretching the limits of her dress. Her berry-wine-colored lips stayed puckered after each sip. Her dark shiny hair was flowing down one side of her shoulder and rested comfortably on her breast. Not bad at all, Clint thought.

The tall busty waitress came over to their table with her little black apron covering only the most important parts. She was all teeth and grins when she approached the table.

"So what will it be for you gentlemen tonight?"

"Does that choice include you?" Kurt's deep baritone voice came over the rhythmic bass of the music.

Eddie chimed in. "Yeah, I'll take one of you served with whipped cream." His glasses sent off a glare.

"Man, damn. Your game is so weak." Kurt shook his head back and forth. "Can't take you no damn where."

"We'll have four of whatever's on tap." Clint spoke quickly to get rid of her. When the waitress moved, the young lady across the room was back in his view. She was sending all kinds of signals. Ordinarily, he wouldn't have been too receptive. But right now, he could feel every thought she was thinking. He could feel her warm breath whispering in his ear. He could feel her hands all over his chest with questions that could only be answered in person. And he definitely had a few questions of his own. After the third beer he ordered his feet to move in her direction. When he asked her to dance, he was glad a slow jam was working. He didn't have the energy for all the gyrations that were in style. Pulling her close to let his hands run up and down the crease in her back, he put his face in all that hair and took a deep breath. She smelled sweet, simple, nothing too exotic. Clint could deal with this.

"So what's your name?"

"Kandi," she smiled and moved her arms closer around his neck. "What's yours?"

"Clint."

"Nice to meet you, Clint."

"The pleasure's all mine." He stuck his face back in her hair. Sometimes the smallest pleasures can fix the biggest problems. Right now he had a sensuous woman in his arms, moving slow next to him, letting him know he was capable, desirable, and, best of all, still alive. What more could he ask for?

The alarm clock went off at five. It was still pitch dark in his room. He slapped it to the floor and rolled back over to finish his sleep. His elbow landed on something that didn't feel nearly as hard and pointy as the bogus mattress he was lying on. He sat up to inspect what he had bumped into, pulling the sheet away slowly. He could see the dark silhouette of her body. With all his acquired cerebral skills he could not remember her name. Casey, Kassie, Cathy, nothing sounded familiar. So he took the desperate man's approach and started feeling around in the darkness for her purse. The floor was scattered with pieces of clothing and shoes.

Finally, he came across a velvet pouch that was no bigger than his fist. He picked it up and moved slowly to the bathroom, trying desperately not to wake the phantom in his bed. He closed the door first, then felt the wall for the light. Her license was the first thing that fell out when he dumped the contents into the sink. He kissed two fingers and gave the man upstairs props for saving his life *again*.

"Kandi." He called her name with confidence as he shook her bare slender shoulder. "Kandi." She stirred a little with a soft moan. "Hey . . . Kandi . . . I hate to wake you, sweet thing, but I have to get up out of here and go to work." He had no place to go but back to bed, but the quicker he got rid of her, the better.

She rolled over, reaching out for his neck. "You go ahead, I'll let myself out."

"Uh no, that's not going to work." He picked up the light blue dress that reminded him of fresh cotton candy. "Here you go."

He grabbed what could be found of her ensemble and led her to the bathroom.

She came back out minutes later with one shoe on and limped toward the bed.

"Here it is." He held it up for her to grab but she didn't take it. She held up her foot in pointed-toe fashion for him to slip the shoe on for her.

"So what kind of doctor are you?" She spoke from the edge of the bed while fastening her shoe strap. He noticed that even without the berry-wine-colored lipstick, she was entrancing. Her hair was still lying over one shoulder. He wondered how she did that, kept that sexy thing going so strong. At least he was sure it wasn't the alcohol that had made her so appealing.

"I actually haven't decided what I want to specialize in." He knew, but that was just a little bit too personal. He hadn't realized they had gotten that far in the first place. The only conversation he remembered was the one that had gotten her into his bed.

"Do you need a ride?" She was standing in front of him. Her bare legs were toned and tempting.

"No. I have a car." He laced up his Air Jordans, last year's birthday present from Venus.

"Oh. I wasn't sure, since I drove last night."

He stood up. They were chest to chest. "Thank you . . ." Clint kissed her softly on the forehead, ". . . for driving me home."

"You're welcome. Anytime. Do you want my number?"

"Ah, yeah." He tore off a piece of his student loan bill and gave it to her with a pen. She handed it back and kissed him on the lips.

"I have to work today, too, so maybe you can call me this evening."

"All right. Maybe I'll do that." Clint wasn't really interested, but he felt compelled to ask, since she knew so much about him. "What is it that you do?"

"I'm a teacher, third-graders. I thought about the older kids but they're just unmanageable these days. Third-graders are right at that age where they listen and still have a little respect to give. They're a great—"

"You know what, I'm running late. I'll call you." Clint led her to the door. Once he was sure she was gone he flicked the lock in place. He sat back down on the edge of the mattress and started taking off his shoes. He didn't have to go into the hospital today, or anywhere else for that matter. Watching her walk out that door was a triumph. In the old days he would've thrown one more in for the road. She was *too* fine. She reminded him of Venus with all that pretty hair and those sexy lips. The old Venus that smiled a lot and laughed too loud. He had noticed the change in Venus a while ago, but couldn't slow down to do anything about it. Every ounce of energy he had to spare was in this residency program. None of it came easy to him. He felt like he'd been fighting for his life each and every step of the way. If she hadn't been there to catch him every time he was falling, he probably wouldn't have survived. She'd smooth out all the wrongs and make them right just with the touch of her hand or the sound of her voice. He wished he could turn things around, just make them like they used to be. All he needed was one more chance.

When he'd met Venus, she was a dream. He had his very own "little white girl" without taking the hit of her actually being white. To top it off, she was educated and independent. That kind of thing just didn't fall from trees in the area where he'd grown up. Venus was definitely a stand-out kind of girl, the kind you wouldn't mind spending the rest of your life with, but even still, out of nowhere, it's time to get married. She put it out there like it was test time. And Clint didn't like to admit it, but it *was* time. After four years of living it, you may as well be it. Yet he couldn't help thinking about all his buddies who had taken the plunge. Without notice, they were wrapped so tight they couldn't get an edge. Like homeboy, Joree. Ever since he and Dee Dee tied the knot, he couldn't come out and play. When the guys would call him up to shoot hoops, he'd have no game. Then there was Marcell; his lady shut down access to the eight-bedroom hacienda in the Shenendoah Valley like a landlord with an eviction notice. Clint, Marcell, and Kurt had driven there just to kick it after some make-you-wanna-scream-and-holler exams. Marcell's wife thought they were up there doing dirt when they were just trying to get their rejuvenation on. She busted in accusing them of bringing women. When there were none to be found, she started questioning their heterosexual status. It was a crazy scene. But that was the kind of thing that happened once a woman received her ownership papers.

Although Venus wasn't the type who would turn all ignorant without notice—she had more class than a man knew what to do with—he'd seen something take over a woman once she got the deal cinched. All the things that were in the script suddenly become rewritten.

Clint had seen it happen firsthand with his big brother, Cedric, who had raised Clint and his twin sister, Alison, since they were ten years old. Their dad went out for a crazy run, where he'd get his hit and come back home, sometimes not until the next day, but he'd always make it back. Not the last time, though. Cedric played it off for a while, said Pops was down at County General, sick. But Clint and his sister knew he wasn't in the hospital. *At least Clint knew.* Clint had spent all day, up and down every hall, looking inside every room, smelling foulness and degeneration. He looked tirelessly for two days straight and his father wasn't there. In the southeast side of Washington, DC, he couldn't have been in any other hospital. His insurance wasn't in force since Capital Steel had let him go for no shows. Moms had cut out long before that. She told their father she had to "better herself" and needed some time away. Needless to say, she bettered herself right out of three kids. That left Clint, Alison, and Cedric to fend for themselves.

Cedric was only a kid himself, but he didn't want to see his little sister and brother go live with their cousins in North Carolina. "There was already too many of them."

Cedric met a woman, sixteen at best, who was coming over with fresh-baked goodies and treats specially made for Clint and Alison. She'd come over and clean, making their two-bedroom place feel like a real home. It felt good, too. Some mornings she'd be in the kitchen setting it off just like their Moms used to do with biscuits, eggs, and bacon. Cedric would get served up in bed *Love American Style*, while Alison and Clint did their damage in the kitchen, eating four and five pieces of bacon each. It was the land of milk and honey. But it all came to a screeching halt, when out of nowhere, one week after Cedric's eighteenth birthday, the two were married. It was like Alison and Clint were Hansel and Gretel and she was the wicked stepmother and the evil witch all rolled into one.

Every time Clint let it flow through the memory banks, it made the hair on his chest stand up a little straighter. After Cedric headed off to his job as a press operator at the *Washington Post* in the mornings, Alison and Clint were stuck with *Evilena*. The sweet smell of bacon and sausage was replaced with a lit pack of nicotine and tar. Their small domicile turned into a constant gray haze. The only time they could breathe was when *Evilena* went out for more cigarettes. She had stopped cooking and cleaning altogether and would bite off their heads if they moved past the line of their bedroom door for a glass of water, let alone food.

With Cedric working twelve- and fourteen-hour shifts, they had been stuck with her, yelling and cussing that she wished Alison and Clint could go live somewhere else so she and Cedric wouldn't have to put up with their "stupid asses." By the time *Evilena* was done, they answered to *lil mutha fucka* and *triflin' cow* like they'd had name changes. Alison was more affected by the whole scenario. Clint noticed her pattern of shying away from anyone with authority, teachers, neighbors, or adults of any kind. She shut down entirely for a good five years.

Although Cedric was rid of Althea, *her real name*, within six months into the marriage, that's not the kind of thing Clint could easily forget. The damage was done. When the word *wife* came to mind, all he could think of was the bride from hell. *That bitch had gone crazy soon as they'd said "I do."*

Are
You
All Right?

"What'd you do? Oh my God. Venus, what'd you do?"

"Something I've been wanting to do for months, years."

I rubbed my hand over the moist texture. "It feels so good." I had a nice long weekend to adjust to the nakedness and I was feeling confident.

"But you cut it all off. I mean that was kinda drastic, don't you think?" Sherri had one foot in my office. The other half was standing in the corridor. As the receptionist she had to appear as if she was minding the fort, even though she spent a good amount of her time with her head stuck in my office telling me about her grown boys at home who didn't know how to clean up after themselves. *Just unleash them on the innocent.*

"It was all or nothing. So—" I ran my hand down the back of my head again. "Do you like it or not?" I asked, honestly seeking her approval.

"You're wearing it, girl. It's a look everybody can't pull off, but you're wearing it. See, my head is too big for something like that, not to mention, my behind. But you got that petite little figure. Um hum. Yeah, you can pull that off. It looks good."

"Thank you, Sherri." I gave the signal that I'd had enough by turning my attention to the report I was working on.

"Has John or Lenny seen it yet, your new look?" Sherri asked, with hopes of being the first. Lenny Kramer and John Donnely were the owners of this great establishment. I knew Sherri was dying to be the first one to announce my new do. She made it her business to try to be more important than she really was by being the information bureau. Who was seen yelling at who, where so-and-so went with so-and-so.

"No, I don't think so." I had come to work early to avoid all the first stares. I let out an exasperating sigh to let her know I was annoyed by the fact that she was still there. This time I picked up the phone, pretending to make a phone call. She left silently.

"Knock knock." Ray Chambers slid in and shut the door behind him. "Hello, Venus." He pulled up a chair instantly without an invitation. For some reason, Ray thought he was the resident arbitrator and psychologist. He always inquired about my health and well-being. All of our conversations were one-way. He avoided questions about his personal life. In fact, no one, not even Sherri, seemed to know his story. His Native American features were a trap as far as I was concerned. Underneath his soft eyes that turned into small slits when he smiled was just an average white guy whose loyalties remained in the right wing.

"Good morning, Ray. What can I do for you?" I leaned directly into his view so that he couldn't move his eyes around my head without being too obvious.

"I like your new look."

"Thank you, Ray."

"I just wanted to see how you were coming along with the research on the Beatrice Brand Foods Survey. We're going to meet some time next week." He was relaxed, keeping his gaze on my eyes. He was better at this game than I thought.

"Oh, it's coming along. I had Elliot do the data entry yesterday, so we should be getting some numbers out by the end of today. So whenever you're ready is fine with me."

"Great, great." He smiled. "Okay then. I'll talk to you later." He rose up and headed toward the door. He stopped and turned on the heels of his loafers. "Are you all right, Venus? I mean, is there something you need to talk about?"

"Ray, I'm fine. Why do you ask?"

He moved toward me and leaned on the back of the chair. "I just wanted to check on you. I wasn't sure if it was my imagination or if you were having some problems you might want to discuss."

I smiled for him. "I promise, you would be the first one I'd tell."

"You're fine, I mean everything is going okay for you? You're not depressed about anything? You know I will keep the strictest confidence."

I walked around my desk and stood in front of him. I straightened his bright yellow tie that was blinding me. "Thank you for your concern, Ray. I'm fine, really. It's just a style, not a statement of some kind. I'm not trying to be a radical feminist or anything."

"Oh, I wasn't referring to your hair." His eyes finally focused on my head. "It's different, I like it." He put his hand on my shoulder for a brief instant, then turned and left.

I had that icky feeling of my space being invaded. I needed air. My hair was my business, but I knew everyone would make it theirs.

"Sherri, I'm going down for a donut. I'll be back in a few." I moved swiftly past her.

"Sure thing, sweetie."

Now I was sweetie. Was I that pathetic looking? I didn't have the energy to put her in check. The elevator doors opened before I could push the down button, and John, Lenny, and about six others from the office stood there completely speechless. I stepped back to let them get off first, but no one moved.

"Good morning." I spoke a little too loud.

"Good morning," John finally muttered. The others followed suit. I stepped on the elevator and only breathed once the doors were tightly shut. I could see myself in the reflection of the chrome doors. Yes, it was me. I was the same person I was Friday when I'd left here. I'd taken a little more care in my makeup application since I had an extra twenty minutes to spare not fighting with my hair. My eyes seemed a little wider, more intense, almost like an infant who searches for understanding in everything she sees. My nose seemed suddenly too broad, but I knew that was just an institutionalized flaw of my thinking.

I stepped off the elevator and headed toward the sunlit doorway. When the gush of cold wind hit me, I felt a tingly sensation that ran through my body. I walked one block to the Pastry Pantry and bought the biggest donut in the glass case and two dozen more for the morning meeting.

The walk back was brisk, but the frigid air didn't hurt this time. I was too tense to feel anything.

"Hey, Sherri, has the meeting started yet?"

"I saw a few go in that direction, but not everybody."

I headed toward the conference room with the box of donuts in one hand and my bag with the cinnamon roll as big as a saucer in the other.

I put the donuts in the center of the large cherry wood table. Several managers were already inside and didn't waste time grabbing the pastries and mumbling "thank you" through full mouths. I took my usual seat. Saige, our comptroller, walked in after me.

"Hi, Venus." She went straight for the donuts. Her excess poundage wasn't concerned with my new look. Jenny, the new girl, smiled at me and sat down. She chose a chair at random, Ray's seat. I snickered at the awkwardness it would cause.

Dominick Santos, the only other minority besides Sherri and me, came in. He gave a quick wave and sat down on the other end of the table. Lenny and John finally arrived and started the meeting. Each person from their department gave a heads up. When it was my turn to speak, I rose slowly, feeling like everyone was staring at my hair. My words came out thick and jumbled. Ray's face was covered with worry. When I ended my brief presentation by asking if there were any questions, his hand flew up.

My knees went wobbly. "Yes?" I crossed my arms over my chest in defense mode, ready to hear an inquiry about my hair.

"Are there any more of the donuts left with the little sprinkles on top?" He winked at me.

I thanked him with my eyes, grateful for him breaking up the tension I'd created.

The truth was, I'd never really be free until I stopped worrying about what other people were thinking. I could cut my hair bald, get tattoos and a nose ring, but it wouldn't mean anything as long as I was looking for acceptance.

⊚   ⊚   ⊚

And Then
There Was
Kandi

KANDI PULLED THE DRESS OVER
her head and tossed it in a ball to
the floor of her closet. She only had
time for a quick shower. She wished she'd had time to talk to Lena some
more. They had already worked up a good little profit for Ma Bell on
the cellular phone. It had been an expensive call, but she had to tell Lena
about the rest of her evening. The first thing Lena wanted to know was,
"What got into you to make you leave your best sistah friend stranded at
H-Town with no way home?"

"Oh, don't even play that game with me, girlll." Kandi spoke into the
palm-size phone, compliments of Tyson Edwards. "I knew you and
Freddy had hooked up way before I headed out the door. When I went

to tell you about this tall, dark, and handsome lil chocolate thing I met, you were too busy. I mean really, you and Freddy looked like you were going to grind holes in each other's legs. And don't try to deny it, 'cause I was right there next to you getting my own swerve on." Kandi let out a sinful giggle as she drove with one hand on the steering wheel and the other holding the small black phone pressed to her ear.

"So who is he?" Lena had asked. "Or should I say, who is he trying to perpetrate?"

"Lena, I think I'm in love. I know it's a cliché in the worst kind of way, but there is no other way to say it, umh, umh, tall, dark, and handsome. And guess what."

"What? Wait, you're breaking up. Are you going in a tunnel? Wait. Okay, go on."

"He's a doctor." They both started screaming into each other's ear at the top of their lungs. Kandi was glad the morning traffic hadn't started up yet. Someone driving alongside of her would have thought she was crazy for sure.

"A doctor?" Lena asked incredulously. "Are you sure he's not lying just to get in those panties?"

"I'm more than sure."

"I should've known he was a find. You've never just gone off with someone like that. I was about ready to call the police this morning."

"Oh, puhleeze, girl, you weren't thinking about me. If you were, you wouldn't have waited till this morning to send a posse."

"I'm serious. When you get home, you'll hear all the messages I left you. I was giving you till eight this morning to check in, then I was calling the pokies."

Kandi laughed for another few minutes listening to Lena swearing her allegiance on the other end of the phone. "I'm sorry I worried ya, mocha love. I'm very much alive and kicking. Or maybe not, maybe this is all a dream. I've finally met a decent man, and it's all a dream."

It was Lena's turn to laugh. "So what's next? Did you guys make plans or anything?"

"No. Not yet, he's going to call me." The silence echoed in Kandi's ear. "I know how tired that sounds, but he is. I know it. This guy is not the average hop-a-long-cassidy. He's real. Sincere."

"Kandi, when are you going to stop believing everything you hear? That's why Tyson's had you dangling on a hook for so long."

"Oh, you mean like how you believed Freddy when he said he couldn't give you his phone number because he lived with his mean mamma and she didn't like phone calls to the house? Or maybe you're referring to something like the one Freddy told you when he could never spend the entire night because of his religion. And after all that, you swear you didn't know he was married till you saw him playing good Christian at church, sitting with his entire family, wife, babies, and all. And you're still letting him play house, so don't start in on me about being a pushover."

"Kandi, you can be so cold."

"I learned from the best," Kandi barked out.

"I'm serious though. Don't put yourself so far out there. Just be a little cautious. You and me both have made enough mistakes to last a lifetime," Lena whined on the other end of the phone.

"I'm not thinking about Tyson, or Freddy, or any of those other lying married fools. This one is for real. They're not all pitiful, Lena."

"You poor naïve little thing." Lena spoke softly at first. "Dogs! All of them, they're dogs! Just remember that."

"You are certifiable, Lena." Kandi guided her car into the parking garage and turned off the ignition. "Over and out, Agent Scully. I'm home now. I've got thirty minutes to get out of this hoochie dress I wore last night and become *Ms. Treboe* to about thirty rugrats."

"Okay. Just remember what I said. Don't put all your prayers in one basket."

"I know, I heard you. I'll talk to you later." Kandi clicked off the phone and headed up to her apartment.

She dressed and showered with the previous night still heavy on her mind. Before walking out the door, she pressed her fingers on all of her miniature elephant statues, some carved in oak, ivory, a few in brass. She'd always collected them, even as a child. They symbolized luck and good fortune. She thought it was about time for them to start working.

Kandi had a better than usual smile painted on her face when she walked into the Dearborn Elementary School. It had been a while since she had felt elated over meeting someone new. The odds of meeting a man with long-term-status possibilities in a nightclub were like a million to one. But when she'd laid her eyes on the delicious creature sitting across from her last night, she'd known right away there was something special about him. He wasn't on a quest or mission. His mildness indicated he didn't really want to be there at all.

Kandi never had a problem attracting men. That wasn't what she was worried about right now. Her problem was keeping them. And in some instances getting rid of them when they hadn't proven themselves to be worthy.

"Good morning, Kandi." Sue Bellington was unlocking her classroom door as Kandi sassed by, bouncier than a Monday required.

"Morning, Sue. Are we still pulling our classes together for the *Mufaro's Beautiful Daughters* film?"

"Sure. Two o'clock is good for me."

"Perfect. See you in the library." Kandi's coffee-brown eyes were glazed like shiny dark marbles.

"You sure are happy today. What's got into you?" Sue inquired with a smirk on her face, rubbing her expansive belly. In her eighth month of pregnancy, she was as wide as she was tall.

"I guess it's just nice to finally see the sun peek through those clouds." Kandi walked through the Dearborn halls with a pep in her step, not conscious of the loud echo she was making with each click of her heel. She tried to tell herself to calm down. She wanted to be reasonable. She knew better, but Clint was completely on her mind. When he'd told her he was doing his last stretch in medical school, that was the whipped cream and cherry on top of what was already a delightfully tasty sundae.

Kandi knew this was the best time to catch him, before the dollars started rolling in. Once a man started raking in the big bucks, he thought he could have any woman he wanted. And Lord only knew how difficult it was to tame a man with too many choices. Look at Tyson Edwards. He was married and still had too many women, one of them being Kandi. He'd been fairytaling her along for well over a year, telling her as soon as he acquired enough backing he was going to walk out of St. John's and start his own cosmetics company. For a while she believed Tyson. He talked a good strategy, especially the part about being able to marry her once he didn't have to depend on his wife's daddy. She'd been going through the motions with Tyson mostly because there really hadn't been a better offer. He came through, always in the nick of time. By week's end, when she was ready for a nice quiet dinner with all the amenities, there he was. He'd been her good-time sponsor and kept her mind off the fact that she was approaching thirty and still had no prospects for a future. That was, until she'd met Clint. Unlike the other men she'd dated in the past, he was a full package: good looks, a serious profession, and a sweetness about him that made her anxious to be held in his arms again. Right now all she could think about was how to make that happen. The recess bell snapped her out of her daydream. She looked down and had scribbled *Dr. and Mrs. Clint* at the top of her notepad unconsciously. Mrs. Clint what? She didn't even know what her new last name was going to be.

"Miss Treboe, may I have a bathroom pass?" The little redheaded gnome with pale freckled skin was standing in front of her desk.

"Sure Gary." She reached in her desk and handed him the small pink-and-blue rock she'd painted last year.

"Miss Treboe."

Kandi didn't bother to look up past the red mass of hair that was still blocking her view. She knew the face that belonged to the nasal-toned whiny voice. "Yes, Missy?"

"Can I go to the bathroom, too?"

"Missy, when Gary gets back you'll be next."

Another hand went up. "Yes, Leticia?"

"Miss Treboe, Josh said he likes you."

"Well, I like Josh, too." The rest of the class started giggling. The silent reading had been interrupted like a systematic tripping of the dominoes. Now the whole class was rustling in their seats and getting squirmish. Pretty soon everyone would have something to say whether it held any value or not.

"Okay, guys, it looks like everyone has had enough of reading. Let's line up and get some fresh air."

Kandi led the class outside to the playground area. The dampness from the previous night was still sitting on top of the grass like a white sheet. She looked up every now and then from the bench she was sitting on to yell a few words of safety. She didn't have the energy to be super teacher today. She had been on her toes trying to give this new man everything she had last night. Kandi didn't want him to forget where it came from.

If I Woulda Coulda Shoulda

I WONDERED HOW MUCH MONEY men spent monthly on personal maintenance compared with women. Where was the justice? It was all an evil plot to keep women off track, to never catch up.

I headed for the closet to begin the ritual of deciding what to wear. I didn't want anything too close around the neck. A new wardrobe was needed with this buzz cut. The straight-leg Donna Karan pants and box-cut Armani jackets didn't do justice for me now. I needed to show that I was still one hundred percent woman, right down to my hairy little legs. A little cleavage and thigh action would clear up any doubts.

I picked up the phone. "Hey, Wendy, what's up?" I spoke to my best bud about once a week. She was pulling double duty as a working mother and wife, so our talks were brief and straight to the point. "You want to do a little shopping with me on your lunch break today?"

"You're going to stay in the district, right? I only have an hour for lunch and that bitch Sarah is back watching my every move. She'd chain me to my desk if it was legal."

I laughed, knowing she had a serious concern. "No problem. I just want to pick up a pair of those new close-fitting pants that are out now. They're something I swore I'd never sink to, but I need an overhaul in the closet and I gotta start somewhere. How are the kids?" The pause was indefinite, so I tried again. "What's been going on in the Harris household?"

"Stop running through here and get your damn pants on," I heard her scream with her hand over the phone, but it still penetrated my eardrum.

"I'm sorry girl, these kids are getting on my last nerve. I'll meet you in front of O'Toole's at twelve." She hung up the phone without a good-bye.

I finished dressing and stuck a piece of dried-out breadstick in my mouth before heading out the door. The trash men were out and had blocked in my car momentarily. When I finally got a chance to pull out, I gave them my usual wave. They stared at me for a few moments before responding hesitantly. I could see their mouths moving in unison. The one with muddy brown skin flashed a half smile before turning to talk to the shorter, lighter-skinned one hanging on the back of the truck with his body swallowed by large black overalls. They both waved, while talking to each other out the sides of their mouths.

"Go to hell," I muttered to myself through clenched teeth. I hoped they could read lips. As many times as I'd given them respect and acknowledgment for no other reason than being *black men*, they had the nerve to pass judgment on my shaved head. If we were having a judging contest, they would've lost points long ago for missing teeth and keeping an outdated Jheri curl alive past extinction.

I was angry and that's not a good way to be on Route 66. The flood of people trying to get into DC on this two-lane highway was a joke. I turned up the radio and listened to the morning show with Olivia Fox and Russ Par. I flipped it off after hearing Mary J. moaning about someone being her everything. She'll suffer the consequences of making a man her "everything." I almost hit a silver blue Explorer as I attempted to exit. The horn startled me out of my trance.

I was thinking about the dream I had the night before. The dream started out with the familiar white cream, cool at first, being slathered all over my body, and I mean *all over*, and then turning hot, burning small holes in my skin. The figure standing over me as I lay on the white plastic-covered table asked, "Is it burning yet?" When I tried to speak, the sound wouldn't come out. I couldn't tell whoever it was that I was ready. That my body was searing with the heat of the chemical.

I shuddered with the thought. I didn't expect to have that dream ever again. Not since I'd taken action with the clippers. I ran my fingers across the nape of my neck. It reminded me of the feathers on a baby bird. I took my free hand and massaged my neck a little more. I missed Clint for those purposes. He was the best when it came to gentle massages, from my feet to my back and shoulders, even the whole body at times. Now I was working on myself. It wasn't the same.

By lunchtime I was ready to pack it in and go home, but I remembered my shopping date with Wendy. I grabbed my purse and tried to keep a low profile as I made my way out of the building. The sun was bright, making me reach for my sunglasses. Walking to O'Toole's was quicker than driving during the lunchtime rush. I was greeted by the host, who started to lead me toward the busiest area of the restaurant. I reached out and tugged his sleeve to point to the outdoor patio tables.

"I'm sorry, we don't have anyone on duty in that area yet." He checked his watch. "Not for another half hour."

"That's fine. I don't mind waiting." I wanted to sit as far away from people as possible. No matter how hard I tried to feel confident, I truly believed everyone was staring at me.

He seated me on the patio, handing me a menu. "I'll go ahead and take your order."

Thank you for being a mind reader, I thought, as he brought back the chicken and iced tea I'd ordered. I looked up and noticed Wendy coming toward me. She walked right past me. She stopped and then paced a little looking up and down Ninth Street. She looked at her watch, then straight ahead.

"Wendy," I called out. She turned around and looked right through me, sitting on the patio of O'Toole's restaurant. I waved first, then removed my Ray Bans. Her dark square sunglasses hid her honey-brown eyes, but I knew they were bugged out of her head. Her mouth fell open and she inhaled some air, but still no voice.

"It's me, girl." I smiled. "Well, don't tell me what you think. That's all right."

She did an about-face and walked around to the restaurant's main entrance pretending to be too ladylike to step over the white chain-link fence that encircled the outdoor seating area. Her thick scent of syrupy sweet perfume mixed with baby powder permeated the air around me.

"I can't believe you did it. You got balls. You got some serious balls." She stood over me, examining the contours and dips of my oval-shaped head.

"Well thanks, I think." I pushed the half-full platter of fried wings and celery to her. "I saved you some."

She sat down slowly, but quickly snapped out of it when a waft of the chicken caught her attention. She grabbed one of the tiny wings and plunged it into the accompanying blue cheese dressing.

"It looks good on you, but I still can't believe you did it." She removed every sliver of meat, giving it a last suck before throwing the bone down and grabbing another.

"I can't believe I did it either." I put my sunglasses back on just in case I momentarily welled up.

"What'd Clint say?"

"His opinion is the last I care about. I sent him packing over two weeks ago. Don't you listen to anything I tell you?"

"You did what?" She stopped licking her fingers. "You threw back a prime catch like Dr. Feelgood? Do you know how many sharks are out there, swimming the waters for a fine-ass man like that, and you go and throw him back in?"

"It wasn't working out." I leaned across the table so no one could overhear my shame. "I've been primping and polishing for him for over four years." I held up four fingers with my unpainted nails. "Not even a ring, Wendy. I'm sick of waiting."

"I don't care if you got to wait four more. You just don't go giving up no doctor, honey!" She raised her hand as if she was speaking the gospel. "I guess you weren't paying attention when the world announced 'the man shortage.' The drought is only going to get worse."

"It's too late now. My pride is at stake." I replaced the Burnt Clover lipstick that had been wiped off with the grease of the spicy chicken. Our area was filling with the lunch crowd. I could feel eyes boring into my scalp. I looked around to see who was staring, but there was not one soul looking our way. "Are you ready? We've got shopping to do, remember?"

She threw down the last bone and wiped her hands. "Tell me something, did you guys break up before or after you cut your hair?"

"Before. Why? What difference does that make?"

"Girl, you know how men feel about hair. We've had this discussion too many times for you not to know."

"Yes, I do know. Trust me, hair or no hair, he wasn't willing to commit. I held on as long as I could, Wendy. I couldn't do it anymore. I couldn't keep pretending I was happy just to be in his company. I needed more. So now I'm just happy with myself."

"Are you really?"

"Ecstatic," I lied. "I mean, really, you know how long I've wanted to stop the madness. I was only holding on because I knew how much he'd disapprove. I told you about those reports I read, how those chemicals we use are absorbed into our skin. I swear I think I'm going insane from having used that stuff for so long. I read another study on black girls and white girls, how forty percent of the black ones go into puberty way too early and start their periods at the age of ten and above. And only ten percent of the little white girls started their periods that early. And you know the earlier you start your period, the higher your chances are for ovarian cancer, and a number of other problems."

"How is getting your hair straightened going to make your period come early?" Wendy asked, almost afraid of the answer. I knew she was tired of my continuous preaching of one poison or another in our environment. My addiction to information always led me on research journeys. Last week it was the bleaching process of coffee filters, the week before that it was the cell phone rays penetrating our brain.

"It's not the relaxer, it's the stuff we use to keep the hair bouncing and behaving afterwards, like hair grease, fatty acids, animal protein. That's what those grease-laden hair products are made from, and I'm convinced that mess is absorbed into our system. We have been putting those products on our scalps since the turn of the century. Do you see little white children padded down with grease in their hair? Once it's absorbed into our bloodstream, our bodies can't tell the difference between oh-so-lovely-hair oil, and the saturated fat in a bowl of potato chips; it just knows there's fat. And what causes a young girl to begin menstruation, I'll tell you, it's fat. When her body reaches a certain percentage of body fat, the carnage begins. Then there's high blood pressure, hypertension—"

"Venus, you're right."

"I know I am. This is serious."

"Not about that. I mean about the fact that you are truly going insane." Wendy stood up, placing her sunglasses back over her light-tinted eyes. Her own black tresses were in long relaxed layers over her shoulders. I followed closely behind Wendy's long shapely frame and noticed the approving glances that a group of businessmen were throwing her way. I couldn't help but wish I was being admired as well.

"Oh yeah, that'll work." Wendy looked me over as I twisted and adjusted in the mirror. "Now you need a pair of four-inch-high hooker pumps to go with them."

I laughed out loud for the first time since my hair had been cut. "They would really think I flipped my lid if I walked into the office with these tight-ass pants. Did I tell you how everybody was tripping? Their mouths just about hit the floor when they saw me."

"Well, Venus, it was a shock. I mean, when you do something drastic like that, it's natural for people to assume you're a different person, or at the very least in a different state of mind." Wendy moved to the left side of the three-way mirror and started fingering her hair while she talked. "Damn, I'd just be nothing without my hair, and I admit it freely. I don't know how many times I've panicked when too much came out in the comb. Sidney would have a conniption fit if I came home without this hair. He sits in front of the TV when *Soul Train* comes on watching all those weaves flinging and booties twisting like it's the Super Bowl. And then there's the *BET* channel, Black Educational Training for all the future hoochies of America. Don't mess with him when he's getting his groove on with Rachel."

Wendy and Sidney had been childhood sweethearts and married for a full decade, and I couldn't remember her ever having anything nice to say about him, yet they were joined at the hip.

She hadn't noticed that I was already back in the dressing room doing my best not to hear her. I couldn't take it anymore. When I came out, she was still looking in the mirror finger-combing her hair.

"Where are the pants?" She looked me over from side to side to see which arm was holding them.

"I'm not going to get them. They're not my style."

"You're kidding. They looked good on you. I'm serious, Venus."

I had already started moving toward the escalator.

"Venus. Wait."

The store was filled with lunchtime shoppers, mostly women, strike that, only women, seeking out clothing that would make their mates happy, no doubt. I could hear Wendy behind me grumbling about the fact that she could've used her precious time more wisely than watching me play dress-up in Nordstrom's department store. I let her ramble on while I was thinking *if I woulda coulda, shoulda*. My father used to sing it to my brother and me every time we started whining about something we hadn't achieved or if the tide didn't flow in our direction. I could almost hear my father louder than the classic pianist centered in the middle of the store. "Stop making excuses for yourself. If I woulda, coulda, shoulda, the final words of a poor man." If I would've left Clint alone, not pressured him, maybe he would've come around. If I could've been more patient. But four years, four long years. He should've bought the ring.

"Are you listening to me, Venus?" I felt Wendy's long fingers gripped on my shoulder. "You're scaring me. You've been acting pretty strange lately. We've got to talk." She looked down to adjust her gold watch. "I don't have time right now, but call me tonight when you get home. I mean it, Venus. Call me." Wendy disappeared past the cosmetics and accessories.

@   @   @

Three Wrongs
Don't Make
a Right

"SHERRI, WHO IS HE?" I LEANED OVER THE OAK
veneer into her space, keeping my eye on the
well-groomed specimen walking swiftly down
the hall with John and Lenny trailing on his side, sadly trying to keep up.

If anyone had the 411, it would be Sherri.

"That's Tyson Edwards. He's here from St. John's Cosmetics. He's
the son-in-law of Clarence St. John. Girl, where have you been?"

She kept herself busy typing, not missing a beat as she spoke. "St. John's
just bought up the black hair-care line from Revlure. Don't you read *Jet*
magazine? It was in the business section for at least three weeks in a row."

I was glad she hadn't looked up to see the expression on my face. I
didn't even know *Jet* was still being published in the nineties. Twenty
years ago, that was what one read to stay in the know. I couldn't wait to

lock myself in Aunt Sandra's bathroom when we would visit her in Fox Hills. She received her weekly publication of *Jet* faithfully with stars of *Good Times*, *The Jeffersons*, or occasionally, a music group on the cover. I'd separate them chronologically in a neat little stack on the floor and peruse them one at a time to find out what our black celebrities were doing and who they were doing it with. I'd always get interrupted by someone needing to use the bathroom at the exact moment when I'd found the "picture of the week." These days you could get that information from the mainstream magazines like *People*, *Style*, and *Us*. And the new generation had all the hip-hop publications like *Source* and *Vibe*.

Sherri continued talking. "See, it's usually those big white companies buying up our businesses. But not this time." She let out a little grunt. "No, not this time."

She stopped typing to answer the phone. I had already beelined to my office. It was exciting news, but I didn't know for whom. My head was whirling with possibilities. I made it known to John and Lenny more than a year ago that I wanted to move into an executive account manager position. There'd been no change. But this seemed like the perfect opportunity. If we were signing on with St. John's, that opened the door for a much-needed conversation.

I sent a quick e-mail to Ray. He would take it personally if I bypassed him. He lived for a groveling employee. Me needing him would make his day.

Ray,
    Let's have lunch tomorrow. Please make time for me.
    It's important.
Venus

I clicked the send button and started making out my list. I know the product line. I've used the products. I am the product. I reached for the result of all those products and my hand landed on the baby-fine after-math. I rubbed my nearly bald head and went into a miniature panic. This is not happening. I laid my head on the edge of my white Formica desk and inhaled and exhaled slowly. It doesn't matter. I repeated it over and over. I'm still the best person for the job.

The reply from Ray was instant, almost too quick. The little cartoon caricature waddled across the screen holding up a sign "you have mail." I wondered what Ray really did all day in his Olympic-sized office.

Venus,
    Why wait for tomorrow? I don't have any plans now.
Ray

The phone rang simultaneously.

"Venus Johnston," I answered professionally, even though the short double rings indicated an in-house call.

"It's Ray, Venus."

"Oh, Ray. I was just reading your e-mail. I didn't mean to snatch your attention right away. It can honestly wait until tomorrow."

"No, it's okay."

"All right. Have you been to the Beijing Park Restaurant over on Fifth?"

"No. They just opened up, right?"

"About six months ago. The food is good, though." I pulled out my pen to write the time on my calendar out of habit.

"I'll swing by your office and we'll leave from there."

As we passed the front lobby I told Sherri I'd be back around three-thirty. I didn't think it was strange when Ray said he would be out for the rest of the day. I waited inside the downstairs lobby for Ray to pull up with his vintage Volvo. The rain hadn't stopped coming down since morning.

He jumped out of the car with an umbrella and escorted me to his car. Having the door opened for me was a small courtesy I'd forgotten about. He got in on his side bringing the smell of rain and the familiarity of Aramis.

"You knew that message you left on my e-mail was going to eat at me all day. I had to know what was on your mind. You can't pique my interest and then expect me to wait patiently till tomorrow." Ray guided the car up Constitution Avenue.

I stared at his mane of black-and-gray hair neatly trimmed around his ears. I really hadn't noticed before, but he actually had a strong Richard Gere thing going for him.

"It's not anything juicy. I just heard through the grapevine that a new account was coming in, and that there *might* be a need for a new account manager. I wanted to be first in line. I've got the skills, and experience." There, I said it. My hands were tingling and my face felt warm from the rush of self-consciousness that comes from blowing your own horn, but at least it was out there. I did my part.

"I didn't know you were interested in becoming an account manager." He looked over my way, but turned before I could meet his gaze. I caught myself looking at his profile again; his defining feature was most certainly the strength of his jaw and chin.

"John and Lenny knew. They may have forgotten. I brought it up to them when Jessica left the company back in January. I thought they needed someone to replace her, but they never did."

He pulled into the covered garage across from the restaurant. What little light the day offered was replaced by a blanket of darkness. He turned on his headlights and followed the orange reflection cones to the lower level. I didn't want to speak again while he seemed to be concentrating on finding a parking spot. He slid the gear and pulled the final brake and turned off the engine. The parking spot he chose was a good walking distance from the elevator and it was obvious no one else found this side appealing. I reached for the door handle and his hand landed on mine.

"Wait." The weight of his arm and shoulder pinned me back. "Let me get the door for you."

He got out, ran around to the other side, and opened the door. He extended his hand and I took it. He pulled me straight up so my feet never touched the ground. Suddenly, I was out of the car being held face-to-face with Ray. He squeezed me tight with one arm around my waist and used the other to fondle my behind with a slickness that shocked me, more so than the actual act.

The kiss was hard at first, until my lips were pried open. His tongue searched the inside of my mouth looking for a connection. He slid me down the length of his body, still pressing me hard against him. I could feel him surging somewhere near my waist. When I could feel the ground underneath my feet, I took a dizzy step back. His breath and wetness were still on my face. I wiped the moistness away with both hands. He came toward me again but I pushed him back.

"Ray, stop."

"Why? Why are you pushing me away?" His voice was low and dark. Unrecognizable, not his usual mild manner. "Venus, I've known for some time how you feel about me." He moved toward me again. "The feeling is mutual."

"Wait a minute. What are you talking about, how I feel about you?" I pushed him back again. If the fear I felt was showing in my face, I'd be an easy victim.

"I don't think you need to worry about someone seeing us. Is that what's stopping you?" He reached for my head to pull me toward him. I slipped underneath his arm only to feel him pull me back by the arm.

"What the hell's going on, Venus? Don't tell me this is not what you had in mind for our *lunch date*." He let the words flow through his half smiling, half serious face.

I spoke phonetically like I was talking to one of the Haitian students I had tutored in the past. "Ray, if you believe I have feelings for you, I mean anything beyond our professional relationship, you're wrong."

He looked flabbergasted. "I don't believe this. *Our professional relationship*, you've been after *me*, for Christ's sake!" The spray of his words landed on my lips. "Nothing more than a professional relationship? I'm not crazy, Venus. Don't play that game with me. What, what is it? You think I'm going to tell?" Ray's voice softened while he cupped my face with his hands. "It'll be between you and me. We can go to the Berkshire. It's two blocks away. No one will see us. I swear."

I surprised myself by actually considering it, imagining the feel of his stainless raw body, naked, against mine. My face meshed into his dark thick hair, the perpetual smell of a fresh Herbal Essence shampoo. His moist lips the color of bubblegum searching my body for a place to suckle. Would he be different from the intense energy of Clint, of every black man I'd ever experienced? I blinked the picture out of my mind.

"Ray, I'm sorry for the miscommunication. Let's just call it a misunderstanding." I slowly guided his trembling hands down away from my face. I eased myself into the car without turning my back to him. My heart was racing. The sweat forming on my head had nowhere to hide. The humidity in the garage had made it impossible to breathe.

He started the car and drove recklessly out of the parking garage, into the light of day. I rolled the window down and let the rain spray my face. The rush of air hit me as if I'd been submerged underwater for too long. He let me out in front of our office building and took off, screeching his tires as he pulled away. I noticed a few people staring. I wondered if anyone could sense that his hands were still on me, my cheek, squeezing my butt. Maybe I was wearing my fear and humiliation like a cloak. I walked quickly through the lobby to the garage and to the security of my own car. I sat while I tried to figure out what to do next. I knew that I had subconsciously given him the green light. It came from underneath. It dwelled in a place that begged for approval. Somewhere deep inside I needed Ray at that moment to tell me I was desirable. I could only point the finger at myself. I knew I wasn't responsible for his style of doing things, but I definitely would have to swallow his motivation. I was a victim of my own hidden agenda. When my eyesight cleared from the fog of tears, I began my drive home. Thank God it was Friday.

The ringing of the phone woke me. Clint's voice was on the other end sounding angry.

"So now you seeing homeboy from your office?"

"What are you talking about?"

"I stopped by your office today, wanted to see if we could do lunch—just in time to see you get the white glove treatment by homeboy. So what, you seeing him now?"

"I don't know what you think you saw, and besides, it's none of your business who I'm seeing." I slammed the phone down and pulled the cover over my head. My eyes were still stinging from the last bout of tears, but I couldn't hold it in. I cried harder from the thought that anyone seeing Ray and me together could define us as a *couple*. Did I have that look on my face? Was I smiling like a giddy young girl on her first date?

The phone rang again and I let the machine pick it up. Three more times it rang, and three more times I knew it was Clint. How could I explain what I'd just been through? Neither Clint, nor anyone else, would believe I was an innocent victim, knowing how easily a woman can give mixed signals and how hard it is to slam on the brakes once the light says green. I was better off keeping my mouth shut, and burying it deep with the rest of the bones I had hidden.

Clint slammed the phone down, enraged. Still, he had no right to call her on it, even after what he saw today. He remembered Ray Chambers from last year when Venus invited Clint to her company Christmas party. Ray Chambers spent the majority of his idle chitchat in Venus's face, talking too close. Clint personally didn't play that touchy-feely mess. But he didn't want to embarrass Venus in front of her office stiffs. She was straight corporate around those suits and ties.

He'd seen her transformation go into action every time she was around the pointed-toe club. Her voice would lower into a cryptic monotone. Her laugh would come out fake and hollow when one of them let out a joke without a punch line. If that's where she wanted to be, he couldn't stop her. Clint never could get into the split personality thing, acting and talking one way around family and friends, then turning into someone your own mama wouldn't recognize just to have a conversation with some white folks. He'd never seen the advantage to it. Once Clint had learned that all white people didn't smell like the Downy fabric softener he'd seen in those commercials, he lost the enchantment. He felt no urge to try to impress them.

He played with the torn piece of paper with Kandi's number scribbled on it as he sat hunched on his badly sunken-in sofa. He didn't know much about her. She did say she was unattached. That was more than enough information. It wasn't like he was looking for a long-term relationship. He just needed someone who could preoccupy his mind until Venus became a faint memory.

Clint held the scribbled telephone number uneasily in his hands, contemplating the decision to call. It had been a while since he had to use his one-liners. What should he say that wouldn't make him look desperate? He knew it was against the brotherhood rules to call a lady before twenty-four hours had passed, hell, in most cases a solid week. He would be breaking the players' code of conduct, showing too much interest too soon. He didn't want to come off like a brother without skills. If a lady thought you were too desperate, she'd run in the other direction no matter how much he had working for him.

Maybe Venus was reacting to too much attention. He'd been calling her and sweating her, making himself look like a fool. It was only natural that she would keep pushing him away. He'd had enough. Here's to new starts, he told himself as he picked up the phone and dialed the number on the small piece of paper.

"Kandi, how ya doing, this is Clint. Hope you didn't forget me already."

"No, are you kidding? Actually I wanted to call you but I didn't get your number. I had been hoping you would call and when I saw that the machine wasn't blinking I got worried that maybe you weren't interested." Her voice was like a soothing drink, the kind that intoxicates you before it reaches your stomach.

"I was thinking we should get together this evening. Are you free?" he asked with a fabricated confidence.

"Sure. What'd you have in mind?"

I don't know. Maybe round two. That's what I'm thinking, but I'm not going to be that crass.

"Do you like gumbo, crab, catfish, that kind of thing?" he asked.

"Now you're talking."

"Frannie's, this place in Maryland. They've got some Creole food out of this world."

"I'm there. Do you want me to pick you up?" she asked.

"No, let's make it a real date this time. I'll pick you up."

The drive to pick up Kandi was spent listening to every sad song available to humanity. Why on this night was it baby-take-me-back, please, night? It seemed like every station had a brother with a heartbreak on programming. He lowered the volume so he could hear himself think.

It was scary being alone. There was too much time to analyze all the stupid things he'd done in the past, like letting Venus go. That was probably the biggest mistake he'd made in long time. She was everything he'd ever wanted: beautiful, smart, educated. What more could he have asked for? He could feel the regret the minute he had picked up his jacket and walked out her door. But how much longer was he going to sit up there and let her tell him he would be nothing without her? Marry me or else. How much longer could he take the "you owe me" speech? He was the one busting his ass around the clock. He was the one making the grades and doing the time. He couldn't think of anything that compared with the mind drain he'd experienced in the past four years. Medical school was an up at dawn and not down until way past dusk experience. Any creative thought he ever had was replaced with suffixes and prefixes of Latin lingo, meshed with organic molecules, slashed with scientific credo, "to not believe anything, unless it could be proven," putting faith, charity, and love at a cruel disadvantage. He had given Venus what was left, which obviously hadn't been enough. ". . . And one step further and my back will break, if my best isn't good enough, then how can it be good enough for two, I can't work any harder than I do." George Michael was singing the story of his life. Clint turned the radio off as he pulled in front of Kandi's building.

She was standing in the lit lobby with her face practically full-fledge against the glass doors. Her black leather jacket cinched at her waist and showed off her long shapely legs in black leggings and matching ankle boots. He parked a ways up and walked back to the lobby door. Kandi's face crept into a smile when she saw him approaching. She quickly tried to mask her anticipation by stepping away from the window and turning to admire the outdated wallpaper.

"How ya doing?" He felt awkward greeting her with only a kiss on the cheek after the no-limit sex they'd shared the other evening.

"Fine. Good to see you. I didn't want you to miss the building. It's easy to pass this place."

"Aah, is that it? Maybe you just couldn't wait to see me." His confidence was on a steady rise.

She let the full smile she'd been suppressing bloom.

"I am *very* happy to see you." Kandi's full lips spread the distance of her face. She grabbed his hand and they walked to the car.

He didn't take the chance of turning the radio back on. He slipped in a tape of Cassandra Wilson. No one could tell what she was singing about.

⟲   ⟲   ⟲

Just
Another
Bad Dream

I'D BEEN SOAKING IN MY OVAL TUB all day. My hands and feet were shriveled up but I didn't care. The smell of the lavender oil in the water was keeping me there, tranquil, quiet.

It was all being interrupted by Sarah yelling into my answering machine. Her loud brash voice could carry through concrete.

"Venus, it's me. Pick up. Venus de Milo. Call me when you get in. I need to pick up your deposit for the African American Positive Association awards dinner. Remember AAPA? We've missed you, girl. Call me."

I dunked my head several times into the warm water. I could do that now without worrying that my hair would look like a wet rat after getting out. *Yes, this was certainly what I called freedom.*

I wished I could wash away the last month of my life and just start over, but it was impossible to change the past. I guess Clint had given up on me. Now I was feeling the loss.

Before, I was brazen, life was a new frontier waiting to be conquered. I had high hopes for this adventure called freedom. Almost the way you feel when you get your first apartment and you tell your parents "so long." The high comes crashing down as soon as you realize there's nobody around to scold or reward. With it comes the realization that the people you were so desperately trying to get away from are the ones who gave you definition and character, a daughter, a friend, a sister. All the things that describe who you are. You can't be a daughter without a parent, you can't be a friend without friends, you can't be anything without the other. It's the yin and yang of life, and I was here without yang.

My yang was probably out discovering that all women do not need a full glass of wine before they can get their groove on. He'd probably also discovered that his English grammar *is* perfect and didn't need to be corrected as often as I'd led him to believe. It would be so typical that some cleanup woman would come around and dust off the diamond I'd been polishing for over four years and think she'd done something extraordinary.

Once again I pulled myself underneath the warm bath water and stayed a few seconds longer this time. If I was crying, I did not know. I assumed the stinging pain in my eyes came from the fragranced water.

I don't know when I decided to get in my car and drive to Clint's place, if it was in between my head soakings, or after I'd consumed my midnight snack of a whole can of sticky caramel popcorn and washed it down with two liters of Pepsi. Sugar was the root of a lot of my evil. Tonight I wasn't out to do evil; I just wanted to see what the other half was doing. I had on my Howard University sweatshirt and sweatpants that were five times too big. My baseball cap sat low on my forehead; even on the smallest notch it was still too large. I purposely didn't wear any makeup or earrings. I was taking advantage of my ability to look androgynous, with my boy haircut and sloppy sweats. I was undercover. If Clint saw me at a glance, he wouldn't know who or what I was.

I had to show ID to get through his parking structure. No big deal, it wasn't written in stone anywhere who came through at what time to see who. I parked and walked quickly through the thick dark air to his brick building. I really didn't know what I was going to accomplish. What kind of satisfaction, if any, would I get from staring at his yellowed front door or hazy stained window, or what kind of satisfaction would I receive seeing him with another woman? Wasn't that what I was looking for?

I crept up each stair quietly. When I got to his door, I knocked softly. It hurt my knuckles so I used my key ring to tap again. I jumped when he swung the door open and stood there, rubbing his face and eyes. He looked me up and down before letting me in. I guess my disguise was a success.

"V, what's up?" He genuinely wanted to know.

"Hi. I was in the area and thought I'd stop by." I couldn't help but stare at his dark tight chest. He was wearing a pair of white knit boxers. The contrast of the white against the twist and turns of his muscular dark thighs made my knees shaky.

"Come on in. Just in the area at five in the morning, huh?"

Ignoring his sarcasm, I stepped into the dark stale room and immediately felt sorry for him. I sent him from the comfort of my ethnically decorated abode, to this equivalent of a roach motel. His sofa bed was extended and ruffled with pasty white sheets and a brown knotty blanket. My first instinct was to pull it all off and do a load of laundry.

"No maid service?" I asked.

He let out a gruff laugh. "No luxuries over here."

"I just wanted to apologize for the way I've been acting. I know I haven't been very reasonable to you." I kept my hands stashed in my sweatshirt pockets, with my fingers crossed. I just wanted this bad dream to be over and for us to start all over.

He was truly surprised by my apology. He sat down still rubbing the back of his neck.

"Damn, V. To tell you the truth, I don't even know what we were fighting about." He came over to the rickety little chair that couldn't hold one more pound of weight, his or mine. "I missed you." He leaned into my face and kissed me. It was brief but effective.

I kissed him back, this time longer. His hands found their way around my waist, massaging the lower part of my back and slipping into my pants. I didn't want him to stop. He wasn't the only one that could do a little traveling. I started with his chest and around to his wide back and down his backside. His mouth never left mine, but still, we found our way into his scrambled bed. I tossed the sloppy fleece and turned into a naked feline, crawling all over him, licking him in spots I hadn't licked before. His lean muscular body was so finely tuned. There was no area unpolished. He gleamed in the faint light that crept through the ragged curtains. He pulled me down on top of him, then rolled us over to take control of my body. His large hands circled my hips and waist. The moment he entered me, I wanted to scream. I held on tight as he took his time, rocking us back and forth, holding me tighter. I didn't want it to end. This was where he belonged, inside of me. He let out a hoarse moan, gripping my thighs with his hands. I braced myself for the power of his final thrust. He sent his body hard into mine. I didn't want to let him go. I didn't want it to be over.

I stayed nestled in his big chest with my legs entangled in his. It felt like a retreat. My safe asylum.

"Did you almost give up on me?" I spoke into his chest, playing with the sparse hairs.

"Nah. I knew you'd snap out of it." He kissed me on the forehead and let his large hand encompass my whole head.

"I'm glad. I don't think I could've made it without you. I think I'm about to have a rocky time at Donnely Kramer."

"Why, what happened? Is it homeboy?" His body tensed, making his chest and arm muscles protrude slightly more.

"Kind of, but it's not what you were thinking. Ray Chambers and I do not have a relationship and never have. But . . ." The words were getting lost in my throat.

"Tell me." He pulled me up so we were face-to-face.

"We kind of had an incident. I mean he came on to me and I pushed him away. That kind of thing can get real complicated in an office. I just don't know where it might lead. I don't even know if I'm going to have a job Monday morning."

"Damn, V. Homeboy pushin' up on you? What'd he do? I mean was he touching you, did he try to kiss you?"

"Something like that."

"You don't have to put up with that shit. Man, I'd get tossed out on my ass if I pulled some shit like that. I knew he wasn't no good. I knew it."

"I know, but this is different. I mean . . . with him being as high up in the company and everything." The part I left out was that I'm the one who left the door open for this mess to happen in the first place. The guilt I felt was eating a hole in my gut.

"V, I know you. And, when you get mad, Miss Demure turns into the Incredible Hulk." He hugged me tight. "Just let it go for right now." He planted more kisses on my smooth, velvety head. I felt loved and cared for, something I missed terribly.

We stayed in his bed until my tender body couldn't take it anymore. The springs in the mattress were making permanent markings on my thighs.

"Are there shower facilities in your barrack?"

He smiled and rolled over, as if it wasn't a serious question. There was just no telling what was in that bathroom. I pulled the scratchy brown blanket with me and tiptoed on the cold floor to the bathroom. It wasn't as bad as I'd feared. There was a shower door, instead of a mold-infested curtain; I was grateful for that. I leaned in and turned on all three knobs since I couldn't tell which did what.

I stepped inside and let the steaming hot water pound me. I used his oatmeal soap scented with *Michael Jordan* cologne. Once again I was bathing myself, trying to wash away my thoughts. I let the water hit my face full force. Even after the intense lovemaking Clint and I had just experienced, there was still a significant hole that wouldn't fill. I knew this feeling well, just like getting on a bike and riding, or the ease of talking to a friend after a long silence. You just jump back in and pick up where you left off, like no time had passed in between. Yes, I knew this feeling too well, and it wasn't acceptable. I didn't want things to go back to the way they were. Clint and I had met on common ground, here, in bed. Our bodies came together, but our minds had not. We were still operating under separate expectations. Nothing had really changed. We were still deadlocked on life's choices.

I stepped out of the shower, dripping.

"Clint, I need a towel." I yelled out again, "Clint."

He opened the door, holding an abused, traveled-looking thing.

I took it and patted gently. I didn't want to leave any skin on the towel. When I bent over to dry my calves and ankles, a black shiny object wedged between the sink and toilet caught my eye. I recognized it as my own. St. John's makeup line was the only one that used this packaging with the black plastic case and the silver and gold exaggerated "S" symbol. It looked like it belonged to me, but I'd never been in this bathroom before. I opened it, hoping it had been mixed up in Clint's things when he moved out of my place.

The too-light shade of peach was a slap in the face. It was a color I would never own, not even by accident. I closed it and laid it on top of the closed toilet seat. When I opened the bathroom door I could hear his voice get lower, before hanging up the phone.

"How was your shower?" He came over and kissed me between the eyes as I stood with the shredded towel not completely making it around my dripping body.

I looked at him, straight through him, and said, "Fine." That's it. That's all I said. Just fine. Everything is just fine. I kissed him good-bye after I got dressed and told him I had a lot of work to finish at home. He said he was back on rotation tomorrow morning and this was our last chance to spend some quality time together. He wanted to come home with me and spend the rest of his time off at my place. I don't know what I said after that.

All I remembered was being back home, alone, staring at my bronze and taupe sponge-painted walls, trying to find all the points where there was too much paint, where the first application started. On some spots where too much paint had landed and dried, I had conveniently placed the art of Henry O. Tanner and Synthia St. James. Gold frames surrounded my investments, lending them even more value. It was all so perfect. And with all its fine detail, I was still disappointed. I wanted to add more white to the walls, to brighten them up. The room was too dark, no matter how wide I pulled the curtains, or how bright the bulb was in my lamps, it was still too dark. I decided I must paint, start over, with a new canvas. I stared at the walls until my head became heavy and I dozed off.

The cream was slathered thick. The hand dipped into the large white tube to scoop some more. "Relax," the voice says. "Is it burning yet?"

The massage feels good, rubbing, smoothing.

"It's hot now," I say. "You can rinse me, it's hot now. Please."

I scream, "It's hot, it's burning."

The voice only laughs hysterically, insisting just a few minutes more, and then I'll be ready. But by then it'll be too late. Please get it out. It's burning.

I was awakened by Sandy's moist breath. She sniffed my face, grazing me with her wet nose. "Thank you, girl." I reached over and scratched her behind her ears. "Thanks for waking me out of that one," I whispered while patting her on the head. I reached up and patted my own, confirming there were no red patches where it felt like my head was on fire only moments ago. Just another bad dream.

Never Kiss
and Tell

WHEN HE SAW THE COMPACT sitting there, right there, in plain sight, he felt like he'd swallowed the whole damn canary. He knew Venus had laid it there. Clint could kick himself for not having picked it up himself the first time he'd seen it. It must have fallen from Kandi's purse when he dumped everything out in the sink the other night. Hindsight is twenty-twenty. Who knew Venus would ever darken that bathroom door?

Venus didn't say a word, but leaving it there, sitting like a work of art resting on an easel gave him instant understanding. She didn't give him a chance to state his case. When he and Kandi got together, he and Venus were considered null and void. He wasn't doing anything wrong. But here Venus comes, all after the fact, showing up with her goodwill and apology. Now, it's his fault, even though she's the one who initiated this whole mess. What was he supposed to do, sit around on his hands and knees begging forever?

Clint picked up the phone and left the first message. "I'm sorry about what you found in the bathroom. I know how it looks; you're wrong."

The second message was almost as pathetic.

"V, you know I'm not like that. I was sure we were through before I even met someone else." After he hung up, he wished he knew her code to the machine so he could erase it. The third message was to cover up the second one.

"V, I met someone, but there ain't nothing to it. Please call me." And the fourth message was to cover for the last one. And on and on, it seemed like there was no way out. He couldn't clean it up no matter what he said. He should've just denied everything, "*don't know where that thing came from, could've been there when I moved in.*" But Venus was no fool. She mastered the lie detection skills a long time ago. One truth could shatter glass faster than ten lies. The math didn't add up.

Yeah, I met someone, she's fine I'll give her that, damn fine, but she's not you. I love you and I don't want to fight anymore. I'll even go further than that, let's get married. Hell, I'll marry you tomorrow, let's just stop playing games. That's what he would say if he had the guts. He didn't though. He didn't have the strength, or the weakness, to give himself over that way. He cleared the lump in his throat, made peace with himself, and called Venus one more time. This time no machine, it only rang twenty times. *I give up.*

Kandi was hoping he was just worn out from all the fun and late hours they'd been keeping the last couple of nights.

"Girl, what'd you expect? You gotta make them work a little." Lena shoved another set of clothes to the right to get a better look at the selection.

"It wasn't like that, Lena. There was no game playing. We went out to dinner last night. He was a perfect gentleman. He didn't ask to come in afterwards. He walked me to the door and kissed my hand goodnight and left like a prince on his horse." Kandi adjusted the Ann Taylor bags on her arm so she could thumb through the clearance rack in Macy's.

"Well, I guess he got what he wanted the night before and didn't need anymore." Lena had a way of telling the hard ugly truth. She simply left out tactfulness.

"That's my point. He didn't have to take me to dinner last night. He didn't even have to call for that matter. I just can't figure him out. We had the perfect date. Then when I call, he doesn't have time to talk."

"Maybe he *is* just tired. What's there to figure out?" Lena was holding up a lime-green suit from last season to her chestnut skin highlighted by her blond and gold streaked hair. "Just give him some time. He'll call. Stop stressing out over this guy. You've known him for what, twenty-four hours, and you expect him to devote his every waking hour to your presence?" She reached over the rack and put her hand on Kandi's arm. "Get a grip, honey."

Kandi was trying to stay cool and not think about the night before when Clint had practically hung up on her when she'd called to tell him what a great time she'd had on their one official date. Lena was right, she was expecting way too much.

"I'm trying to be sane and reasonable, but I'm afraid he's going to get away. It's the same philosophy for shopping, if you find a great deal on the rack, if you don't scoop it up today, it might not be there when you come back for it tomorrow." Kandi knew she wasn't making sense. Comparing him to an off-the-rack bargain was nuts. Anyone could see Clint was quality in the making. He was a man, solid and grounded. Whatever was holding him back would have to be dealt with gently, one step at a time. The layers were thick. It was obvious he would be no easy catch.

"You're right. I've got to have this." Lena held up the bright lime-green jacket to her body again.

"Lena, it's not true in all cases. Please don't buy that suit."

Lena sucked on her teeth and rolled her eyes, restoring it to its home with the rest of last year's collection. "You watch. This style is going to come back this spring, and I'm going to kick your butt for talking me out of it."

Kandi suddenly wasn't in the shopping mood anymore. There was so much work to be done.

Stop, in the Name of Love

AFTER MUCH THOUGHT AND CON-
templation, I walked straight into
Ray's office and told him we
needed to talk. He surprised me with a single white long-stem rose and
told me he was sorry. It was as if he knew I was going to be the first person he saw on that Monday morning. Before I'd even sat down he
reached inside his desk and handed me the flower.

"I didn't want anyone to see it, so I hid it in the drawer. May be a
little bruised."

"Ray, this wasn't necessary." I sniffed it carefully. One of the yellowed petals floated to the floor.

"Yes, it was. That's my gesture of friendship. I overstepped my bounds
and I apologize. You were kind enough not to punch me in the face,

which is what I deserved. I had a long weekend to think about it." He leaned back in his chair. He was waiting for my next move.

"Thank you. Your apology is accepted. I'm sorry too for being—"

"You didn't do anything. Let's just drop it right here. I'm going to talk to John and Lenny first time I get a chance. It's the St. John's account. That's the one you were referring to, correct?"

I sat down in one of the wide-back chairs in front of his desk, sinking deeper into the cushion than I expected. "Yes. What do you think my chances are?"

"Frankly, Venus, I don't know. I honestly haven't been given any information on this account. I usually don't get things past my desk until after the deals are already made. The only thing I can promise you is that I'll put in a positive word about your interest."

"Thanks, Ray. I appreciate it." I stood up and hesitated. I put my hand out. We held hands in truce for a few seconds longer than necessary. I walked to my office holding the white rose as if I'd just been crowned Miss America.

"Good morning, Venus."

"Good morning, Sherri. How are you?" I knew better than to ask that question but I was feeling generous.

"Girl, my sixteen-year-old, Marcus, brought home some little tramp last night. I almost knocked him senseless. Told him he was going to have to take that somewhere else, 'cause I wasn't having it. I asked that little girl if her mama knew what she was doing, out here in the middle of the night. She just looked at me, like I was talking some foreign gibberish. Just no respect. I don't know what the world is coming to, she couldn't have been no more than thirteen or fourteen, with her little tight pants and stomach all showing. That's why the Lord never gave me a daughter, 'cause we'd be fighting, rolling on the ground, before I let a child of mine walk out the door dressed like a prostitute. I mean, really, have you seen the clothes these children are wearing when they go to school, high heels, miniskirts— Oh, good morning, Dominick."

She paused for him to walk by. "He sure is a cute little something. Venus, how come you don't give him the time of day?"

"Sherri, he's not my type."

"Oh, excuse me. Not rich enough for ya." She threw up her hand in a snooty fashion and commenced to answer her own question. "Maybe not, but he sure is a little cutie. If I was ten years younger, I'd put a hurtin' on him myself."

I giggled all day at the thought, picturing Sherri tossing Dominick around like a Kewpie doll.

She went back to her station and started answering phones and storing information into that computerized rumor mill of hers.

I started putting together some ideas for the St. John's account. I knew it was premature, but I wanted to be prepared when I had a chance to speak to John and Lenny. I chipped at the white paint that was lodged underneath my cuticles from sponging white paint all over the walls.

I drifted in thought, wondering what Clint's conquest looked like. She had to be very light skinned to be wearing that awful color blush. I knew his type. I was his type at one time, my slick relaxed mane worn with a part on the side, with the thick lips, lush dark eyes, and the reconstructed arched brow. I cringed at the thought. She probably resembled the lighter-shade Barbie named Aisha or something. I tried to concentrate on the task at hand. Making mental pictures of Clint's possible women choices was destructive.

When the phone rang I picked it up on the first ring, glad for the distraction. It was Sarah, asking me if I was still going to the African American Positive Association awards dinner.

I hesitated. If I said no, I'd have to explain about Clint and I breaking up. If I said yes, I would get out of a long unnecessary explanation, but I'd be committing $250 for tickets that I had no plans on using.

Wendy came over about an hour early, ready to go, and nearly fell over on her stiletto heels when she saw me, fresh faced, with only a dab of lipstick and some eyeliner. She was determined to make me shine, especially if she was going to be my escort. "Natural beauty doesn't exist, sweetie, unless you're still counting your age by months."

I was wearing a gold sleek clingy number I had bought last year. I had dressed without the excitement that usually comes with preparing for a night on the town. I hadn't wanted to go, but when Sarah had squealed on the phone that I was a nominee for volunteering at the King Jr. Community Center, I felt obligated. Someone out there thought of me as a stand-out kind of gal and I didn't want to cause any disappointment by not showing up.

Wendy did the finishing touches on my makeup.

"You look gorgeous, Venus." She dusted a light powder over my face while I sat with my eyes closed, thinking of various excuses for Clint not being on my arm. Wendy was my date even though getting her to come took a promissory note to watch Tia and Jamal while she and Sidney took a weekend off. That was an easy trade. Her children were my children, at least until I had my own.

"Okay, you can look now."

The person staring back at me was someone I didn't recognize. Was that my nose looking slimmed down by magnitudes? Were those my eyes, large and erotic? Not that I was chicken liver to begin with, but this was amazing. Wendy stood next to me like a proud mother sending her daughter off to the prom.

"Wendy, you are an artist, girl."

"Looks good, doesn't it?" Wendy licked her thumb and went toward my face.

"Uuh uh, what are you doing?" I had to stop her by grabbing her hand. "Please don't put your saliva on my face." We both laughed.

"I was just trying to get that little smudge off your eye." She leaned in over me. "Right there."

I felt the moistness and let out a howl. "Wendy, you are nasty."

The valet driver opened my side first and gave me an approving once-over with his eyes hung low. He watched my candlelit shimmering Hanes leg stretch out of the too-high slit as I stepped out of the car. Wendy and I walked into the huge banquet room with seating for hundreds, maybe close to a thousand. I couldn't tell. It had been a while since I'd been to a formal gala.

On every white linen tablecloth sat a centerpiece of roses with beautiful china and crystal goblets traced with gold. Wendy was impressed as well. We both stood in the middle of the floor filled with pride that our people were capable of such class and sophistication, and that we could actually afford to be a party to it.

Wendy turned to me, "Is this place laid out, or what?"

"It's nice, very nice." The lighting was set low with the chandeliers overhead imitating candles. I had a sudden wish for Clint to be by my side. He would love this.

"Let's get our seats so we can watch the rest of the people come in." Wendy kept the small seating assignment card in her hand, looking at it, and back at the tables, as if she couldn't remember it if she tried. "102, 107 . . . there it is, 111." We were positioned near the front center of the room. There was no one else at our table yet, so it looked even larger.

Wendy wasted no time getting her compact out and checking her makeup. I fidgeted with the swan-shaped napkin.

"What would you like to drink, madam?" A clean-cut young man approached us, dressed with a black bow tie and white shirt. He held a tray with water and coffee.

"What are my choices?"

"You can have anything you want, water, coffee, something from the bar."

"I'll take a Chablis."

"And I'll have the same," Wendy added.

Guests trickled in. The room was filling up nicely. The shimmering dresses and black ties gave a regal ambience. Elegant spiral curls and French twists held up with sparkling combs were the flavor of the evening. I caught myself wishing I had a few dangling curls of my own. But Wendy assured me I looked like the actress married to Will Smith. Even better, she added, "You've got my finishing touch all over your face."

The jazz trio started mixing tempos and rhythms. It was more than music, it was the setting. A full-figured diva was crooning sultry tunes that blended in with the bass of the cello.

"There she is." Sarah was walking over with her arms out preparing for a hug. "You made it." She stood a shoulder and head taller than me when I stood. "You look mah-ve-lous," she mocked in her deep raspy voice that most men found sexy.

I turned to introduce her to Wendy. They politely shook hands, but I knew there was no chemistry. Sarah's loud voice and even louder cleavage always made other women take a step back. She had the kind of personality and presence that demanded space and attention.

"Hi, I'm Sarah Philips, the secretary for AAPA."

"Nice to meet you." Wendy went back to surveying the clientele as they entered the room.

Sarah turned her attention back to me. "Where's Clint?"

"He couldn't make it, he's on call."

"Well, he's missing something fierce tonight because you look good, girl! I'm proud of you." She eyeballed my modest hair while she was speaking. "Takes a strong sister to make that move. I hope you win tonight. You really do deserve it." She squeezed me with her long, strong arms.

"Thanks, Sarah. Thanks."

"So what is this club you're in, Apple?" Wendy asked with one eyebrow up.

"A-A-P-A stands for African American Positive Association. That's why we're here, remember?"

"Well, do you have to shave your head to be a member?" Wendy was referring to Sarah's short natural style that she'd worn ever since I'd known her. Sarah had only recently bleached it blond.

"No, smart-ass, you just have to spend some time doing something for someone besides yourself." I gave her a little kick under the table.

"Well, in that case I should be a member, because that's all I do is serve others, dinner, breakfast, clean laundry, beer, and you know what else. Need I go on?"

"No. Please spare me."

I finished the last of my wine and appreciated the small buzz. The group that was seated at our table seemed a tad uptight, but I was hoping for better once they'd sipped on a little bubbly.

Wendy had become engulfed in a conversation with the older woman who sat on the other side of her. I tried to keep my attention focused on the music, even though the noise level had increased significantly from the time we arrived.

"Welcome, everyone, to the third annual AAPA awards dinner. We are so pleased at the turnout this evening. And as you know, your donation for tonight's dinner supports a very good cause, which is sending more of our young people to college—"

I stopped listening when I saw Clint standing in front of me, practically blocking my view, pulling out a chair for a woman, and then sitting down himself. I stopped breathing, I don't know for how long, until I felt Wendy's elbow go into my ribs. "Did you see what I just saw?"

I ignored her question and stared straight ahead to the stage where Sarah was wrapping up her introduction.

"Please give yourselves a round of applause."

Everyone stood up clapping. I took the opportunity to look the two of them over carefully. He looked like a million bucks, wearing a tuxedo and one of those shirts that didn't need a tie. I could see the diamond stud in his ear, the chandelier lights bouncing off the small nugget. He looked well, which made me feel sick. His accomplice was everything I'd pictured her to be, wearing a strappy black dress that showed off too much cleavage and a wide Quaker behind. Her hair was pushed up with long tendrils hanging down the back. Clint held her chair for her and she touched his arm gently to thank him.

I sat down a few seconds before everyone else. Everything felt heavy; my arms, legs, and even my lungs felt like there was something compressing them. Wendy sat beside me and gave the silent, are-you-okay stare. She didn't take her eyes off of me, until I responded. I must've given one blink for yes, because nothing would come out of my mouth. She slid her full glass of wine in front of me. I drank it gratefully in one swallow.

"Do you want to leave?" Wendy whispered in my ear.

"I can't. I'm fine. Really."

She placed her warm hand over my numb blocks of ice and squeezed some life back into me. What I really wanted was to dig my fingernails into Clint's neck and shake him violently. Watching him gasp for air would have made me feel better. But instead, I took a deep breath, asked for this seething anger to turn into strength, and pasted a stupid, *it's-all-good* grin on my face.

I poked at the stuffed game hen on my plate. I stabbed it a few times with my fork pretending it was Clint. I had to be told several times by

Wendy through her gritted teeth to sit up straight. When the waiter came by to take dessert orders, I asked for one of each. I had a saucer with chocolate cheesecake, carrot cake, and some kind of whipped dessert with a long French name. Wendy saw the assault I was about to make on my stomach and leaned near me.

"Please don't embarrass me tonight."

"I won't. I promise." I ate slowly, savoring each bite of the creamy cheesecake. It was delicious. This was my reward for being humiliated in public. Once I'd polished it off, I began working on the carrot cake. I looked up with my fork loaded and ready for launch, when I felt a tap on my bare shoulder.

Clint was standing awkwardly over me. "Hi."

"Hello." I put the large chunk of cake down. "What are you doing here?" I pretended I hadn't seen him when he first came in an hour ago, and hadn't been watching him the whole time carrying on conversations with everyone around him.

"I was invited by a friend. I saw your name in the program as a nominee for the Crystal Honor. That's nice. That's great." He tapped his thigh with his hand.

"Yes, it is." I gave him my plastic smile.

"I hope you win."

"Thank you." I watched him get as far as the other side of my table before I started working on the carrot cake. Wendy grabbed my hand and took the fork out of it. "If you still love him, quit playing games."

Maybe it was too much wine, because suddenly I could hear Diana Ross singing, "Stop in the name of love, before you break my heart . . . think it ooover . . . think it ooover."

This was a big deal for me. I dusted a spot on my mantel to place the heavy plexiglass statue that was supposed to look like crystal. The inscription read, *Venus Johnston, 1997 Volunteer and Leader in Excellence.*

I was proud of myself. This probably wouldn't hold much value on my résumé, but it meant a lot to me. When I spoke at the podium, I noticed Clint staring at me like a proud papa. I actually used him as my center point to not get nervous in front of all those faces. His date wasn't too happy about that. I assumed he had already filled her in on basic details from the way she had her mouth twisted. She'd look at him, then back up at me while I was at the podium.

Bumping into her in the ladies room only added to the tension. I decided to introduce myself properly to the prom queen. She made sure not to look me in the eye, but I already knew that trick. Her attempt to invalidate me didn't work. I commented on her beautiful gown, asked her where she'd gotten it. She mumbled something about having it so long she couldn't remember. After I spent too much time washing my hands and putting on lipstick, I told her it was nice meeting her and if she ever wanted to talk again I was sure Clint had my number. I could hear her sucking in all the available air in the room, gunning up to speak as I left. I thought about what Wendy had said the rest of the night. Any more wasted time and his name would be changed to *Ken* to go with Ms. *Barbie*.

What he ever saw in her I will never know, Kandi thought as she sat next to Clint on their drive back to her apartment. Venus Johnston gave a speech like she had won an Oscar or something at the AAPA dinner. Kandi twitched restlessly under the strap of her seatbelt as she thought back to Clint's face sitting there all goo-goo eyed, watching Venus offer up melodramatic thank-yous. Kandi couldn't figure out what the attraction was. In her eyes, Venus was just an itty-bitty little thing with nothing going on, especially in the looks department. Kandi would give her a two out of ten on a good day. Well, maybe a five, but that was only because of her small waist. Take away two for not having any hair, and she was demoted to a three. Kandi gave her one more point because of her smile. Men love those big take-me-I'm-yours smiles. But that's it, a four and no more.

Kandi glanced over at Clint driving silently. Maybe he was over her. It's so hard to be objective when you've got something at stake. Kandi would have clocked that little squirrel if she wasn't wearing her good stuff. Venus was standing there all smug in the ladies' room, commenting on Kandi's dress as if she needed her approval. The nerve. After that encounter, Kandi marched right out of the ladies' room and over to Clint, where he sat in satisfaction with himself, and asked him point-blank if there was something she should know about Miss Venus. He turned and looked at Kandi like she was getting too personal. The hairs may as well have been standing up on the back of his neck. He gave her the look of an animal about to pounce to protect their young. The defensiveness he'd shown was her gag order.

Ordinarily Kandi wouldn't do the catfight thing. She'd step aside and say, "he's all yours," and then watch the man come crawling back like they always do. But not this time. She didn't want to be a second choice, or an alternate. She didn't want to chance losing Clint.

She sensed he was the type of man who gave one hundred percent, the all or nothing kind. He poured his heart and soul into every word he spoke. She'd come to believe he was incapable of lying like most of the scoundrels she'd known. That's how she knew whatever Clint had shared with Venus must've been on the up and up. He wouldn't even give Kandi the satisfaction of saying something typical like, "she didn't mean anything to me," or, "we were together, but it's over now." Rather than speak an untruth, he chose to stay closemouthed on the subject.

Clint stared straight ahead into the darkness, driving along quiet with his own thoughts.

"Are you sure you don't want to stop and have some coffee somewhere?" Kandi reached out and touched his thigh, as close to his private area as she could without being outright whorish.

"I wish we could, babygirl, but I told you I have an early day tomorrow. I really shouldn't have even gone out tonight." He touched Kandi's hand that was lying on his thigh. "It was worth it, though. I had a good time." He tried to cushion his rejection.

"Even after seeing her there?" Kandi asked cautiously. She couldn't hold it in any longer. She needed to know what he was thinking.

"Look, Kandi, I told you. That's not even something we need to be talking about."

She could feel the muscle in his thigh tighten. She pulled her hand away. "Not a problem. Discussion closed."

Insecurity was drilling a hole straight through her heart. She knew the nasty mess that it would make if she didn't seal it up and quick.

If she really thought about it logically, she was stressing over nothing. It was she who he'd spent the last couple of weeks with on his days off. Last weekend they drove out to Richmond and she'd met his older brother, Cedric, and his family. Clint's nephews were the cutest little boys. Staring at those little brown faces, all she could think about was how Clint's and her own children would look. Cedric had those same narrow almond-shaped eyes and deep dimples like Clint. The little boys had them, too, just like little clones.

Kandi and Clint pulled into her parking garage. She assumed he would spend the night, but he kissed her gently before turning to leave once her door was unlocked and open.

"I'd stay if I could, babygirl. But I've got a long day tomorrow."

She watched him walk away. Wanting him was taking a toll on her. Wishing for more than pecks on the cheek and consoling hugs had left her feeling defeated and restless. She couldn't understand how he could spend all the time he did around her and not want to make love. What was he waiting for?

Kandi closed the door and immediately felt the force of someone else's presence. She felt for the light switch next to the door, throwing it on, lighting the entry like a stage.

"Well, don't you look pretty. Hot date?" The voice came out of the darkness shooting fear into Kandi's being. Tyson came up and wrapped his strong hands around her waist.

"What are you doing here?" She peeled back his hands.

"I thought I was always welcome. Has that offer been amended?"

"Slightly. I think it would be better if you called first, that's all."

"Whatever you say, Kandi. You make the rules. I'm in no position to make demands, like you've told me a thousand times." He pulled her into his chest. The scent of his cologne made her dizzy. "Do you want me to leave, then call so I can come back?"

Without waiting for her to answer, Tyson turned her around and kissed her on the back of her neck, massaging her with his tongue. He slipped her straps down around her shoulders and started pressing kisses into her skin. His familiar touch, his scent, drew her to him even though she tried hard to fight it. His hold on her lay somewhere between his dark lush lashes and his lean bronze body and the small hope that he actually did love her.

Kandi knew where he would touch her next. She anticipated the movement of his hands and the pressure she would feel from the building of his desire. She knew she should stop him, if not for her own self-respect, at least for the hope she had in a future with Clint.

She told herself one more time wouldn't hurt. After tonight, she promised to herself, after tonight she would end it completely with Tyson.

But for now, she let his tongue wander along her body leaving wet warm spots on her black satin chemise gown. She shuddered after having been deprived of touch for so long. She kissed him back, sucking gently on his bottom lip. He picked her up and carried her to the bed where he began pushing up her dress. He slipped his hands inside of her and played gently pushing her to a point of no return. She tore at his clothing, pulling his silk sweater up over his head exposing his wide smooth chest.

"Who's going to love you like this?" he whispered in a husky voice in her ear. "Huh, who's going to love you like this?" She bit down on her lip to control the moans that were rising out of her with every penetrating strike of his body. A rippling sensation started in the deepest part of her and climbed higher into a crescendo as they moved in rhythm. His body lifted and dove deeper into hers, but she had already left the scene. She was soaring, watching as he reached the height of his pleasure. He rolled over, giving short sighs of relief.

Kandi curled up wishing she could rip out the part of her that wanted him, that allowed this to happen. She listened to more of his promises and plans until he fell asleep. He used her as his sounding board, like she used him for self-rejuvenation. After all, if someone like Tyson Edwards wanted Kandace Treboe, she had to be something special.

Driving around in his 850 Mercedes with the phone pressed up against his ear, he was the portrait of the black businessman made good. His flawless persona was the result of his weekly trips to the barber, a personal tailor for his suits that cost thousands of dollars, and five-course meals prepared in four-star restaurants. What he lacked in morals, he made up with good looks and good manners. His belief that he was doing nothing wrong by being here with Kandi instead of his wife probably was handed down by his daddy, and the daddy before him. A long-standing belief, "women were put here for one thing and one thing only," was probably instilled in his daily living, as one learns how

to say please and thank you. A natural thing you pick up from existing,
like breathing, involuntarily.

She watched him sleep in pure bliss. He probably didn't have a care
in the world at that moment. And suddenly she detested him. She made
a promise to herself, she would never let him have her again.

Truth or Dare

I was sitting at my desk thumb-
ing through reports when Clint's call
came through, catching me off guard.

"Can you tell me something?" he asked.

"Sure, what is it that you want to know, Mr. Fairchild?" I was wearing my professional hat. I knew how it annoyed him when I pronounced
every consonant and vowel.

"When did you stop needing me?"

I let out a long sigh. "You know that's not the case, Clint." I leaned
back in my chair, cradling the phone close so my voice wouldn't carry.
How many times would we have this conversation, and he still not get
the point? "You're the one who doesn't need me, and you made that
perfectly clear."

"Just because I haven't tied the magic ribbon around your finger?"

"It's not just the ring, Clint. It's the whole package. You never even hinted that we were going to spend the rest of our lives together."

"I never said I didn't want to get married, V. You just assumed. All I asked you to do was wait until I got my stuff together. You know what I go through, what I'm going through every day, trying to get through this program. I can't concentrate on too much else." His voice was sincere.

"The truth is, I'm tired of waiting. I've been more than patient. I'm tired of waiting for a sign or miracle that tells me 'this is it.' That's what an engagement ring is, a promise for the future, and you couldn't even do that. I just had a feeling I would be waiting indefinitely, and my life will have passed me by. You're forgetting I'm a little bit older than you. I don't have a whole lot of time left to get on the mommy track."

"Well, I don't see you getting there any quicker without me."

"Oh, what's that supposed to mean?" I was sitting up straight now. He had my attention.

"I'm just saying, I don't see no new daddy prospects hanging around anywhere."

"What are you saying? 'Cause honey, I can get a man." My neck was moving involuntarily. I had to read him his rights. "You are not the only man walking this earth."

"I'm not saying you can't. I'm just saying it doesn't look like you're trying too hard."

"And how would you know?" My temper was rising. "I might have someone waiting at home for me right now. I could've had the best date of my life last night."

"I doubt it, V. You wouldn't have been at the AAPA dinner with Wendy on your arm if you had it like that."

"Don't doubt it and don't dare me. Because I am very capable of getting someone, anyone. What . . . you think 'cause I cut off all my hair men won't find me attractive?"

"I never said that."

"That's what you're implying."

His voice went low, the one he used for seducing, "I don't believe that. You're just as beautiful now as the day I met you."

He was trying to get control of me, the situation that I'd become.

"Let's just kiss and make up." He paused. "I want to come home, V."

I wanted him to come home, too. I wanted to make a great dinner of all his favorite foods, snow crab, corn on the cob, broccoli with long stalks all smothered in pats of rich butter. I wanted to show him how fat Sandy had gotten since she was a puppy. I wanted to show him the wall I painted, and how I rearranged all the pictures. But I couldn't. I could not give in. If I did, it would be a sentence of an undeterminable amount of time.

"It's not that simple, Clint. I wish it was."

I hung up the phone realizing my office door had been open the whole time. I knew Sherri had gotten an earful. She was probably out there transcribing the whole conversation. Not that anyone around here gave a flying frog what was going on in my life. I may as well have been invisible. All this week Ray hadn't had more than two words to say to me. I assumed he was feeling animosity toward me after he'd found out I addressed John and Lenny about the account management position without him. Probably feeling I overstepped the chain of command.

John and Lenny practically run in the other direction when they see me coming, most likely assuming I will approach them about the promotion again. I asked Sherri if she knows anything. For once she knows nothing. I was stuck doing the analysis profile for Gary Marshall, who is officially the account manager for St. John's, for now. I hadn't given up on changing that status quo. I was more determined than ever to make it happen. The only thing getting in my way was a small thing called reality.

I headed out for the day. I stood in the hallway and pressed the button for the lobby. After stepping in I watched the elevator close and then reopen abruptly to admit another passenger.

"Sorry about that, I have to catch this one or I'll be late for my next appointment." He bent his elbow hard, letting his Rolex catch my attention. "You work around here?"

I stared up at this magnificent creature called man, and could barely speak. "I'm the research analyst for Donnely Kramer," I managed to whisper.

He turned to face me. "I'm Tyson Edwards."

He held out his hand. Not a hard day's work in his life was my assessment. Nothing worse than a man with softer hands than your own. "Nice to meet you. You know my company just signed you guys on as our new advertising team."

I took my hand back. "Yes, I know. I'm the one doing the research reports—you know, the number crunching, who's buying what and when."

He smiled, like that was a little more information than he needed to know. The elevator doors opened. "Nice meeting you." He nodded quickly and walked away.

"Nice meeting you, too," I called after him as he was pushing through the large double-glass doors. I suddenly needed a thick Hershey's bar. I have to admit I was salivating. He looked good enough to eat. I had seen him from a distance, but even up close he was truly gorgeous. His smooth flawless skin and those long black lashes would put the Cover Girls to shame.

I headed to the garage to get my old faithful Hyundai. I had a three o'clock doctor's appointment that I didn't want to be late for again. I was seeing a therapist at the suggestion of my brother, Timothy. He's the only other person I told about my dreams. He thinks there may be some hidden message that needs to come out. He thinks there is a hidden message in everything since completing his thesis on *Subliminal Conversations with Our Higher Selves*. This is his fourth degree and he still had no real job. I told him he's the one who needed a therapist. But after giving it some thought, I figured it wouldn't hurt. Maybe I could flush out some other demons hiding in my closet, kind of a two or three for one deal. This was probably the one and only secret I kept from Clint. I didn't want him having something to blame my decisions on. He already accused my every thought of being a product of the white man and my sheltered middle-class environment. He really would have had a field day with Dr. Quincy Parish. He's the perfect example of Dr. Freud before the age of forty. Instead of white hair, his is bright sun red. But everything else is Freud, right down to the black horn-rim glasses.

As I pulled my car closer to the exit gate, I noticed Tyson Edwards with his back facing me, talking to the garage attendant. I drove around slowly so I could get an idea of what was going on from their facial expressions. I rolled my window down. I had to ask.

"Can I be of assistance, Mr. Edwards?" I called out.

He walked over to my car. "Oh, it's you. No, I'm sure everything is going to be fine. My car is just missing."

"Your car is missing? You mean, it's been stolen?"

"That's what I'm trying to find out. People usually don't take the keys when they're stealing a car. I told this young punk, who suddenly doesn't speak English anymore, that I don't want to have to call the police. Things could go a lot smoother if I get my car back without involving the police." He was squatting next to my door, we were face-to-face. No earring, no hole for an earring. One of the few and the proud. The last of the Mohicans.

"I'm so sorry about this. I know Manuel. He's always been very nice to me, maybe I can talk to him."

"Would you try?" He stepped aside and opened my squeaky car door. I walked over to the concrete hut and gave Manuel my we-are-all-brothas-and-sistas speech. He stuck to his story of not knowing what happened to the car. He said he took ten minutes for a bathroom break and didn't notice anything strange when he got back. He was shaking and nervous. He said he needed this job, and he knew it would be the end of him if anyone found out a car got snatched on his watch.

I walked back to my car where Tyson was standing. "I think it's really been stolen. You're going to have to call the police."

He threw up his hands, "Unbelievable. This is just un-fucking-believable. I've had that car for all of two months, and it gets stolen."

"I can give you a lift. You said you had to rush to another appointment back in the elevator. Do you need me to take you? I can drop you off somewhere. It's not exactly luxurious, but it's very dependable."

"Would you? I don't want to put you out of your way, but I need to be at a meeting that's about twenty minutes away and I'm already late."

"No problem, really." I clicked on my seatbelt, started Betsy right up, and was thankful for my miracle. I had Tyson Edwards's undivided attention for the next twenty minutes.

"Girl, I think I met my babies' daddy today. There's only one problem. He's already married to somebody else."

I knew what Wendy was doing with her every breath. This one, a sigh and then a clearing of the throat, was the signal of eye rolling. She had all kinds of different smirks that went with her tongue clucking. A complete sigh was a frown.

"As if that's ever stopped anybody before," she pronounced loudly, probably staring at her husband, Sidney, when she said it.

"No, no, no. I am not the man stealing or borrowing type. But, girl, if you saw this man, you would know what I'm talking about. His skin is like baby skin, just smooth and tight, no blemishes, no hair, just fine. No, excuse me, I meant, FFFINE. He's the CEO of St. John's Cosmetics, and he just signed us on to do their advertising."

"Okay, so he's fine, but he's married, case closed. I don't suppose you mentioned your conspiracy theory to him. You know about how all their chemicals and oils are saturating the brains of our black youth. How St. John's is contributing to the poisoning of our bodies, how we're all going to die of hypertension because our hair is shiny and straight."

"No. I did not. We only talked briefly and that's no way to start a relationship. I was too busy staring at his eyes."

"I was just checking, you seemed adamant on being heard on the subject, so I was just checking." She let out a devious snicker. "So what's going on with Clint?"

"Nothing is going on with Clint. He's still telling me I'm the one that made this thing crash and burn. And it's just not true."

"What happened with that Tyra Banks look-alike? Are they a couple now? Did you ask what was up with that?"

"None of my business. Don't know, don't care."

"Venus, please. Stop pretending you're not still in love with Dr. Feelgood. He's going to get away, mark my words."

"As far as I'm concerned, he already got away. They'll probably live happily ever after and have babies."

"Yeah, she looks like the type that'll name 'em Spring and Autumn . . . and Summer. I hate that one." Wendy gave off a small cough of a laugh.

I didn't think it was funny. I was only being facetious; I didn't need Wendy to give them names, that made it seem too real. I poured myself another cup of spearmint tea and spent the rest of the night thinking about Tyson Edwards.

I never made it to my appointment with *Dr. Freud*. Needless to say, it's my loss, since I have to pay whether I show up or not. But it was really my gain. Tyson Edwards, the key to my impending promotion, was truly interested in everything I had to say as I drove him around. I told him about my ideas for positioning the St. John's makeup line to women over forty, and starting a whole new line for the eighteen to thirty group. Something fresh and youthful.

At first I caught him staring at me like I had no real clue, but once I got going, I was on fire. I told him about my experience with all his company's hair products and makeup firsthand. I ignored his glances at my bald head, as if I was mistaken.

I explained how he was going to have to break everybody up and stop assuming just because we're African American, we all think alike. He responded that he had a department that handled all their brand and product decisions, he just needed Donnely Kramer to create the ads to sell them.

That's when I went into my spew about it being one hand washing the other, how he had to bring these two groups together, the marketing and development. Duh . . . who doesn't know this? But I kept talking. I didn't shut up until we pulled in front of the St. John's thirty-floor deluxe office building. He offered to pay me for the ride, like I was a taxicab. I told him it was my pleasure. I couldn't help feeling a little insulted by that gesture. But I stored it where it belonged and stayed focused on the fact that he now knows I exist. I gave him a business card as he was getting out of the car. He kind of stared at it like it served no real purpose, but he took it anyway, like it was the right thing to do. Watching him walk into his building, I caught myself wondering what was underneath his suit. That's when I knew for sure I was long overdue for some human contact.

⑥   ⑥   ⑥

Twilight Zone

FOR THE FIFTH STRAIGHT DAY MY stomach was rumbling and doing somersaults like the circus had come to town. I'd been popping antacids all day and nothing had worked. The only relief would come when Ray started answering one of the twenty e-mails I'd sent him about the reports on the Simmons Mattress account, or decided to leave his door open long enough so that I could stick my head in. I felt like he was avoiding me like the plague. It wasn't my imagination. These days I wasn't feeling very liked around the office or at home. Even Sherri hadn't troubled me with a visit. Was it possible to miss even the things that bring annoyance, in longing for the familiar?

I'd left messages for both John and Lenny asking for a light informal meeting to see if they'd made a decision yet about the account manager position, with no response. If I wasn't still making it home every day to feel the warmth of my cocker spaniel, I'd think I was in the Twilight Zone. "Where is everybody!" I'd scream at the top of my lungs, and keep screaming while Rod Serling came out wearing his usual coal black suit with his shiny black hair parted on the side and melted to his head.

Rod Serling would give his overall assessment of my situation in the flat monotone voice he used to introduce every episode of the weekly program. "A young woman caught in the spiral of the corporate ladder. Trapped by her ambition, aspiring too high, too quickly? Will she learn the value of staying in her place? For what would the world be without the little people to do the grunt work, and the big people taking all the credit?" He would turn around and look at the black-and-white scene of me trapped at my desk, then shake his head in pity before returning to talk into the camera. "We will find out in the Twilight Zone."

I couldn't go on like this. That's all I knew. My belly was going to explode with the acids of self-doubt and confusion. Where did I go wrong? Was it the confrontation with Ray in the parking garage? It seemed like we were back on solid ground, the rose, and the apology. Or maybe it was the brainstorming session that I took upon myself to have with the CEO of St. John's.

The CEO of St. John's? Would I have had the same spunk and determination to corner him with my ideas if he were not black? Did I completely overstep my bounds by just assuming I could have my way with his time and attention because of our imaginary association? Did he walk in here the next day and demand I be terminated for talking too fast and driving too slow and taking up his time?

The intercom buzzed, interrupting my thoughts of drinking the last drop of Mylanta sitting in the bottle on my desk. I reached for the phone and answered as if the governor were calling to give a stay of execution.

"Yes."

"Venus, it's John. Are you available for a two o'clock meeting this afternoon? Lenny and I would like to meet with you. Shouldn't take more than an hour . . . tops."

"That's fine. Will we be meeting in your office or the conference room?"

He muzzled the phone before answering. He could only be conferring with his left brain, Lenny. "My office. Okay? See you at two."

This was it. Finally. I was relieved. I didn't care what they had to say, I only wanted them to say something. If I was going to be kicked out on my duff, so be it. I just needed to know so the suffering could be put to an end. Someone like me can't live without a constant source of information. Information is my power, my sustenance. Some people need cigarettes, or caffeine. *I need to know*. I looked at my watch and wrote down "2:00" on the calendar on my desk. The month of December was blank, no meetings or appointments scheduled. My life was the sum total of my desk-long, desk-wide monthly planner and it was completely empty, except for the 2:00 I'd just written, and the lunch date I'd had with Ray that turned out to be a bombardment. I scanned the rest of the days with my finger and stopped at Christmas.

I had completely forgotten about the beginning of the holiday season. In less than two weeks I'd have to face my parents. They would see me without my armor, without Clint, without my hair. They'd just see me.

After chipping off the tips of every fingernail, I started my walk to John's office. I walked right past Sherri, who must've been wearing blinders because she hadn't looked up to see who was passing her air space. I moved slowly but steadily past Ray's double doors that were shut tight. Two doors down, I passed Saige in the accounting department training another new girl that no one bothered to introduce to me. I continued walking but I couldn't feel my feet. For the first time in a long time, I admired the mauve and teal walls filled with an extensive collection of watercolor paintings. I decided right then to add some mauve to my walls at home, maybe sponged. I'd do it this weekend.

I stopped in front of John's door and knocked lightly before letting myself in. "Hi, it's me," I said as I slid in the door.

"Come in, Venus. Have a seat." John was sitting at his desk that is too large for his body. I turned to close the door and saw Ray sitting casually with his long legs crossed. He smiled and gave me a wave. I decided to sit in the chair instead of on the couch where Ray's arms had taken over the entire span of the backrest.

"We're waiting for Lenny and then we'll get started." John's voice broke through my mind-reading attempts on Ray. I still couldn't figure out why he had been avoiding me all week and now sat there as if nothing was wrong.

"Oh, I'm not in a hurry," I said, trying to sound as carefree and relaxed as possible.

"I didn't get a chance to e-mail you back on that Simmons report, Venus, but yes, I did receive it. It looks great." Ray's poor attempt to make small talk only made me more distrustful of him. I wanted to tell him that was over four days ago and I really didn't give a rat's tail what he thought.

"Thank you," I spoke between my sparkling gritted teeth.

"So, Venus, whatcha got planned for the holidays?" John interrupted my telepathic efforts once again.

"I'll probably be going back to LA to see my folks for a couple of days." I interlocked my hands around my knees to stop them from shaking. "And you?"

"I really don't know. The Missiz makes all the plans in our house. I haven't been given the agenda yet." He leaned into his phone and pressed the intercom. "Lenny, are you joining us?" There was no answer, but the door opened suddenly.

"Sorry I'm late. How ya doing there, Venus?"

"I'm fine, Lenny. How are you?"

"Good, good, can't complain." He moved quicker than John. They were both in their early forties, but John always seemed like he was on his last leg while Lenny exuded the life force.

"Well, we're all here, so let's begin." John pulled out a thin file from out of his desk. Out of nowhere, Ray and Lenny were holding the same type of manila folder.

"Excuse me, John, um, do I need any of the information that you have there? I don't seem to have a copy."

The beating of my heart was too loud. The sound was making me strain to hear myself speak.

"Actually, I don't have another copy. Maybe you can look on with Ray."

I turned in his direction and made myself comfortable next to him on the couch. The heat from his body was a complication I would have to endure. I was determined to see what was in that file.

"Okay, are we all set?" John asked. "If you'll notice, Venus, this is a little list Ray went ahead and compiled for us of maybe the last ten or so analyses you've run this past year. You could say it's a year-end review type of thing. We just wanted to go over some of our findings with you." He cleared his throat and began speaking even slower. "If you'll notice to the right of each report, we have a percentile that tells us the accuracy of the findings." My eyes steered to the right and then quickly scanned down. Twenty percent, eighteen percent, six percent, twenty-one percent. Nothing over twenty-five percent. They were trying to make me look incompetent. Pure and simple.

"Exactly what are these numbers trying to say, and what did you use to measure them?" My voice wavered a little. I looked Ray straight in the eye when I spoke, but he looked only at John and Lenny when he replied.

"Well, I simply took the reported sales of the product and cross-referenced it with a random sample of the consumers who purchased the product, and measured their profile with the one given in your analysis."

"I can't see how that kind of measurement should reflect on my reports. There are just too many variables in the purchase of a product by a consumer. Too many to even name. I mean that's an area that hasn't been touched in even the largest companies. I don't understand why you're suddenly attempting to judge my work by this standard." My hand was visibly shaking so I let go of my end of the file. I dropped my hands down into my lap.

"I mean we're in the business of advertising. How the product is sold, when, and where isn't our responsibility, and you certainly can't expect it to be purchased only by the people who are targeted." The room was silent. I looked them over one at a time. They must've been gearing up for plan B, collaborating in their utter stillness.

Lenny spoke first. "You're right on a few points, Venus. Yes, you're right, we can't say exactly who will buy the product, but we can predict a certain amount of reliability. And that's your job, to tell us who that certain amount will come from. We just think these figures are a little low. We're not asking for a miracle overnight. If you could just put in a little more effort in your analysis. We'll give you whatever you need to make it happen. A better software program, another body perhaps. You tell us."

"Well, I guess I'll have to put some thought into it. This being the first time I've heard of a problem, I'll need a little time."

"That's all we ask, Venus." John rose up and walked me to his office door.

"Lenny, Ray." I nodded to them and left the room. I don't know how I made it to my office. I fell into my chair and lurched forward. The pain, the sharp cramping was unbearable. I grabbed my purse and headed out to the elevator.

It wasn't coming fast enough. I pressed the down button harder with every pulsating jab of my stomach. I could feel Sherri's eyes on the back of my whole body, from my heels to my exposed scalp. I pressed again on the elevator button and it opened. I got inside and moved into the corner to get out of her eye view. Once the door closed I let out spasms of tears. The loud echo of my own sobbing scared me. I cried loud and hard, ceasing abruptly when the elevator stopped moving, and quickly wiped my eyes and cheeks before the doors opened. I didn't want anyone to see the mess I'd made of myself. Here I'd been thinking of being promoted, moving forward, and they were on a completely different page. According to them, I needed help. Not up to par.

I drove home with my eyes rimmed with redness and burning. I cussed Ray, John, and Lenny. I didn't understand why Ray hadn't warned me that this was coming. Actually I did understand, and quite well. He'd probably been planning some type of retaliation from the first day I'd rejected him. Just because I didn't want his nasty hands all over me and his tongue down my throat, now he's trying to get rid of me. How could I have been so naïve? The apology, the promise to talk to John and Lenny about the St. John's account, it was all a smoke screen. I beat the steering wheel again with both hands. "Son of a bitch." I reached up and pressed the remote button. My antenna brushed the door from entering too soon. I closed it before the engine was off and wondered if this was how accidents happened. Coming home from a job where people treated you like gum on a shoe, staying in the running car just a little too long for solace, listening to the rest of your favorite song . . . and they call it a suicide.

I stomped my way up the stairs into the house.

"Please tell me this is just another bad dream, Sandy," I whispered into her warm layer of hair as she kept trying to lick my face. "I need a hug, girl. Give mama a hug." I squeezed her gently and put her back down on the floor. She jumped up and down, ruining yet another pair of panty hose, not that I cared. I leaned back in the large leather chair with my legs outstretched and used my fingernails to dig holes in the small snags. I pulled until my legs were covered with strips of black nylon. I looked like I felt, all torn up.

"Hi Mom."

I didn't want to start crying again so I planned to make it brief. If she heard even the smallest amount of tension, she'd ask, "What's wrong, baby?" and then the tears would overflow like Niagara Falls.

"I'll be flying in on the twenty-second. I don't have the exact time yet. I'll call you with that a couple of days before I come."

"Is Clint coming with you?" She had to ask.

"No, he can't make it. He's not going to have enough time off to fly all the way out there and back in time for work. I don't even think he gets Christmas off." I couldn't think of any other excuses.

"I think we're going to have dinner over at your Auntie Katha's house this year." She moved on, ignoring what I'd said about Clint. She could always see straight through my half-truths.

"Auntie Katha makes the best pecan pie." I went along with the change of subject.

"Timothy has found himself a new lady friend. He says he's bringing her with him. Must be special if he wants us to meet her."

"They're all special, Mom. Stop hoping for a miracle. He's never going to stick with any of them."

"You don't know. You never know what the future holds."

"You're right, I don't know. I don't know much of anything these days." I shoved the kitchen towel into my mouth to hold in the cry. Here I go. Damn.

"Venus, baby, what's wrong?" That's all it took for the dam to break. I couldn't hold it in a second longer.

"Oh Mom, I've just been making a mess of things, my job, Clint. I feel like I've been walking around and living in the Twilight Zone. Clint and I . . . we're not together anymore."

"What happened? Tell me and stop all that sniveling."

"I just told him if he didn't want to get married, it was over. I was tired of wasting my time. He's been putting it off for so long, I just started not to believe in him anymore. I mean, he was going to have me waiting for him forever. I had to move on with my life."

"That's it? He didn't run out on you or hit you or nothing like that?"

"No. He hurt my feelings, though. I mean, he broke my heart."

"He hurt your feelings?"

"Yeah. All this time we've been together, he hasn't even proposed or given me a ring or nothing."

"Venus, did you tell him how you felt before you told him you were tired of being tired?" She knew the answer before she asked, but as a mother, it was her duty to make me spell it out.

"Well . . . he knew. He knew, it wasn't a secret that I wanted to marry him. He just kept putting me off. I wasn't putting up with his broke butt for nothing." I let out another stack of hiccups mixed with tears. "When he showed up for my birthday with a puppy instead of the ring I'd been expecting, I just lost it. I told him to either commit to marrying me or get out. And he left." Reliving that day made the tears flow uncontrollably.

"Venus. Stop it. Stop crying! I can't talk to you with all that sniveling in my ear."

I stuck the towel in my mouth again and clamped down hard.

"If you're so misty eyed over this, why don't you tell him you made a mistake? Fix it. Don't just sit there wallowing. Tell him you made a mistake."

"That won't fix it! Telling him I made a mistake. He's the one making the mistake."

"Okay, Venus. Do whatever you need to do. In the end it'll always turn out how it's supposed to anyway. It always does."

"Are you sure?" I snuck one more sniff in. "I hope that's true."

"Oh it's true, ma'dear. Things always work themselves out. I promise."

"I love you, Mom."

"I love you, too, sweetie. See you in a couple of weeks."

We hung up. And for a while I believed what my mother had said, that things always worked out the way they were meant to. Clint would eventually recognize how wrong he was. He'd see that all I wanted was what was best for both of us.

⟲   ⟲   ⟲

Too Through

THIS HAD BEEN THE LONGEST FOUR weeks of his life. Clint didn't think Venus could hold out this long. He just knew she was going to break down by now, but she had thrown in the towel. All this time, he'd been holding out for her. He could kick himself for being so stupid.

The last couple of weekends had been spent keeping Kandi at bay. He knew it was easier to let go when the physical aspect didn't get out of hand. Once he started putting it to her on a regular basis, she wouldn't let go easily when the time came. So he hadn't slept with her since that first time, the first night they'd met.

Last Saturday evening was one of the hardest. After they had dinner he was kicking it on the couch watching *Star Trek* reruns, and here she comes sashaying around with a little red thong, one-piece thing all up her nice round ass. He couldn't see straight for all that body talking to him. He had to get up and out of there, quick.

Babygirl is fine. Tiny little waist, nice round bottom, with those perfect tits that stand at attention. Makes a brother want to salute.

He shook the vision out of his head. When he'd told her that he had an early day and couldn't stay, she just about cried. Her face dropped. It wasn't even about her. He wished he could tell Kandi the truth—*you know just in case Venus wants to get it together, I gotta be able to make a clean break. I don't want to hurt you, but I'm still in love with V.*

She'd kick him straight in his nuts if he told her the truth. He sensed Kandi had one serious mean streak flowing through her.

Clint overheard her cussing some old G out on the phone. Whoever she was talking to must've been begging, because she was straight out ruthless, telling him to go screw himself, or his wife, whichever he preferred. Clint stayed in her bathroom and pretended he didn't hear anything. With all the house cleaning Kandi had been doing, telling old boyfriends to step so they could be together, he felt guilty. And what if he did end up back with Venus after all the changes Kandi had made for him?

Damn.

Forget about that "hell hath no fury like a woman scorned" business, that was an understatement. There was nothing worse then a black woman who thought she'd been dogged. On any given day, Howard University's campus parking lot had at least one car driving around with love-don't-live-here-anymore vandalism. Slashed tires, scratched hoods, broken windows. Luckily, Clint had never found himself in that situation. Without a doubt it had been luck, because he'd broken his share of hearts in the past, but none of the breakups had escalated to madness. Sheila, his lab partner in Organic Chemistry, got close when he'd ended the relationship coincidentally around the same time as the semester was ending for his junior year. She'd confronted Clint while he sat with

Dr. Yorba, his mentor, who happened to be congratulating him on how well he was doing. "You would've gotten an 'F' if it hadn't been for me," she had screamed in his ear. "Next time choose someone else to fuck over." She knocked over his iced tea onto the table, where it spilled over onto the crotch of his pants. He jumped up from the cold, bumping into her. She responded by shoving him hard in the chest, causing him to fall over Dr. Yorba. He was grateful he didn't own a car at the time. The embarrassment subsided within a few days. By Spring Break, it was forgotten.

The light danced around the walls from the candles that were lit. Kandi placed them all around the bathtub, in various shapes, big and round, small and square. She pulled out every candle she had collected over the years, and even bought some new ones for this night. She laid out the cream-colored silk and lace negligee on the bed. She placed the black one next to it. She stared at them both trying to decide which one was more flattering to her cinnamon-dusted skin. It was winter and her skin had already lost the healthy glow it developed in the summer. The red and purple were definitely not an option. She played eeny meeny miney mo to decide between the black or cream color. The cream won. She put the black one back on the satin hanger and shoved it into her overstuffed closet.

Kandi put the wine next to the tub in a bucket of ice with two glasses. It was a fantasy picture, the candles flickering and the wine chilling. She turned up the heat on the thermostat so that she wouldn't freeze walking around half naked. Tonight there would be no excuses. She went to great lengths to find out Clint's work schedule, something he never seemed to know, so she called one of the shift nurses who had befriended her after they had chatted like old friends. Clint wasn't on call and he didn't have to be back at the hospital for two solid days. She sprayed the perfume on herself and into the air.

One more for luck. She let a cold burst of perfume sink into her panty line. The phone rang. Her heart double skipped.

Please don't let him cancel, she thought while rushing to the phone.

"Hey girl, it's me." Lena's voice was a saving grace.

"Hello, lady. What's up?"

"No, the question is, what's up with you? How come you can't call anybody anymore? You just forgot about your best girl over here."

"I swear I've been working overtime trying to get some kind of response out of this man."

"Puhleeze. There is no need for you to have to work. You know what I'm saying. You have the body, the hair, the everything—"

"I know, Lena. But I told you, he's still stuck on his little chicken-head ex. If you saw her, you would be as baffled as I am. She has like no hair—bald as an eagle—and I ain't lying."

"Well, if she's that bad, why are you worried?"

"I don't know. I can't explain it. He's a lot deeper than that surface stuff. I may be able to win him temporarily with the looks, but she's got some kind of hold on him. I think they've been through a lot together. That kind of thing is hard to break through."

"Well, work with what you got. And you've got a lot. If he can't see all the good things you've got going, he's blind and he doesn't deserve you anyway."

"I hope he can see just fine tonight. I'm going full throttle, I've got the candles, the music, wine."

"Have a nice time. Promise not to forget about your homegirl." Lena sounded worried.

"I promise. Really. I'll call you and let you know how it goes."

What Kandi couldn't explain to Lena, she couldn't explain to herself, either. Why was she working so hard to get this man to want her? He didn't have a problem when they'd first met. He was all over her that first night, like a man who'd been starved a little too long. Maybe that was it, maybe he and his little freaknik were still doing the do. All the excuses about working and studying weren't genuine. That had to be it. He and Venus were still seeing each other.

After turning the bathtub water off, she looked up at herself in the mirror over the sink. She cleared the steam. The person staring back looked like one of the models in the Victoria's Secret catalog. Perfect hair, eyes made up, cheeks highlighted, lips full and burgundy. But there was a flaw in this person, something that prevented men from choosing her, making her their everything.

She had followed the rules. She had attended college, got a degree in education, and became a professional woman, independent and well read. From the age of fifteen Kandi had sworn she wouldn't end up like the rest of those Roosevelt High girls, with a baby before voting age, and no one but themselves to depend on. No one but themselves and the state, that is. She joined the Deltas, to separate herself from the common BAP. By grade school she had set her goals to be married by the age of twenty-five to a Denzel look-alike who believed the only thing worth living for was her, a large house in suburbia, and two kids and a Volvo. Where did she go wrong when someone like Venus Johnston could be a better pick than herself?

She closed her eyes hard to restrain the urge to cry. She didn't want to ruin her work of art. The intercom bell rang, snapping her out of the why-me-oh-my party. She rushed to the intercom panel.

"Who is it?"

"Clint," he confirmed into the speaker.

She pushed the button, letting him in, then quickly ran and put on a robe and threw the negligee back in the closet. Something told her she was overdoing it.

"Why didn't you use your key and let yourself in?" She looked at him through half-squinted eyes.

"I . . . I can't stay. I wanted to come up and give this to you." He held out the set of keys and the card key that opened the parking garage .

"What's this about?" She knew very well what it was about, but couldn't believe it.

"Kandi. Sit down for a minute." They both walked over to the couch.

"I know I've been tripping lately. I've just had a lot on my mind. The one thing I said I wouldn't do is hurt you just because I'm tripping." He tapped himself in the chest with a solid fist. "It's not fair. So . . . maybe we should just chill out for a minute. You know. So I can get myself together."

"Okay, if that's how you feel." She heard herself say. She thought in an instant she was going to be sick. She could feel the rush of liquid moving through her jaws, filling her cheeks. The rush of nausea hit, then backed down just as quickly.

He lifted her chin to look her in the eyes. "Are you going to be all right, babygirl?" He could see the flush of red in her face that wasn't there before.

"No." Her voice seemed loud and awkward. "No. I'm not all right. I've been trying to make this night and every night perfect for you, just so you and I can be together, and I'm sick of your excuses. Now you tell me it's just not going to work out right now because you're tripping. So what are you trippin' off of, your ex-girlfriend, Venus? Or maybe she's not your ex, maybe she's still present and accounted for." Kandi stood up and shouted in his face. "I cannot believe how stupid I've been. You have been running around here pretending that you're too tired to spend one intimate night with me, all the while you've probably been sleeping with her."

He stood up. "Kandi, I gotta go. I'm sorry. I didn't mean to hurt you." He walked to the door. "I'm sorry," Clint whispered while pulling the door closed.

She didn't cry, not until she was finished saying what was on her mind.

⊙   ⊙   ⊙

Pickaninny?

THE SMOOTH FIGURE GLIDING A few steps in front of me could only belong to one person. The suit hung on his body like it was made while he stood. I quickened my pace to make the elevator with him. I stood by his side without saying a word. When the elevator cleared out a bit, he looked down at my silky head and spoke.

"Well, hello Miss . . ."

I looked up at him and smiled. "Johnston. How are you, Mr. Edwards?"

"I'm well, thank you. How's all that research work going?"

"Great. Just fine." I batted my eyes and threw him a half smile. "I know this is probably inappropriate, but are you free for lunch? I really think you could help me out with some of the basic information about your company." I figured I had nothing to lose. I was already on the hit list. May as well have the Last Supper.

"Oh, I thought you already had all the answers."

"Forgive me if I came off a little obnoxious. It's a nasty habit I've been trying to break. Quick lunch, Mr. Edwards?" I gave him my shy humble pie face, the one that any pro could see through.

"Actually I am free for lunch. It'll have to be early though. Eleven-thirty all right? I should wrap things up by then." He peeled back his sleeve to let the light bounce off his crystal timepiece.

"That's perfect for me. I'll meet you in the lobby." We stepped off the elevator and went in separate directions.

Sherri gave me a rehearsed "how are you" and went about her business. I gave her a full-scale "good morning" and knocked my knuckles on her station while I hummed and picked up my mail. I was feeling good for a change.

The best defense against self-pity is looking good. Fortunately, I had worn my gray silk and wool blend suit with the big lapels, the skirt tailored to show lots of leg action and a floral chiffon scarf to match. I had put special effort into my wardrobe, makeup, and, yes, even hair. I brushed the fresh sprouts down with a little cream and gloss. It was laid against my head in shimmering perfection. I even caught a few stares from Dominick as I was striding through. He couldn't be more than twenty-five years old, and I was not trying to raise another boy into a man like I did Clint. I bet he had that Latino stamina though.

I had to catch myself from that fantasy. Lately no one had been safe from my vivid imagination, the kid who delivered the pizza over the weekend, one of the rec-center counselors where I hadn't been spending enough time lately, and the worst was the young bagging clerk at Weis. I knew he'd busted me staring at his chest in that too-tight T-shirt he was wearing. I thought about calling Clint for a safe romp, but I didn't know about it being too safe anymore since he'd been seeing *Barbie*. I really didn't know where she'd been or who she'd been with.

I pulled out my envelope ripper and started my routine of opening all the mail at once and putting it in a pile then taking everything out of their envelopes, forming a new pile, and then reading everything in the stack. The process was halted when an envelope without an address or stamp caught my eye. On the front it simply read *Venus Johnston* in bold black letters. I took the small folded notepaper out. The drawing was in dark heavy felt pen. The round stick person with a huge head was probably supposed to be me. The little squiggly lines drawn up in the air coming from the round circle head were assuredly my hair. The word scribbled at the bottom said *PICKANINNY*. I looked inside the envelope for anything else that might have been put inside.

Suddenly, I felt scared. If it was meant as a joke, it wasn't funny. I got up and shut my office door and leaned on it for a moment. I tried to think rationally, one by one, who could have sent it. The most reasonable choice was Ray. I couldn't imagine anyone else feeling strongly enough about me to get this type of response. Clint, possibly. The thin line of love and hate could have been crossed. I stared at it again. I sat down at my desk and flattened it out completely, staring at it, waiting for it to tell me the story of its existence. The lined notepaper was cheap, it had perforated holes on the side, so it came out of someone's notepad. I smelled it, the pungent odor of the ink was still there. I rested my elbows on the desk and laid my head in my hands. Who hates me this much?

I got up and marched up to Sherri's desk.

"Who left this here, Sherri?" I held up the plain white envelope with my name on it. "Did you happen to see who left this?"

"No, I didn't. Was it in your regular mail?"

"Yes, but it's not mail, there's no address or stamp on it, so it had to be hand delivered."

She looked at the envelope again. "I've been here since eight-thirty, and no one hand delivered anything this morning. Someone could have put it in your box last night."

I turned and walked away. I returned to my office and closed the door behind me. I wished it had a lock. I didn't feel safe.

I took a chance and called John. He picked up on the first ring.

"John, I need to speak with you, now if it's all right. It's real important."

"Sure, come on in."

I put the picture back in the envelope and walked with it pushed up my sleeve. If I ran into Ray in the hall, I didn't want him to see it in my hand.

John was sitting at his desk that reminded me of a toddler's high chair set. His slightly curly dark blond hair was highlighted by the sun shining through the window behind him. It almost looked like a halo over his head. I knew better.

"Someone put this in my mail today. It was personally delivered. There's no address, only my name. That means it was someone with access to our offices." I laid it on his desk. He opened it slowly, turning the picture sideways, then back straight, not quite able to make out what it was.

"Pick-a-nin-ny. Is that what that says?" His face turned a crimson red.

"Yes." I stood at his desk, but couldn't keep the tough girl façade up and fell into the chair in front of his desk. "I asked Sherri if she saw anything or knew where it came from, but she has no idea. That *is* a racial slur, John."

"I know the term, Venus. Unfortunately, there isn't anything we can do about it without a witness. We just can't point any fingers."

"I think I know who did it."

"Who?"

"Ray. He might still be angry that I rejected his sexual advances."

John's face started shading again just after he'd regained his normal pale beige tone.

"What are you saying, Venus? Exactly what happened?" He put up his hand. "Wait, hold that thought. Lenny, could you come in here please?" He released the intercom button and leaned back in his chair with his fingers holding on to the desk edge.

Lenny walked in a few minutes later. "What's up? I'm kind of in the middle of something next door. Make it fast."

"Go ahead, Venus." John sent Lenny a preparatory glance.

"Ray Chambers made a sexual advance toward me about a week and a half ago. I didn't say anything then, because he apologized and we basically agreed it was a mistake. But now I think he's taking out some kind of revenge on me."

John held up the picture. "Exhibit 'A.' Venus thinks he drew this and left it in her mailbox."

"He's the only person who could have done it," I interjected, trying not to sound too pathetic, sitting there in my good suit and all, but it was true. Who else could've done it?

"Whoa, wait a minute," Lenny let out an exasperated rebuttal. "There's about twenty-five people who work in this company, not to mention the possibility of someone in the building. That's another thousand or so suspects. Let's not jump the gun."

"Well, the other thousand or so people didn't have me hauled up in the parking garage groping me." His lack of understanding was frustrating.

"Venus, let us talk to Ray and find out what's going on. Don't mention this to anyone else. We'll take it from here." Lenny slipped the piece of paper in his coat pocket and went back to his meeting.

My head fell forward into my hands. I was good for at least two hours of tears, but suddenly remembered my lunch date with Tyson Edwards. Misery would have to wait. I stood up and brushed my suit out, as if I could remove all the nastiness that surrounded me.

"Will you let me know what happens, John?"

He filled me with assurances and escorted me out of his office.

When I rounded the corner, I could see Ray standing next to Sherri's area. She was filling his ear and he was giving her the trust-me smile. I slipped into the ladies' room, hoping he'd pass quickly. I couldn't be late for my meeting with Tyson Edwards. I noticed myself in the bathroom mirror, pressed up against the salmon-colored door like some secret agent, and decided I needed to get a handle on things. I walked up to the vanity mirror and leaned in close to examine the efforts of this morning. I went in the stall and pulled off a piece of the cover sheet tissue and used it to press away the oil that had built up on my perfectly made-up St. John's face. In an instant I was fresh, looking as good as I started out before all this trauma took place.

I took a deep breath and marched out of the bathroom, made the hard right around the corner and didn't care if Ray was still there or not. When I finally had enough nerve to look up, I could see Sherri typing away, alone. I wanted to knock that fake hair bun off the back of her head, and ask her whose side she was on, consorting with the enemy. Instead I darted past her and into my own office, closing the door behind me. I grabbed my purse from under the desk and peeked to see if the coast was clear before heading back out. I walked toward the elevator, passing Sherri.

"Will you be out for the rest of the day?" She spoke audibly, but I pretended not to hear her.

I tightened my jaws in order not to give her the tongue lashing I felt she was due. The elevator opened and I stepped in and moved to the corner, feeling foolish trying to dodge her scrutiny.

There was no trace of Tyson Edwards in the lobby. I looked at my watch and realized I was fifteen minutes early. Waiting in the parking lot would lessen my chances of being seen by anyone from the office. As I rounded the corner, I heard my name being called. I turned around to see Ray walking quickly toward me. I bolted through the steel door that led to the parking garage.

"Venus," he called out louder from behind, causing me to stop in midstep. Why was I running from him? If anything, I felt like clawing his eyes out. He should've been running from me.

"You're a hard lady to catch up with."

I turned and met his eyes with contempt. "I didn't hear you calling me. I'm kind of late for an appointment."

"Well, let me walk you to your car."

"That's all right, what can I do for you?" I stood firm.

"I just wanted to know if everything was working out okay, see how you're doing with the suggestions Lenny and John made yesterday. I wanted you to know I had nothing to do with that. They came to me out of nowhere and had me run those reports. That's why I couldn't get back to you on your messages. I was on a time line."

He kept his hands shoved deep into his pockets to show he was harmless. "That's all I wanted to say."

He was waiting for a sign that I believed his bogus excuse.

"Okay, well, I gotta go." I looked at my watch and turned toward the direction of my car. I knew he was still standing there. I listened intently, but still heard no footsteps but my own.

"Venus," he called out. "Come see me when you get back from lunch."

I raised my hand and gave a parade queen wave.

"Sure thing. I can't wait," I mumbled to myself.

My car was stuffy when I got inside. I checked my watch again. Eleven-thirty on the dot. It was already time to go back, but I waited a few more minutes to make sure Ray was completely gone. These new pumps I was wearing had logged some miles today, I thought as I trotted back through the steel door and inside to the lobby.

"There you are." His words were slow and mellow.

Slightly out of breath, I was unable to speak back to the handsome creature, acknowledging him only with a smile.

Tyson Edwards touched me lightly on the elbow. "I guess you know I didn't park here this time." He led me outside where I gratefully inhaled the fresh cool air. He waved his hand and a black Town Car pulled up. He opened the rear door for me and I scooted in to the farthest side. He got in after me and took a seat, bumping knees with me. I left mine there. I didn't want to be rude.

"The Hyatt, Kevin."

I looked out the window and mouthed the words "oh no" to myself. I hoped he didn't think we were going to have that kind of lunch.

He must have read my mind. "They have an exquisite restaurant there." He spoke, instantaneously alleviating my fear.

"Oh." I kept looking out the window. The heavy scent of his cologne filled the air. I didn't dare touch anything, or roll down the window. I took short necessary breaths.

"You like seafood?"

"Uh huh." That was an intelligent answer.

"This place makes the best seafood." Within minutes we pulled up to the curb, where a young valet opened his door. This was the same place the AAPA awards dinner was held. I felt somewhat better for having a clue.

He guided me by my elbow. His touch was doing sinful things to my body. I was already in a bad state of needing a fix. Feeling him so close opened up off-limit zones. I couldn't tell if the cold air had put my little friends at attention, or if it was him. Either way, the fabric of my suit was brushing against my bra sending miniature sparks. The maître d' showed us to a wine-red velvet booth that seemed to engulf our bodies. It was almost the size of a small private room. I sat first while he took off his jacket, revealing his lilac shirt under the darker plum silk tie and matching suspenders.

He slid in across from me.

"Your menu, sir."

"That won't be necessary. We know what we want."

I gave a polite smile and didn't argue while he ordered for both of us. I couldn't help but feel like Cinderella, although this wasn't a date, merely me trying to make a business contact. I was networking and needed to keep a clear perspective. If I could stop staring into his soap opera star face and do a reality check, I'd be fine.

"So, Miss Venus. What kind of great ideas do you have for me today?"

"Thought you'd never ask." I scooted in close so he could hear me. "If I may continue from the last time we met." I laughed shyly. "I know I told you about separating the lines of cosmetics and hair products to be marketed to different groups, but let me break it down for you. If you took the same product and packaged it four different ways, you'd have four times more probability of it being sold."

"I'm listening," he said with a smile that sent darts through my body, whipping around and ending in my first chakra.

"It's that simple." A warmth moved through me, causing my thighs to squeeze together. Networking, that's all. "The same product marketed to teens, young adults, eighteen to twenty-five, women twenty-five to thirty-five, and then your over-forty market. Same product with four different looks. Sure I wear my favorite color lipstick that I've been using since college. But what's going to happen when I think this color is outdated for me, too young? I'm not only going to change to a new color, I most likely will switch to a new brand. One that says, this is for you, more mature, more elegant. You see?"

He clasped his hands together over the table, making his wedding ring visible, a thick gold band with three midsize diamonds slanted through the middle.

"It makes sense. I like it a lot. So what are you doing spending your time as a number cruncher with all this creativity running through your veins?"

"I ask myself that daily. I love my job, don't get me wrong. I just think it's time for me to move on. I've discussed it with them. I wanted to be the account manager on your project, but it wasn't doable."

"Oh yeah?" He tilted his head to the other side and squinted through his low thick lashes.

"Yes. I thought I'd be perfect for this account. Believe me when I tell you, St. John's has a lot of my money." I rattled off on my fingers all the products I've used faithfully. "I swear, I just cut off at least two feet of hair, all by-product of St. John's."

He laughed. "You did what? I don't believe you."

"I'm serious. Look." I pulled out my wallet and showed him my DC driver's license. It was a picture taken three years ago, but it still represented my story.

"Wow." He spoke under his breath. "Impressive." He slid the wallet across the table.

"Wow, what?" I asked.

"Just wow." He was squinting again. "You had it going on. What made you do that?" He pointed to my hair.

"Disenchantment, you could say." I snapped my wallet closed and put it in my purse.

"So you took it out on your hair, huh? That is something I will never understand about women. Even being in this business, I can't figure out why women's global world outlook is attached to their hair." He raised his arms to the shape of the world. "If something happens in a woman's life, the first thing she does is change her hair. A new job, a divorce, any little tragedy, and the hair gets it." He started laughing in a low chuckle.

I laughed with him but I was still reeling from his first response. I *had* it going on.

"It's your hair or your life." I played along. "Come out with your hands up." I subsided the laughter long enough to think of a sensible answer. "Honestly, I think it has a lot to do with how we grow up. Little girls get it on a regular basis, you know, every day they've got to do something with their hair, ponytails, barrettes, you name it. We're fussed over by our mothers for the special events. Taken to the beauty shop before we can walk good. And it just goes on and on. Every stage of our life is defined by how we look."

"Boys, too. Little boys have to sit in the barber chair, get a little something something taken off the sides, special occasions, Easter Sunday. Women aren't the only ones that went through that. Come on. This is something untouchable. It's bigger than the both of us." He cracked himself up.

I accepted the second glass of wine he poured. "Seriously though, I think black women have it the worst. We hate our hair, starting from the day our mothers sigh in exasperation in our little baby ears, "what am I going to do with all this nappy hair," then come the braids, the pressing comb, the relaxers. After every experiment is exhausted, we're still left hating our hair. We sit up and watch those "bouncin' and behavin'" commercials with the little blonds shaking their heads, and we wish that it was us, but it'll never be. Then there's companies like *yours* that do the same, except with black models who've spent hours being made over, truly over, and it becomes our goal to live up to those standards."

"Oh, so now you're trying to blame the companies that make the product. I think you'd fit into that category, Miss Johnston."

"Guilty as the rest of the world. I don't deny that the advertisers are partly responsible, but we're just trying to give the companies, like yours, what they need to sell their products. And what sells is what's popular and beautiful. I didn't make the social rules, I just live by them."

"Till now?" He pointed slightly to my hair.

"Yes. I've rejected the system and I'm darn proud of it."

"Are you really? Do you really feel better? Does it make you feel prettier, smarter, even sexier?"

I had to think for a minute. I didn't have a good reply. In all honesty, I was fighting daily to feel good about myself, but I didn't know if it had anything to do with my hair, the weather, the stars aligned with Mars and Saturn, losing Clint. I just didn't know.

"That's a loaded question, Mr. Edwards. Let's just say I'm proud. I did something I wanted to do without thoughts of repercussion. That alone is a rush, to take charge of your life and to stop doing what's acceptable and pleasing to everyone else. I admit I don't enjoy being dismissed and ignored by the opposite sex now that my hair is gone. Just like your remark, 'I *had* it going on,' as if *now* I don't exist or I'm invisible." I spoke with total disdain. "No, there's nothing fun about hearing something like that. It doesn't make me feel desirable or sexy knowing that you see me with such shallowness. But I'm learning. Every day I receive a lesson that teaches me that I can't let what others think define me."

After I stopped talking, I identified the culprit, the empty wineglass, sitting in front of me. When my eyes crept up to meet his to form my apology, it surprised me that his expression was neither shocked nor appalled. In fact, he looked completely impressed.

"You're right, I'm sorry for insulting you." He said sincerely, sliding his hand out to shake mine, "Tyson Edwards. Nice meeting someone truly as beautiful as yourself."

When he attempted to refill my glass, I slid my hand over the top. We ate and talked more.

I couldn't help but think how lucky his wife was. I'd seen her in pictures in the *Essence* magazine. In the shadow of his flawlessness, she was an average-looking woman. She had soft round features, very likable. Still, nothing compared with her better half. He asked me what my background was, where I went to school, and all that name-dropping stuff I never was any good at. I explained my beginnings, from a small suburb in Southern California, with a mother who stayed home all her life and a father who worked in his same social worker position for thirty years until he retired. Tyson, like me, would never know that kind of stability in one career. We both agreed that was an extinct ideology.

He spent the rest of the lunch talking about himself and his upbringing in Virginia. He painted the perfect Cliff and Claire Huxtable scenario, but I could see he was dealing with some deeper memories that probably weren't so perfect. He spent a lot of time staring down at his plate when he spoke of his doctor father and schoolteacher mother. I matched him story for story in the area of life's lessons, going to school where I was told by teachers not to try too hard, that they understood if we didn't do so well, meaning me and the other five percent of minorities that made up the school population. That only served as fuel to make me try even harder. My sweet reward was the "A" they had to mark across my page. I ended up attending the University of Southern California with a full academic scholarship.

He talked of being the all-city pro in his high school for basketball, only to be cut from the team after the first year in college. We agreed the real world was a lot different from the one our parents painted for us. Too many dreams, and not enough resources to make them come true.

Although he admitted to having everything a man could want with his position and status in the business arena, he'd always have to prove himself. It was known he had only attained his success by association. If he hadn't married the heir of St. John's, where would he be? It was most evident in the way he flashed, made sure you saw the gold, the Benz, and now chauffeur-driven Lincoln Town Car waiting out front. He wore his insecurity literally on his sleeve, back, and wrist.

The afternoon ended much too soon. He told me he would see what he could do about influencing John and Lenny without stepping on any toes. I knew he would. His car dropped me at work, and he reiterated his goal to see me on the St. John's account. I gave him a thumbs-up and watched his shiny car drive off. Why did all the good ones have to be married already? I inhaled deeply and began mentally preparing myself for the tension in the office. It was only two. I still had a full day ahead before I was through.

I'm Innocent

WALKING INTO A CONVENIENCE mart was like stepping into a scene from *Bad Boys*. The shop owners see a black man and immediately put one finger on the steel trigger hidden underneath the counter while the other rings you up. *Damn, all I wanted was some gas and some chips. Mutha fucka staring at me like I wanted to rob him. When will people stop tripping?* He walked back to his car feeling like there may have been a gun pointed at his back. It's not like he was running around with his pants hanging off his hips, with gang colors wrapped around his head. He had on a simple Fila fleece with some wide-leg Hilfigers. You couldn't get any straighter than that, but all they see is a black man with the potential to get violent.

Clint pulled into Cedric's driveway, stiff from the hour and a half ride. The two-story colonial home already had Christmas decorations, white lights hanging like tiny icicles from the roof, a pine tree wrapped with multicolored lights, and carved-wood deer stationed out front. Cedric was definitely making family life look worthwhile.

He pulled the overnight bag out of the back seat. He needed this break from the hospital and that uncomfortable sofa bed. Cedric had extended the weekend invite to Kandi as well, but Clint had to break it to him that they were history. Cedric was disappointed, making his point that Kandi was a pleasant sight and did wonders for his libido. Clint had told him he should be quite content with what he has at home. His wife, Shelly, had the likeness of a TV mom, with her bright eyes and attentive smile. She and Cedric had been married a little over ten years and it seemed they were still going strong. Although, in the back of Clint's mind, he could always see Cedric's first wife, Althea, breathing fire and making demands. He could never be sure what went on behind closed doors and only hoped Shelly was as genuine as she appeared.

"What's up, man?" Cedric and Clint hugged for a good five minutes. Clint held on the longest. He needed the comfort of unconditional love, and he knew he could always depend on his big brother.

"You two come in and quit letting out all my heat." Shelly came down the stairs and gave Clint a hug. "Where's that . . ."

"Kandi," Clint filled in.

"She couldn't come?" Shelly asked concerned, but still relieved.

"Nah. Things aren't quite working out."

"So you're back with Venus?" She asked hopefully.

"Not working out there either."

Shelly pushed her hand into his chest, "You shoulda asked her to marry you like I told you. Now you let her get away. Hardheaded boy." She disappeared down the hallway, mumbling about men not knowing what they want and chasing their tails in circles without the faintest clue of what they'll do when they catch it.

"Rodney, come get Uncle Clint's bag and take it to Daryl's room," Cedric yelled up the stairs.

"I don't want to put Daryl out his room, man."

"He's spending the night at a friend's house. So you got it to yourself."

They walked into the family room where the fireplace pumped out old-fashioned heat from fresh-cut wood. Clint fell into Cedric's favorite chair, knowing he was going to pitch a fit.

"Boy, get outta my seat. You better sit in one of these couches Shelly paid too much money for." He assisted Clint up by his arm and fake tossed him on the couch. "Messin' with my chair."

Shelly walked in with two beers. "I've tried to toss that beat-up old thing out. Every time, he stops the moving men from the Salvation Army from getting it." She washed her hand over Cedric's face. "Big baby."

Clint took a swig of the brew. The ice cold liquid sizzled going down his throat. He took a moment to rest his eyes. A nice fire, a brewsky, and a soft place to lay his head, that's what he needed. He was so tired. It seemed like Venus and Kandi both were stored in his brain, living there, screaming at him, what a no-good-m-f he was. He didn't need that on top of everything else that was floating around up there. Sometimes he felt like a hard drive that had reached its maximum capacity for storing information. Right now he could use one of the thousands of medicines he'd memorized that could soothe a simple headache. *There ain't nothing wrong with aspirin, I take it. Does right by me.* He laughed out loud to himself.

"Clint man, what's on your mind?" Cedric wanted to get in on whatever was so funny.

"Nothing, man. I'm just delirious over here. I was thinking about the program. Sometimes you just gotta laugh or it'll beat you down. I was thinking about all these medications I gotta memorize that'll give instant satisfaction. But there ain't no medicine that can fix a broken heart." Clint took another sip of the beer.

"Oh naw, hell naw, please don't tell me you still whining over Venus. Please don't tell me that," Cedric pleaded.

"I still . . . I don't know. I guess if she had a legitimate point, I could let it go, but it's all bullshit. I never lied to her, never cheated, never did nothing. I'm innocent, man. And all of a sudden it's just over."

Cedric shook his head in disapproval. "That's the problem. You didn't do anything. Anything is better than nothing. Women are like that. They want a little shake, rattle, and roll, once in a while. They don't want things to settle too much; complacency is a nasty word when it comes to a woman. You can't start taking things for granted and expect that she's going to be happy. Gotta shake things up." He tilted the bottle to his face, swallowing the last of his beer.

"How was I supposed to have time to be 'shakin' things up'? Man, this internship is no joke. I didn't have time for the romance game and she knew it. I'll tell you what it was; her schedule was thrown off. I ruined her plans. I didn't propose marriage when and how she wanted." Clint stared straight into the fire. "She didn't give a damn about me, all she was thinking about was *Venus*. She stomped her feet and marched off like a three-year-old that didn't get the toy she'd wanted for her birthday. I tried to talk to her, but she wouldn't hear me out." Clint pushed his fingers into his temples. His headache had worsened from the beer or the conversation, he wasn't sure which. "I'm sick of this game she's playing, man, that's all I know. I'm tired of feeling like I've done something wrong. I'm always feeling like that with Venus, like I can never do what she wants me to do, never be *right*."

"So what are you going to do? Keep running up this hill of ice, or move on? When she comes to her senses, you'll either still be there or snatched up by some sweet, hot thang named *Kandi*." Cedric let the name roll off his tongue. He let a few minutes go by before realizing Clint was zoning out again. "So what do you think?"

"What do I think about what?" Clint asked.

"How long you gonna wait?" Cedric relaxed into his large leather recliner ready for an answer. He'd hoped his brother had more dignity than to keep getting spit on. Back in the day, he'd had the steel-toned body, the sparkling smile, and the woman problems that went along with good looks. Not much time had passed, but it was obvious that becoming a man and a father to his siblings before his time had struck hard blows. Barely forty, and gray hair almost completely covered his head. His strong smile was still there, but his eyes were sallow, the result of graveyard shifts and overtime.

"I don't know." Clint kept his eyes on the fire for some kind of sign, an answer.

Cedric threw up his hands and shook his head. "You're hopeless, man."

When Clint was about nine, he'd told his big brother he wanted to be a doctor, something he'd seen on an episode of *Julia*, where Diahann Carroll's face lit up with admiration and love for her television son, with the news, "a doctor, oh boy." Clint received the same response from Cedric, only he never let go of it. He made Clint repeat it twenty times a day every day. "I'm going to be a doctor." By the tenth grade, Clint hadn't wanted to be a doctor or anything else. All he needed was a paying gig with the city just to get out of the tiny two-bedroom apartment they'd been living in since he could walk. After getting as far as putting in a couple of job applications, he'd decided that breaking his big brother's heart wasn't on his things-to-do list, especially after Cedric had worked so hard to support Clint and Alison. He had to follow through.

Being a natural athlete was his road to an education. When it came time to choose which college he'd attend, it boiled down to the premed curriculum, not their status in the Pack 10. He'd garnered himself a place at Georgetown University by holding the high jump record in the eastern region and was on his way.

He repeated the words every night before sleep, staring up at the bunk bed overhead. He repeated the words to himself in classes while taking tests, he repeated them to himself when a joint fell into his lap at a party, or when a pretty young thing rubbed up against him swearing that she was on the pill. He repeated the words when each and every obstacle stood in his way.

He was going to be a doctor . . . for Cedric.

Clint was starting to feel the haze of the alcohol's numbing effect when Cedric's voice interrupted. "If I were you, I'd just stay low. Stay out of her way. Let her deal with her demons. Without you to blame things on, she'll have to deal with the real problem, whatever it is."

Clint closed his eyes, and for the first time didn't care. He was tired of being goaded into action by someone else's expectations. He felt a big hook in the side of his mouth where he'd been caught like a fish and led around by whoever held the extended pole. It had been passed from Cedric's hands to Venus's with the hook and wire still intact, only this time Venus was on a speedboat. He knew removing the hook would be painful, a little scary at first. Clint couldn't remember the last time he'd made a decision without consulting either one of them. But it was time.

He looked over at Cedric as he lay stretched out in his recliner chair. "Thanks, man."

"Advice is free, my brother."

"Not for advice, for everything. Thanks for taking care of me." Clint let his eyes fall closed once again. He pictured his hands holding on to the hook, he pulled with one fierce grip. It would hurt for a while, but eventually once the shock wore off, he'd swim the waters free of guilt, free of obligation.

Never Promise

CLINT WOULD BE BACK. THEY always come back. She pictured her scalding anger puncturing him with her words. The rage she felt was self-induced and she knew it. Clint had never made any promises. He had tried to maintain a safe distance between them. All along he had been preparing her for this dismissal. She really couldn't blame him at all. Her anger was instead directed at Venus, at whatever mysterious hold she had on his heart. The crackling sound of the postwar intercom put a pause on her thoughts.

"Ms. Treboe, we have a delivery here for you."

Kandi put her pen inside the notepad and closed it.

"What is it, Marcy?" By using first names, she was signaling that the little people were out of the classroom and they could speak freely.

"Kandi, you gotta come see this. Two dozen long-stemmed roses," Marcy's voice belted out.

"I'll be right there." Kandi locked her room and walked quickly to the front office. The plaque engraved on the outside of the office door always made her question why she hadn't tried to get a new teaching job. *Lillian Dearborn Primary founded 1896*, with no upgrades, but built to last. She thought about the new schools that were being built fast as lightning over in the suburban areas. Nice central air conditioning, floors with vinyl, large windows to see the flowers in the spring or snow, in today's case. Yet she was still drawn to this little brick school with the hardwood floors. She walked past the chatting teachers who used their break time as a soap opera digest update. They sat huddled together in their large down jackets and corny snow boots. They mostly talked about the children, who had no manners, or needed to be in a mental institution instead of their classrooms. The conversation would then turn to the status of the parents, divorced, single, or married, and what made the children so screwed up in the first place. Kandi found the conversations cruel and didn't participate in them. She thought it was a shame, the way some of the teachers talked about the kids behind their backs. The same children who trusted them with their secrets and fears were most likely the topics of discussion.

Marcy and Lynn were standing around the larger than life assortment of red and pink roses inside a beautiful crystal vase when she entered the office. Most of the other staff went outside to catch some of the fleeting sunshine, watching the children build snowmen during their recess breaks. Marcy and Lynn were the only ones in the hallowed brick building. It echoed from its emptiness.

"Open the card, we want to know who these came from." Marcy was bouncing around like a teenager. Not surprising, since she was only one year past legal age.

"Now, now, ladies. I can't share that kind of information with you.

Next thing you know, he'll get stolen from me by one of you young beauties." Marcy blushed with her wild wavy hair falling in every direction. Her reddish brown skin glowed from youth, and nothing more.

"Kandi, just read the card, you don't have to tell us who it's from." Lynn, the other intern, spoke with her thick tongue, swollen from a piercing gone bad. Since the Spice Girl invasion, her wild erotic look had become typical. Kandi gave Lynn compliments on her smile and eyes hoping she'd feel good about her natural attributes and shed some of the dramatic accessories. What she really wanted to tell her was to go catch a sale at Sears. But all those changes would come in due time. Lynn really would have no choice in the matter; fitting in, becoming ordinary, happened naturally, like day turning into night.

Kandi picked up the vase and started toward the door. "Sorry, no can do." She could hear Lynn speaking like there was too much spit in her mouth as she started walking away.

"See, I told you we should've peeked."

For a brief moment, Kandi anticipated the note card to be signed by Clint with an apology. That was until she saw Tyson's handwriting on the bottom. It simply read *in time;* that was his reminder to keep waiting. In time, they would be a real couple, not one hiding with stolen days and nights. In time, she would be Mrs. Tyson Edwards, if she were patient.

She tore the card into tiny little pieces and set the flowers on her desk. She grabbed her pen and notebook and headed outside to watch over her class during recess. Her thoughts couldn't help racing back to Clint. She'd let him off the hook for a week at the most. She didn't want to seem too pushy or needy. After a satisfactory waiting period, she'd call. Whatever problems he and Venus were going through that sent him her way in the first place would rear their ugly head again. Right now she'd finish her list of stipulations for taking him back. She noted each one with precision. Number one, they would have to spend at least three nights per week together. Two, all communication with Venus must end. Number three, Clint must tell Venus directly that he has found someone new and to back off. Number four—

"Ms. Treboe, Christopher Lee fell off the monkey bars and now he's holding his arm and rolling around on the ground."

Kandi stuck her pen into the notepad, irritated at the interruption. Christopher Lee's mother had brought in cupcakes and syrupy punch for his birthday earlier and then left Kandi to fend for herself after the sugar high took effect. Kandi wouldn't be surprised if Christopher thought he was superboy for a day and tried to skip handlebars instead of taking them one at a time.

The other children were standing around him, some giggling, and some silent and in shock from the eerie moaning noises that were coming out of him. Kandi gently pushed her way through.

"Christopher, where does it hurt? Do you think it's broken?"

"I don't know. It hurts." He let out more sobs.

"Well, try to stand up, Christopher. Can you stand up?"

"It hurts."

"Okay, sweetie. Just calm down." Kandi looked around to see who would be most diligent. "Missy, run to the office and tell Principal Erin that Christopher Lee may have broken his arm. Don't waste time talking to anyone else. Find Principal Erin."

Missy took her orders seriously and ran off in the direction of the office.

"Can I go with her? Can I?" Kelly wanted in on the limelight.

"Run, go ahead." Kandi turned her attention back to Christopher. She felt guilty for being annoyed at the interruption. But she had been right in the middle of some very important thoughts before this accident happened.

Principal Erin made his way through the small mob of children.

"Looks broken, and I didn't want to move him," Kandi whispered in his ear.

Joseph Erin was a large man with hands to match. He lifted Christopher up with the ease of carrying a newborn infant. He carried him to the office while the children followed like a swarm of bees. Kandi hurried in front to pull open the heavy oak door to let them pass. Principal Erin dispatched orders to call Christopher Lee's parents first and if they weren't home, to gather the medical information off the emergency card and call his doctor. Principal Erin laid the small boy out on the wire-framed cot.

Marcy had the file in hand before a few seconds went by. "No one's home," she waved the card in the air. "I'm calling the doctor."

Kandi sent the other children back to the classroom with Lynn. She took a seat on the edge of the cot and watched the boy continue to squirm. She touched his head and pulled her hand back quickly. The heat from his forehead stung her hand.

"Oh my God." She scooped Christopher Lee up, cradling him in her arms, not knowing where her strength came from and called out, "He's got a temperature."

The office was now an empty hollow box. She looked through the glass partition for Principal Erin. Marcy wasn't sitting at her desk. In that instant, she was all alone holding what felt like a hot steaming rag.

Kandi picked up the flannel blanket at the end of the cot and wrapped him slightly to stop his shaking and clattering teeth.

"What's going on?" Marcy walked back in the office.

"He's burning up. We need to call an ambulance."

"Mr. Erin told me to just leave a message with his doctor because his mother wasn't home."

"I know Marcy, but he has a fever. Call an ambulance."

"Kandi, I can't. The last time I called an ambulance it was for that Spencer boy. I got in trouble, because it wasn't a real emergency, and Mr. Erin was all over me for the cost. The parents didn't want to pay for it."

"What's the problem?" Principal Erin walked in, blocking the doorway with his frame.

Kandi was relieved. "He's got a fever out of this world. I don't know what's wrong with him, but it feels like convulsions or something. He's shaking like he's freezing, but his skin is on fire. We need to call an ambulance. This doesn't make sense if it's just his arm."

He walked over to Kandi and felt the boy's head. "Yeah, he's hot all right, but I don't think an ambulance is warranted. Marcy, call his parents one more time. See if they can be reached."

"Wait a minute. We can call the parents after we call the ambulance. This boy is burning up." The heat from Christopher Lee was spreading into Kandi's body.

Principal Erin turned toward Marcy. "Call his parents." Marcy knew who held rank.

Kandi stormed past him and started walking with the boy to her classroom. "I'll take him to the hospital myself."

"Ms. Treboe, you bring him back in here right now!"

Kandi was already rounding the corner of her classroom. The other children stopped in the midst of their loudness and watched Kandi carrying the sack of weight on her shoulder while searching her desk drawer for her car keys. Lynn rushed to her side.

"Grab my keys, Lynn. Hand them to me."

Lynn picked up the silver elephant with a harness of keys and shoved them into Kandi's hand so as not to miss her target. She didn't question her goal; she could see the determination in Kandi's usually pleasant face.

Kandi pulled into the emergency hospital entrance and ran to the passenger side of her car. The strength she started out with in abundance was now spent. After struggling unsuccessfully to gather up Christopher's slack body, she ran inside to find someone to help. The first person she ran into was a janitor with the name "Sam" sewn on his shirt. She led him out to the car without a word. He picked up the deathly pale, sleeping boy and carried him inside.

"This little boy is having some kind of seizure," Kandi told the receptionist through the glass structure. The lump of fear in the back of Kandi's throat prevented her from speaking any louder. She wanted this to be over, but it was like running down a long endless hallway.

"Bring him around." The receptionist instructed with her brown hand, waving them through the double doors. Kandi followed the janitor who carried Christopher Lee in his arms. They walked to the back where waiting beds were open for more unfortunate incidents.

"Is he diabetic, or have any existing condition?" The chocolate woman was writing on a clipboard.

Kandi shook her head no and answered, "I don't know" when appropriate. "I'm his teacher. This wasn't supposed to happen, we thought he just had a sprained arm, broken or something. I don't know what's wrong with him." The tears Kandi had kept in the tight neat ball finally broke through. All Kandi saw was the rush of white coats and pastel uniforms file past her. Another brushed past her, almost knocking her over. She lifted her eyes out of the confusion to focus and see Clint standing over Christopher Lee, touching him with his stethoscope.

She whispered his name, then backed out of the room, unable to share the same space as Clint. Standing before her, he was Dr. Fairchild, an angel of greatness, someone capable of saving life, giving calm.

The chocolate woman caught her by the arm.

"We need more information from you, ma'am. You want to have a seat?"

Kandi felt her way into the chair and gave as much information as she could to the best of her ability, name, age, what he'd eaten in the last hour. They'd have to call the school for his pertinent data, they kept that type of information there, insurance, who to bill. She laid her face in her hands. Who to bill? This little show was going to cost a fortune, she thought briefly before Clint came out. He walked directly to her as if he'd seen her all along. He kneeled down in front of her for eye contact.

"Hey," he touched her knee. "He's going to be fine. How'd you know?"

"How'd I know what?"

"That he was having an allergic reaction. I think you missed your calling."

"I didn't know. The only thing I was sure of was you don't have a fever with a broken arm."

"He was holding on to his arm because of the wasp sting. Wasp or bee, we couldn't tell which for sure, but it was definitely an allergic reaction."

"Wasp? In this weather?" Kandi let her head fall back.

"I know, but as long as there's a heat source, they'll live and thrive. You may want to mention to whoever keeps up maintenance around there to check out the basement or furnace area for nests."

"I'm just glad it's over. I'm probably going to be fired for insubordination. I wasn't supposed to bring him here. I just couldn't believe that the principal was so afraid of spending an extra dollar that he would let that boy suffer while he tracked down his parents."

"You did the right thing," he assured her. "You want to get something to drink downstairs?" Clint was already standing up, appearing larger than life. He extended his smooth dark hand. The hand that saved lives.

"Sure." Kandi straightened her skirt that had edged its way around with the zipper showing near the front. She wiped away most of the smeared black eyeliner. "How do I look?"

"Gorgeous as ever." Clint gave her a reassuring pat on her shoulder as they started to walk. Kandi felt a breeze of hope when he touched her. The tenseness that had built up with the day's events evaporated.

Kandi felt proud to be in Clint's company. He put his arm around her shoulder to gently guide her. A few of the female staff did double takes as they walked through the corridor. Another one taken off the market, they were probably thinking, by the typical light-skinned, long-hair type. The usual pick of the too-dark brother who'd finally made something of his self. But they were wrong. She wished it were the case, that Clint was hers and she, his. He would be with her if he could. It wasn't his fault, she found herself thinking. If Venus would just let him go.

She slid her arm tighter around his waist and slowed her steps. She wanted to feel the strength of his arm wrapped around her for as long as possible. If only momentarily, she wanted to feel like she was the chosen one.

Go Home

The snow left everything shimmering. The stretch of land on the left side of the road all seemed even and smooth. It gave a certain comfort. A calming effect. I slid on my sunglasses so I could look at it a little longer. The brightness of it with the sun bouncing off was almost too radiant for the eyes.

I had woken up intent on giving this day the benefit of the doubt. Hoping that this day would bring the change I needed. Hell, if I couldn't have it all with the doctor's wife profile, I could at least have the career. After my lunch with Tyson yesterday I was expecting to be put on that St. John's account, pronto. Who would have the nerve not to give the client what he wanted? And at this point, the client wanted me. I could just see Ray's face when he was told I would be an account manager.

He'd have to do his own work, for a change. Make all those numbers measure up, like they wanted out of me. The new stuff would probably land on Ray's empty desk.

I parked my gray Hyundai and gave it a nice pat. Soon I'd be trading the baby in for something new and shiny, maybe a Beamer like the one I'd contributed to for Tina back in my hair-day.

I picked up my mail from my box. Sherri wasn't sitting there. I was glad. I sifted through it as I walked, looking for anything suspicious. There it was, another envelope with my name on it. When I reached my office, I dropped my coat and purse on the desk and sat down, almost missing my chair. I tore the envelope open, cutting myself on its edge. It hurt like hell. And for what, this little piece of paper. *STUPID BITCH.* The words were screaming out at me. I dropped the note on the desk where it landed facedown. The reverse side had a smaller version of the stick person drawn on it the same as the first note.

I picked up the phone to dial John. His voice mail came on and I hung up. I got up and peeked out before heading down the hall to Sherri.

"Sherri!" She kept her head down. "Sherri, are you going to tell me you didn't see anyone drop this off here, either? You're the one that puts the mail in our boxes." I held the envelope up to her. She took her time acknowledging me.

"Actually, I did put that in your box this morning. I found it sitting right here on top of my computer. What is the big deal?" She stood up to straighten her skirt that was riding up her thighs.

"The big deal is somebody is sending me insults and calling me bitch anonymously and I'm trying to find out who it is." I squeezed the tissue tighter around my finger to ease the stinging of the paper cut.

Sherri put her hand over her mouth. "You're kidding me. I know you lying."

"That's why I asked you yesterday. You didn't see who brought the envelope over yesterday, either?"

"Venus, I swear, if I saw anything, I would tell you." She had a new sympathetic tone in her voice.

I looked around, up and down the halls. "Sherri, keep your eyes open, please."

"I will." She detected my desperation and felt sorry for me.

I walked back to my office and left a message on John's voice mail. "I received another offensive note today. I guess you gave Ray a good talking to, huh?" I hung up. What possessed me to talk to the owner of the company that way. Sarcastic, arrogant. It was hypertension. My blood was surging at lightning speed through my veins. I couldn't work under these conditions. The phone rang within seconds after I put it down. I jumped.

"Venus, how ya doin', it's Ray."

"Yes," I said, exhaling hard.

"You didn't stop by yesterday before you left. We need to schedule something this morning, or this afternoon, to get together." He waited patiently for my response.

"I'll look at my calendar and get right back with you." I hung up the phone. Cold drafts of air made the hair stand up on my arms. I dialed Lenny's number, then hung up the phone before it could ring. What if he was in on it, too? Maybe they saw what trouble I could cause with a sexual harassment charge and just wanted to see me gone with the wind under my feet. I had to calm down. The only way to deal with whoever it was, was to not let it get to me. I did a few deep breathing exercises. Stretched and breathed some more. I grabbed the note and stuck it back in the envelope and made a file for it. I titled it Idiot's Notes, where they would be filed if any more came. I wished I hadn't let Lenny take the first one. I closed the file cabinet and concentrated on the task at hand. I had to stay focused on the goal of working on the St. John's account. That was my main concern.

I really had to rethink my strategy. Even if I did get the St. John's account, how could I work for a group that had no respect for me? St. John's probably meant nothing to John and Lenny, who were creating multimillion-dollar ads for the likes of Energizer and Pepsi. St. John's budget of maybe one-tenth of what the larger accounts were spending was probably ranked pretty low on their bottom line. Nevertheless, I had a goal and I was sticking to it. St. John's deserved everything I had to offer. Gary Marshall would do nothing but put together a few greasy head models and float the product around and call it an ad. I had ideas bursting out everywhere, walking, shopping, listening to music, everything gave me inspiration for another idea.

I watched rain fall on the roof of the building next door. It was the next best thing to a view overlooking the city streets of northwest DC. I'd rather be over looking the Potomac River like Ray's office, which reminded me to dial John's office once again.

"Yes." He answered on the first ring.

"John, it's Venus, did you get my message?"

"Uh no, I haven't gotten that far yet. I just got here."

"I got another note."

"Bring it in, let me see it."

"I don't think that's necessary. I already tore it up. I just wanted you to know how frantic I was when I first received it this morning, so you'll have to forgive my harshness when you hear the message I left earlier."

"Was this note exactly like the first?"

"No, this time it said 'stupid bitch,' but with the same drawing on it as the last one."

"Venus, this really might be serious. Maybe you should take some time off. Leave a couple of weeks early for your Christmas vacation until we can get to the bottom of this."

"I . . . I'm all right. That's not necessary."

"I think it would be best, Venus. You are completely stressed out, you're a nervous wreck. Whatever is going on needs to stop, and the only way I can see that happening at this point is if we pull out the determining factors, one of the most important being you." His voice was unusually strong, not like his daily demeanor when he and Lenny played good cop, bad cop. "It's for your own good, Venus."

"John, I have a lot of work to finish here. I—"

"Venus, it's best. I'll take care of whatever is pending. Right now your well-being comes first."

Any other time I would've been grateful for extra time off, but not like this. I hung up the phone feeling removed. What was happening here? The earth was spinning. I could relate to "stop the world I want to get off." This wasn't fair. I was the one being sent the derogatory notes, being harassed. I was sure it was Ray Chambers. Who else could it have been?

I tried once more, calling back within minutes. "John. Hi." Pause. Say it.

"Are you making this decision based on my actions or someone else's? Because I'm really getting the impression I'm being punished for something I'm not responsible for."

"Well, obviously it's nothing you've done, Venus. But this thing has gotten out of hand. We don't know who's sending the notes, but we know who they're being sent to. I'm just trying to take the product out of the equation, and that's you."

"But that's not fair. I shouldn't be punished for what someone else is doing. I'm the victim here."

"Venus, you're under the impression you're being penalized. Not at all. No, in fact it's just the opposite. My first concern is your safety. I have to take threats of any kind seriously. Violence has hit exorbitant levels. The corporate climate has shifted to a zero-tolerance policy. If someone out there hates you, who knows what's next?"

"The someone is Ray. Why is that so hard to believe? No one else has a reason to be this mean, this angry with me. Nobody. Ray is the only one. It makes sense; he wants some kind of revenge for my rejecting and humiliating him." I rested my head in the palm of my shaking hand.

"If we had some proof of that, I would take action, Venus."

"Well, you're not going to get proof by sending me home. He won't have a need to make another move. His goal will have been accomplished. I'll be gone, out of sight, out of mind."

"I think I'm making the best decision, Venus. Let's just leave it at that. In fact, you can start your vacation today." He paused. "All right . . . stop in before you go." We hung up the phone at the same time, except I slammed the receiver down hard.

I grabbed the Idiot's Notes file and my purse and coat and stomped up to the elevator. Before my hand pressed the down button, I turned right back around and headed for Ray's office.

I didn't knock, I walked straight in. "Why are you doing this? Why are you sending me these notes?" I threw the file on his desk and it slid, landing directly in front of him.

He opened it, picked up the half crumpled paper, and then tossed it back in the file. "I didn't send you this. You think I sent you this?"

"Stop lying. I know you did. No one else around here has a reason to hate me. I know you do." My voice wasn't my own. It was low and menacing. "Remember the parking lot scene?"

His intense stare made me angrier. "We put that to rest, Venus. I apologized, and I meant it. I don't have anything against you. I admitted I was wrong." He was trying to make me seem crazy. Paranoid.

"Yeah, right!" I leaned in closer to his face. "I have something against you. I'm being sent home over this shit while you get to sit and do absolutely nothing in this big office of yours. Thank you very much." I turned around and marched out of there, slamming the door behind me.

I was hot, steaming. I was sure my head was glowing from the heat. I could see John coming out of his office wondering what was going on. Dominick and Saige were standing outside of their offices, too. Sherri was peering all the way down from the other end of the hall. Ray came out looking like the innocent victim, standing directly behind me with his sleeves rolled up over his forearms as if he'd just been through a rough time. He raised up his hands implying he didn't know what was going on. John walked over to me.

"In my office now. Please." He added. He looked up at Ray. "You, too."

We both walked in and sat down at opposite sides of the office.

"What the hell is going on? That's all I want to know. Has everyone lost their minds around here?" John pleaded.

"I told you he's the one sending the notes, but you won't believe me."

"I don't know why she thinks I would do something like that. I've been the most supportive member of this team when it comes to Venus." He turned to me. "I have always been in your corner."

"The review wasn't enough, questioning the quality of my work. Now you're out to embarrass and humiliate me all because I wouldn't be with you."

"Is any of this true, Ray? Did you make advances toward Venus, sexual advances?"

"The only thing I did was take her up on an invitation to lunch. If I appeared overly grateful, I'm sorry." He looked at me again. "But I never touched her in that way. Not intentionally."

"He's lying!"

"Venus, please." John scolded. "So you're saying Venus just made it up?" he asked, not sure who to believe. "You never tried to kiss her, fondle her?"

"John, I mean really. I don't need this, if you know what I mean. Venus is attractive in her own sort of way, but really, I am not interested in her."

I was trembling from anger. Now I wasn't pretty enough for him. But I was pretty that day when he couldn't keep his hands off me.

Ray turned to me again. "I'm really sorry if you misinterpreted my feelings. And it goes without saying that I have no animosity toward you."

John put his hands down in his lap as he lowered himself on the edge of his desk. He strained to keep one foot on the ground.

"I don't know what to do here. This situation is scaring me. We're a small company. We don't need this kind of thing here." John looked down at his hands like he was grappling with himself. He needed Lenny for this, but then he spoke the forced words. "Venus, I have no choice. Until we can resolve this, I think you'd better stay home."

The fireplace hadn't been lit since last year around this time, when Clint and I would pull all the pillows off the couch and make out like teenagers on the floor. This time it was just me and Sandy on the thick-piled Berber rug. I struck the long wood-stemmed match and watched it burn before moving it toward the paper-wrapped log.

I'd been off for exactly three days and it felt like three weeks. An extended vacation, at least that's what we agreed it was called. My heart felt like it was caving in when John had said the words. "Me?" I wanted to scream, "why not him?" The smug expression on Ray's face said, *see, I told you I would win.*

I walked out of there with my dignity stripped. I knew I shouldn't have told anyone about the garage incident with Ray. I should've just dealt with it, ignoring the notes, ignoring the fact I felt like a leper before this thing even made headlines. The stomach doesn't lie. It's the Geiger counter of everything that's going on around you. When you hear someone say "trust your gut instinct," it's the truth. Those stomach acids start falling in like soldiers, reporting there's something foul in the mist. Fight or flight, that's what it's telling you. *Get your shit together 'cause there's trouble ahead.*

Ray had probably started an undercurrent right after our encounter in the parking garage. I could just imagine him planting a rumor here and there so it would spread like a fire, like it had a life of its own.

"Venus came on to me. Can you believe it?" I could see him mouthing the words. Sherri, listening, and giving it credence. I imagine as I'm walking toward them, no matter how close I get, I still can't hear anything coming out of Ray's mouth, but I know the look, the looks from both him and Sherri. Each step I take, coming closer, in slow motion, I can see his mouth moving, telling lies.

I had to blink hard to shake away the thought. The feverish heat from the fireplace made my eyes tight and dry. The fire caught easily. I pulled the chain curtain closed on the fireplace. *Burns Fast and Easy* melted away quickly as the fire spread across the packaged log.

◎   ◎   ◎

Just Lunch

"WELL, WHEN WILL HE BE IN?" I kept the phone pressed tightly against my ear. "Ah huh, ah huh. Yes, thank you . . . no that's quite all right, I've already left three messages. I don't want to make it four."

The receptionist gave a small laugh in response to what she took as a joke. I'd been trying to reach Tyson all week. I didn't quite know what I was going to say when I got my chance. I was lingering on a hope that he might be able to show me light at the end of the tunnel. He definitely saw my skills when I pitched to him a week ago. But coming out and asking him for a job, and explaining the mess left at Donnely Kramer, would take an abundance of tact and finesse.

I picked the phone up before the end of the first ring.

"Venus Johnston." I hadn't let go of my professionalism just because I was sitting at home in cotton sweats.

"Venus, I hear you're trying to get a hold of me in a bad way." He gave a faint chuckle, but then turned serious. "How can I help you?"

"Tyson, I'm on vacation so I didn't know if you had come in looking for me. You know, to go over some of the things we had talked about."

"Well, actually, I haven't been able to make it back over there all week. I made a tentative appointment with those two, John and the other . . ." he paused, "Lenny on Monday. You have my word that I will speak highly of you."

"Thank you. I appreciate that, but what I really wanted to know is if you had time for another great rap session. Lunch will be on me this time." As if that would be a deciding factor. Any restaurant I could afford was going to look like Denny's compared with his usual haunts.

"I wish I had time. I have so many things going on right now."

"It'll be worth your while, Tyson. Please. A quick bite. Everyone has to eat. And I know you're not the type that eats on the run. Those ties cost way too much to be dripping secret sauce on 'em."

He belted out a strong laugh. Done.

"All right. How about Wednesday?"

"That's so far away." I crossed my legs and sat up straight. It was better to get into my role. I stared up in the air to forget about the gray sweats and dirty socks I'd slept in and worn for the past two days. "Can't you make it sooner? Wherever your next meeting is today, this afternoon, I can meet you." I held my breath.

"Venus, has anyone ever told you, you'd make a hell of a salesperson?"

"No, but I've been told I can't take no for an answer."

Again, the healthy laugh. I envisioned his pearly whites lined neatly against his prominently shaped lips, eyes turned into little slits.

"All right, all right, enough. I'll meet you at Hunan's, it's across the street from the MCI center. Two o'clock. And Ms. Johnston," his voice got a little deeper. "Don't forget your promise to make this meeting worthwhile, for both of us," he added, hanging up before I could respond.

I parked a couple of blocks down. My taupe-colored Kenneth Cole suit made me look and feel like a million bucks and I didn't want the image ruined by stepping out of my two-toned, gray and rust Hyundai. I walked with care in my leather pumps around the melting ice. It was definitely a day for snow boots and it was way too cold to be out without a coat made with some kind of insulation, but I didn't want to hide what little I had going for me. I saw his white sports Jaguar parked out front.

I walked in and spotted him immediately. The waitress was flirting. She gave a surprised sneer when I stopped directly in front of Tyson's table, as if to say, "this, this is what you're waiting for." I wish I had a dollar for every woman with half a body and a little hair who thought they were better than me. Was it some kind of preprogrammed ignorance that said, a woman with hair was more of a woman than one without? The war of the haves and the have-nots played out silently, only it wasn't about class and money, it was about the symbolism of the sprouts growing out of our heads. I suddenly remembered being chased home from school by a knotty-head little dark girl who told me I thought I was too good and stuck up because of my long lustrous ponytails. I wondered what she would think of me now. Would I be accepted into her world, considered "down and cool" because I cut off the one thing that told her I was different?

I responded to the young woman's disapproving look with my own that said, "yes, and he's all mine." Then I smiled shyly at Tyson while he stood like a gentleman and waited for me to be seated.

Of course, he had already taken it upon himself to order for me, too. I couldn't decide if that was something I would like all of the time. Once the novelty wore off, I'd probably cringe. For now I enjoyed it immensely.

I sat directly across from him. I liked the view. "I'm going to come right out and ask you this, Tyson. Would you hire me? I don't mean hypothetically. Can I come work for you at St. John's?"

"This is a shock. I thought you were happy at Donnely Kramer. What happened in such a short time to make you want to defect?"

"It's a number of things; most importantly, they're not going to give me the St. John's account or any other account for that matter. I just know I'm supposed to be doing something else."

"Something like what?"

"Working for St. John's."

"Doing what?"

"I . . . don't really know exactly where I would fit in, but you know what I'm capable of. I've worked in marketing all my professional life. I've done PR, research, I'm sure I would be an asset."

I couldn't tell when I started feeling like I was begging, but I knew it wasn't a pretty sight.

"Venus, my company just acquired another line, you know that, right? Do you know how many people we had to cut just to make it work? We let go of some awesome talent because we just couldn't have our cake and eat it, too. I think we kept maybe five or six people out of a hundred from the new side, and it was a struggle just fitting them in. Until we see a profit off this new acquisition, we're pretty much strapped. Why do you think we're outsourcing with Donnely Kramer?" He leaned in closer. "It's not because we think they're the best thing since Laurel and Hardy, I'll tell you that. We simply can't afford to house full-time people right now. We get in, they put out, and we're on our way."

The whole time he was speaking to me, I could hear the tiny fella on my shoulder telling me to just slide in on his side of the booth and make promises I couldn't keep, if he'd just give me a shot. I heard the part about not being able to afford a full-time staff, but one person. I don't take up that much room, and for the input, he'd get his return.

"I see. I do understand, Tyson. But you know I can't take no for an answer. You know that, right?"

"That's something we have in common, Ms. Johnston. Since that's the case, I'm going to give you another number where you can reach me without going through the systematic channels." He reached inside his pocket and pulled out a gold pen. He wrote down the number on the back of his card and slid it to me.

"What's this?"

"It's a voice mail, but I check it regularly. Mostly for private calls." He gave me a knowing smile.

"I see." I said as I pushed it into my wallet. I took another sip of the plum wine.

"I've managed to clear my schedule for the rest of the afternoon," he said.

The waitress brought over the grilled shrimp and full grain rice. My stomach started talking to me. I didn't know if it was the smell of the garlic and sesame arousing my senses, or the little guy in there shouting, get ready, alert, trouble ahead.

"Today? This afternoon, you mean? I wish I'd known. I wouldn't have set up the other appointments I made for *this afternoon*." I looked at my wrist where I'd forgotten to strap on my watch.

"Maybe next time, then." His mood was not affected by my rejection. My nervousness seemed to thrill him. He refilled our glasses with the dark sweet wine.

I ate greedily, determined to ignore the rumbling in my stomach. *Look out, trouble ahead.*

It Happened
One Night

SHE SPRAYED HER HAIR WITH A
light mist of oil sheen. Kandi
accepted Tyson's dinner invitation
that had come with more roses. She let him talk her into an evening of
dinner and dancing in New York. She was disappointed that the roses
weren't from Clint. After their short interlude of coffee and muffins at
the hospital, she was sure he'd have a change of heart. But an entire
week had passed since that day. Clint had smiled more than she'd seen
before, giving her the sense he'd been relieved of some of the burdening
problems on his mind. She stayed loose, fluttering around only the subjects that kept him comfortable. Kandi didn't mention Venus and neither did he. Yet she'd heard nothing from him.

When Kandi returned to school the next day, she'd expected a pink slip sitting in her mailbox, but instead she found a thank-you note and compliment on her quick action from the parents of Christopher Lee. The roses were found sitting in her classroom, next to the first batch that had already bloomed. At the end of class Kandi dispersed the roses to the boy students and told them to take them home to their mothers. She told the girls what was left would be kept in the classroom for "us women to admire." They all giggled, making fun of the boys who were told to carry them home with the utmost care. A couple of the boys asked what to do with the rose if they didn't have a mother. Kandi told them to give it to the one person who made them feel the best about themselves. Lucas, the tall skinny one with thick glasses, walked up and handed the rose to Kandi. She was overwhelmed and almost cried. Kandi thanked him and pulled out a separate vase from her expansive collection and set it in water by itself on the desk. It truly was a special rose. Surprisingly, none of the other kids made fun of Lucas for that show of fondness. It was the one thing she could count on, the acceptance and love of the kids. They were her children, even if it was only one year at a time.

Kandi peeked out her bedroom window, the one that overlooked the front of the building. She had her eye out for anything overly polished and looking way too expensive for her neighborhood since she never knew which of his many cars he'd be driving. The dark-colored Lexus parallel parked just as she was finishing with a light brush of powder on her nose and forehead. She slipped on her heels and grabbed her purse. She didn't want to give Tyson a chance to come up, with his next words being, why don't we just eat in.

She met him as he was stepping off the elevator. "Hello."

"Hellooo. Umh . . . you look good. I must say absence has made my heart grow fonder."

They kissed gently on the lips.

"Thank you," she said gingerly, while pressing the elevator button.

"So fast, sweetheart. We've got at least an hour and a half before we have to be at the airport." Tyson swung Kandi around to face him. "No appetizer before dinner?" He placed his soft warm hands on her face, capturing it for a kiss.

"I left the place a mess . . . maybe we can go have a cup of coffee or something." She moved slightly out of his grasp. The tan doors opened and she stepped in first. "Coming?" She cut her eyes.

He gave Kandi a curious look before following her in the elevator. "So, are we going to play cat and mouse all night?" He pulled one of her spiral curls down, letting it bounce back.

"I just thought it would be nice to have an evening out, as we planned."

He nuzzled Kandi on her neck, pushing her hair aside with his nose. "I promise I won't mess up this pretty new hair of yours," he whispered. "I promise." He grabbed her hand and kissed it.

"No, Tyson." She smiled faintly, pulling her hand away from his mouth. "I'd prefer not. I've really been looking forward to getting out of that apartment; the last thing I want to do is go back." She turned to face him with her bottom lip slightly extended for effect. "There's plenty of time for that later."

The elevator doors opened to the lobby. He stepped aside for her to pass, "After you, milady."

"Why thank you, Mr. Edwards." She gave him a curtsy and led the way outside to the cool evening air.

After he seated her in the passenger side, she watched him glide around the front of the car. His dark suit brought more attention to his dramatic eyes. His hair was groomed to perfection as usual. His scent filled the car immediately when he got in. For a brief moment she felt exceptional, like she was his only woman. In certain aspects, she probably was special to him. Finding women to listen to his lies wasn't easy, unless they're being paid to listen. She listened attentively, reassuringly, and without question. He'd told her that before. She was a great listener.

". . . the sad thing is," he finished off the story, "she's actually very smart. I could probably use her at St. John's. But I've already put a lot of the company's equity at risk with this new acquisition. I know that old bastard is waiting for me to fuck up somewhere. Trying to facilitate a whole new department while we've got millions on the line, shiiiit. That would be a nail in my coffin."

"Hum. That's too bad." Kandi stared out the window, or more to the point stared into the window, at her own reflection. She looked closely to see if her nostrils were flared like a bull ready to attack. Venus Johnston seemed to find her way into a lot of her conversations lately. She concentrated to see if her eyes showed any fury.

"Have you made any moves in the direction of starting your own company?" Kandi asked, with her head turned toward him, confident her face told no truth.

"I'm still in the planning stages," he conceded.

"Maybe you can hire her then, when you get it together." Kandi turned back into the reflection in the dark window. Maybe when you get divorced, you and Venus Johnston can get married and work this new company together. Live happily ever after. At least then Clint wouldn't have any more excuses, she thought to herself.

Tyson gave a proud smile at the thought of owning his own company. She smiled back at him.

"That's what I love about you. You're understanding, intelligent, and beautiful. What a package. I can't talk about these kinds of things with Valarie. We've been married for seven years and she has never once asked me about my dreams, my plans. I can't remember the last time we had a conversation that lasted past ten minutes, hell five. You're the quintessential woman, baby. If the world was filled with Kandis, mankind would be upgraded. Threefold!" He slapped the steering wheel. The same hand then reached for her thigh, landing somewhere in the middle.

"I haven't forgotten my promise, you know. I still want you to be Mrs. Edwards. It's just going to take a little more time. You trust me, baby?" He picked up Kandi's hand and kissed it gently, leaving behind moistness from his lips.

She smiled for him again. "I trust you." She let out the held breath as they arrived at the airport.

They parked and walked a small distance in the night air to the small plane. It seated approximately six people, seven with the pilot. Everyone was dressed exquisitely. Kandi made small talk with a strikingly beautiful blond woman. The woman wanted to know what kind of perm could produce such perfect curls in Kandi's hair. Kandi lifted her hand and touched her head as if just remembering what look she was wearing today.

"Oh that." She shrugged. "It's a heat style, nothing permanent."

The woman admired it for the rest of the flight. Kandi smiled at her, but she didn't feel beautiful at all, that was something that had to come from inside. It didn't matter how much glitz and spritz you had going, if you didn't feel good in your heart. It was a waste.

Kandi felt empty. Not just because of Clint. She felt it before she'd met him, years before. The feeling of being trapped in a hole. No growth, no enhancement. Being trapped in this one place and unable to move. It seemed like such a simple plan in the beginning. First high school, then college, then career, then husband and children. It was supposed to go like that, effortlessly. She hadn't asked for anything more than what she'd been promised by mere existence. But here she was, stuck, like her feet had landed in a concrete puddle and it was drying too quickly, faster, to the point where she could barely move. The anxiety in her heart was telling her to get out before the concrete dries, before you settle. But when she tried to move, she became tired, worn out from try-ing so hard. Tired from the weight on the other end.

She caught herself before the tears started forming. Tyson hadn't noticed. He was discussing no-load mutual funds and the stock market with the blond woman's escort. Kandi fanned air into her eyes with her satin handbag, trying to remove the threat of teardrops. She peeked out the small round hole of darkness and looked down. New York was lit up, the city that never sleeps. She pulled her coat close around her neck and put on a happy face.

The restaurant was another one of Tyson's hangouts. He must've known every great chef's restaurant within the fifty states. He never used the establishment's menu, reeling off his special requests, mix this, and don't use that, to the maître d', with whom he was on a first-name basis.

After dinner they walked in the freezing cold air, about a block up the street to a night club. It wasn't the heavy bumpin' rump-shakin' kind of club Kandi was used to. It was a big airy club with too much room to dance. The music was disco, Gloria Gaynor and Donna Summers. "I'm Your Boogie Man" by KC and the Sunshine Band was playing.

It was seventies night, they were told. Almost everyone was dressed in polyester and platform shoes. It was hard to tell if they were costum-ing or for real. Kandi's own shoes were in a platform style. Her dress was clinging to her body and stopped an inch below her knee with a tasteful slit on one side. She fit in quite nicely.

Kandi was on her third Margarita before she accepted Tyson's invi-tation to dance. Once they were out on the floor they were doing the Bump and the Rock. He started doing some old moves that he was probably famous for back in high school. She followed his moves, sway-ing from left to right, turning when he turned, swinging when he did. They were doing dances from *Saturday Night Fever*, moving their arms up and down with index fingers pointed. She hadn't planned on having this much fun. This night was only meant to get Clint off her mind, and to stop sulking.

When they got back to their table, they were both so out of breath they couldn't speak. He picked up one of the napkins from underneath her drink and leaned over the table slightly to pat the perspiration from her forehead. The coolness of it felt good. He moved the moist napkin to his own face and wiped gently. He'd done it again. Something so small, an act of decency so minuscule, removing the sweat off her brow, and she'd fallen for it all over again.

It made her recall the time they'd first met. She was on her way to see her sister in Boston. She was standing in front of the ticketing agent in a state of hysteria after finding out the airlines had given her seat to someone else in standby just before she'd arrived. Tyson had arrived to the gate late as well, but of course they didn't give away the first-class seats. Standing there taking in all the chaos, he felt compelled to intervene.

He handed his ticket to Kandi. "Be my guest. I can take another flight. You seem to be in a hurry."

"No, I couldn't. But thank you anyway." She turned back to the flight attendant, who was completely impressed by his generosity. After she recaptured the woman's attention, Kandi spoke, "Just book me on the next flight."

He interrupted. "I have a suggestion." He pulled out his small brown leather wallet and threw down a shiny gold card. "Why don't we both take the next flight?" He turned to the preppy brunette. "She and I will sit together . . . in first class on the next available flight."

Kandi's mouth was still hanging open. "Really, that's sweet of you, but I can't accept."

"It's my pleasure. Besides, it'll give me a chance to talk with you, get to know you."

Kandi gave a disbelieving low belly laugh, but he persisted.

"A cup of coffee while we wait, that's all I'm asking. If you find out I'm a disgusting ogre, you can sit one row up from me and I promise I'll pretend I don't know you." He flashed a perfectly aligned full-teeth grin. His smile had a boyish charm, innocent but still sexy. His hair was cut so close it laid in small waves across his head. You could tell he grew up as the one all the schoolgirls probably adored for his curly hair and genetic perfection. He was used to getting his way.

"Hey, I'll even let you hold the tickets, like cash in hand. No obligation."

"All right." She succumbed to his plea. He picked up her overnight bag that rested by her feet. They walked into the dimly lit rendition of a coffee shop and sat down at the farthest table.

"So what's in Boston? I hope it's not a husband and four children."

She blushed. "No, it's my sister. She just had her first, it's a boy. I'm flying out there to help out." She stirred more cream and honey into her tea. "And you, any children?"

"Not so lucky yet." He poured more of the raw sugar in his coffee. "So, are you from the DC area?"

"Actually I was born and raised in Tenekin, Tennessee."

"Whew! Small-town girl in a big city. How you faring?" He mocked.

"Great. I came here right after I graduated from Fisk. Haven't left since and that was five years ago."

"So that makes you, let's see, about twenty-seven?"

"About," she added.

Kandi watched his eyes open and close in a slow blink. His thick, shiny dark lashes moved slowly from the weight. "What about you? I get to find out where you're from and what you do since we're playing twenty questions." She was nervous from his presence, but she wasn't letting on. Men this good looking didn't have ordinary lives, she knew that much.

"Oh, that stuff is overrated, don't you think." He winked at her. "Giving the pedigrees and what you drivin', where you workin' . . . all you need to know is that I'm a nice guy who thinks you're a very nice young lady. And beautiful, too. Has anyone ever told you, you look a lot like that singer? I can't think of her name . . . wait. You know she sings real high soprano." He snapped his finger trying to hum one of the singer's tunes.

"Yes. I've been told that, but I think I'm prettier."

"Ooooh, I see." He laughed, he saw through her façade of vanity. "So what do you like to do? What keeps you so fit? Skiing, jogging . . . what?" He gave long approving glances of her toned legs that were crossed and exposed to the right of the table.

She leaned toward him and fingered him to come in close. "It's a secret but I'll tell you anyway. I dance around the house and pretend I'm Jennifer Beals from *Flashdance*."

He sat back up, straight, not sure whether to believe her or not. "I guess that'll do it." He did an admiring once-over. "Do you wear those little cut-up sweatshirts and body suits?" He let out a small groan at the thought.

Kandi sipped her tea and sneaked a peek at his left hand. There was no sign of a ring on his long caramel fingers, no tan line. She probably should have asked right then and there. That would've been the smart thing to do. Instead, she let him wine and dine her for the next few months until she was so in awe of him that when he finally did confess, she said, "I figured that."

What she really meant was . . . of course you're married. *How dare I expect to find someone as good as you without a flaw or two? I mean really, why in the world would I deserve to have my very own Mr. Right?* She was almost grateful for that being his only imperfection. The possibilities of other bad qualities were endless. He could have been bisexual or an ex-convict, or worse, someone with only five dollars left in his bank account and in need of a place to stay.

She let it happen. Kandi had just ended a succession of nowhere relationships and needed a break from her ill-fated wedding planning. What she didn't expect was to be going on year two with this man, this married man. He was her Band-Aid, her quick fix. Evenings like this one always came in the nick of time. Just when she thought she was too through, here he was to save the day, to save her from falling into the thick mire of self-hate and self-pity. Dinner, dancing, and, if she was lucky, brunch in the morning.

She knew she couldn't have everything, never would.

Elementary My Dear

I HAD TO FIND OUT IF ANYTHING eventful had happened in the office during the past week I'd been out. Had Ray fallen over a railing or slipped on a banana peel on the stairs? Wishful thinking. I moved a stack of magazines out of the way to get to the phone. My home had become a giant mouse cage. Newspapers strewn across the floor, the classified sections cut out in shreds, companies where I'd promised myself I would send a résumé.

Sherri answered on the first ring. "Donnely Kramer, how may I direct your call?"

"Hello, Sherri. How are you? This is Venus."

"Venus, girrrl. I was hoping you'd call. Two more of those envelopes came. Same as before. Just your name on them." She spoke in a hushed tone.

"Really? Where are they? I want to see them."

"Well, John's been getting your mail, so I assume he has them." I could hear the tapping of the keyboard. She wasn't missing a beat.

"Did you look inside?"

"Oh nooo. You know I couldn't do that, Venus."

"I know, Sherri. And you never saw how they got there, right?"

"Well, I did see a lady leaving one morning as I was on my way in. She stepped on the elevator as I was getting off. My first thought was that she was looking for you, you know, since we're the only other sisters up here. And sitting right there on the counter like the two before was an envelope."

"You think she left it?"

"It just seemed strange. You know how you just get that feeling. Not to mention that smell."

"What smell?"

"Her perfume. It was kind of lingering over here in my space. You know how sensitive I am. The scent left a trail from the elevator to here."

"What'd she look like?" I was listening hard, while watching the silent talking heads on the television.

"I really couldn't tell, besides her being kind of light skinned. I didn't get any eye contact."

"I mean, was she tall, short, fat . . . what?"

"She was about my height. I wasn't studying her. Girrl, I couldn't tell you nothing about the way she looked. I didn't even give her a thought until she was halfway out the door. I know the scent." Sherri blurted out, "It's St. John's. It is, now I remember. One of the girls was spraying it as a tester around here yesterday. But it wasn't lingering overnight. It definitely came from the woman I passed in the elevator."

"St. John's perfume. Anybody could've been wearing that! Anybody black, and we already know that much. I'm sorry for drilling you, Sherri. I'm just scared. I don't know what's going on."

"Well. I'm keeping my eye out now. The notes have been coming like every Tuesday and Thursday, so maybe tomorrow I can come in a couple of minutes early. I'll be on a sting operation."

"Thank you, Sherri." I actually smiled at the thought of her going the extra mile to be even nosier than usual. "I really appreciate it."

"Gotta go." She cut me off. "Yes and thank you for calling." She spoke clearly and professionally, changing her dialect to one who mastered the King's English. That was my cue someone else had entered her zone.

I hung up and paced around the living room, ignoring the swishing and crackling sound of paper underneath my feet. I had been suffocating in this house. My anxiety wasn't doing wonders for my overall health. But I wasn't getting on the scale to find out how badly. As long as I didn't have to put on any waist-fitting apparel, what I didn't know wouldn't hurt me. I moved around the room in the baggy sweatpants well enough. Who was the woman? I had no enemies. None I could think of. The only possibility would be . . . no. She doesn't know where I work. Or maybe she does. I could have been dinner conversation on one or more occasions. Clint isn't the type who likes to divulge information. Unless he found it necessary to bare his soul before moving on, sort of like a cleansing. It could happen.

I dialed the hospital.

"Hello, I'm trying to reach Dr. Clint Fairchild. He's a resident doctor there, I don't know which department he's in."

"Hold on to be transferred." The operator didn't waste any time connecting me to another unfeeling voice.

"Pediatrics, this is Cora."

"Hello, is Dr. Clint Fairchild available?"

"Let me check." She took a few moments. "May I say who is calling?"

"This is his sister. I really need to speak with him."

"I'll page him for you."

After ten minutes of holding, I wanted to hang up, but his voice caught me.

"Hey, Alison."

"It's Venus, Clint. I'm sorry. I knew they wouldn't track you down unless I said I was someone with some kind of value."

He let out a short sigh, a definite sign of indifference. "What's up, Venus? How're you doing?"

"I'm fine. I'm doing okay. Do you have a few minutes?"

"Not if it's more than a few; I'm in the middle of rounds. You want me to give you a call back?"

"Yeah. That's fine. Call me back." I fell back into the sofa. Sandy was so used to seeing me sitting here, she didn't bother to come and keep me company. She just assumed I'd be sitting in this same spot with the remote in my hand.

Since my suspension, I usually started the day out with the local news. By ten I was watching CNN, keeping up with the latest scandals. After they started repeating the news with five different slants, I moved into the one-hour dramas, Maury, Jennie, Sally, and Jerry Springer. It seemed they were repetitively showing the teenaged girl dressing for success, hooker success, that is. Channels filled with young ladies chasing after men twice their age, getting pregnant, and talking strategy of how to be free of the prison they called home. It really gave a future parent a lot to look forward to. I clicked through the channels without stopping, knowing every commercial by heart. I finally stopped on a new talk show. One I hadn't seen before. Another Oprah wanna-be talking into her mike, posing the question of why fat women can't be accepted as beautiful in this day and age. The various responses were all stilted. One woman stood up claiming that her husband did indeed love her queen-sized bottom and wouldn't have it any other way. Another less obese woman, large nonetheless, asked why their size wasn't sold in *Frederick's* and *Victoria's*. The slim-figured woman with big red hair on the panel spoke at no one in particular. "Big women aren't going to wear a G-string, or any other pleasure-applicable wear. It's too uncomfortable for them." The audience booed and hissed for a few moments. The woman continued, "If you have six layers of skin flapping around you're not even going to see the skimpy lingerie underneath all that . . . fat."

"Excuse me, but how would you know? Have you seen your line of clothing on anyone my size?" The large woman still at the microphone shouted out. "You are discriminating plain and simple."

The rest of the audience agreed. The fashion show began with the extra-large woman walking out in black lace and garters.

I must've startled Sandy with my boisterous laugh. She poked her head up quickly, then put it back down to rest on her paws that looked like mittens. Her eyes told me she felt sorry for my mental decay and my fits of revelation. I began to surf the channels again. Back to Jerry trying to make sense of the senseless. One more face slapping of a sister who stole another's man and I will have waited long enough for Clint's return call.

"That's right. You tell her." I slapped the sofa. "Get him, too. Yeah, uh huh . . . he shouldn't have been with her in the first place. . . ."

I let the phone ring three times, trying to hear the last comments out of one of Jerry's distinguished guests before I answered.

"I thought I missed you. Sorry it took so long. I had to meet with one of the doctors here. Good news." Clint sounded exhilarated. I pictured his dark skin beaming with the contrast of his shirt and tie with his white lab coat making him look distinguished, official.

I pushed the mute button on the remote. "Oh yeah, what's the good news?"

"I was offered a position here, on staff."

I sat up straight. This was good news. It seemed like the day would never come, that all the hard work would pay off, his and mine.

"Congratulations. I mean, if you accept. Are you going to accept?"

"I have a little bit of time to think it over. You know, I don't want to rush into anything. Something better might come through. I was hoping to get with Greater Washington Health. Supposed to be one of the best."

"I see." He could hear the contention in my voice and began to plead his case.

"Hey, it's a hell of a lot better than most of these private groups. They don't pay for your malpractice insurance. That alone could run half a year's pay. GW kicks in a few benefits like pension and vacation and it's like having a regular gig." He paused for my retort. "Kurt got on with Prudent Life. He's got the hookup with six figures. Malpractice paid, vacations, bonuses, corporate style."

"Yeah, but he's locked in. They make you sign contracts. You don't just get all these promises without giving up something in return. Just make sure you read the fine print, Clint." He hated when I used his name at the end of a statement. It made him feel scolded.

"Aay . . . Got it covered. I've worked too hard to get where I am just to be throwing it in the wind. I'm looking out." His confidence was appealing.

"But that's not why you called, to hear about my pending success." He let off a sly hack. "What's up in Venus world?"

I had momentarily forgotten why I called. Listening to his plans was enthralling. We had spent many bull sessions over the years talking about my career path, his future moves, that eventually would lead to our due happiness. It felt like old times. We had been a good team.

"Oh yeah. I have something to ask you. First promise you're not going to get mad." I could already hear his breathing rhythm change when I said that.

"What's up, Venus? Just ask me. Just say what's on your mind."

"Okay. I need to know if you and your new girlfriend, the tall one that was at the awards dinner . . . have you two ever discussed me? Does she know where I work, or anything about me?"

"I may have mentioned you once or twice. No details. Why?"

"I've been getting these abusive notes at my office. One said *stupid bitch;* another one had a stick drawing and written underneath it said, *pickaninny.*"

"So what are you trying to say?" He asked incredulously. "You think Kandi sent them? That's ridiculous. She doesn't know anything about you. How would she know where you work?"

"That's what I'm trying to figure out. Maybe she got a hold of your phone book. Or you could've mentioned where I worked without being aware of—"

"Wait a minute. First of all, Kandi and I aren't together. It lasted about as long as our reunion. Remember that, huh?"

He was still quibbling over the day I found the compact in his bathroom. That one-day stand wouldn't have led to anything more than what it was. Finding the compact only hastened the doom.

"Kandi and I haven't seen each other in a while. We haven't even exchanged hellos in the past couple of weeks. I really don't think either one of us is too heavily on her mind. You know what I'm saying. That's just crazy. No way is she hawking you, V. No way."

"But you don't know, Clint."

"You don't know either. What the hell makes you think it's Kandi, anyway?" His voice was shaken.

"Look, calm down. I was told by the receptionist at work that the person delivering the notes was a black female. I don't have any enemies. I mean, she's the only female, black female, I could think of who would have it in for me."

"Well trust me, V, it's not Kandi. She ain't thinking about you." He took in a jagged breath.

"That's all I called for was your help. I respect your observation. If you think it's not her, then it's not her." My voice went up a few octaves. "It's not her. I'm relieved."

He sucked in his teeth. "You don't believe me. I don't even know why you're trying to front it off like you do. Whatever, V, I don't have time to play Inspector Gadget with you. Call me when you really want to talk. Later." He hung up the phone while I still held it pressed against my face. The click on the other end sounded so definite. Case closed.

That was the end of my hot lead. All I wanted to know was if his good-time Sally could possibly know where I worked. He took it so personal. It wasn't like I was accusing him of any wrongdoing. He didn't want it to be insinuated that he knew a psychopath. Guilt by association.

"Dead end, girl." Sandy managed to cross the great divide of newsprint and magazines to get into my lap. "Now what?" The walls were closing in on me. I was feeling helpless and tormented.

The smell reminded him of vinegar mixed with bleach. His father used to make the concoction and scrub the odor of the drug out of the walls after he smoked in the house. Cedric had come home early from his afterschool job at Mickey D's and walked in with his nose turned up.

"What the hell's going on in here?" Cedric asked the question, but was talking to neither one of the outstretched bodies as they lay in the middle of the floor watching the *Flintstones*. He made his way across the living room in two giant steps and knocked on their father's door. There was no answer. Cedric tried the knob, shaking it and repeating for his father to open the door. When there was no response, Cedric beat the door open with his shoulder and one hard kick.

The thunderous noise heard next was their father and Cedric wrestling and bumping into the walls. Alison started screaming. Clint pulled her out of the way, as Cedric and their father came crashing to the ground next to them.

Cedric pinned his father down by his neck, choking him. "Why don't you just kill yourself? Quit taking the slow way out." His father stopped resisting, but Cedric didn't let up. Alison was in the corner screaming a high-pitched yell to stop fighting. Clint remained on the floor, paralyzed from the fear. At ten years old, he was sure everything, every event in life, was his fault, his responsibility.

"If I ever catch you smoking that shit in this house again, I'll kill you myself." Cedric squeezed his father's tattered T-shirt harder around his bony neck, threatening to choke the life out of him. Cedric rose up not quite believing he'd just threatened to kill his own father, the one who'd raised him, clothed him, and at one point a long time ago stood like an oak, strong, proud, and unshakable. Alison and Clint could hear Cedric's sobs coming through the bathroom door where he'd closed himself in. From then on, their father got high somewhere else, just as requested.

Clint always woke from his dream with the same conclusion, if he could have only warned his father to stop before Cedric had come home. Cedric would have never found him smoking drugs in the house. They would have known where their father was; if he overdosed, he would've been home where it was safe. Clint could've watched his father more carefully. Saved him. That was his ten-year-old mind still talking, still telling him that it was his fault that his father walked out the door one day and disappeared like dust in the wind.

The smell wasn't coming from his memory, though. It was real. The pungent smell smacked him in the face. The room was still dark. He rolled off the hospital bed and straightened himself out. He half stumbled through the door.

"What is that smell?" he asked Jeremy, the nurse sitting at the station outside of the room he had been hibernating in.

"They're spraying on the sixth floor."

"Spraying what?"

Jeremy popped his gum with a loud smacking sound in the middle of each word. "Some kind of bug spray, I assume."

Clint walked away before the snap of Jeremy's gum drove him crazy. Nothing worse than a prissy-foot Negro. White boys dancing on the other side was tolerable. But a brother, that was just too hard a pill to swallow.

"Hey . . . Dr. Grant." He caught up with the head of Pediatrics while she was stepping on the elevator. Her shiny dark red curls reminded him of Annie. She was the epitome of a kid doctor, with her bright face and large eyes.

"I had a question about what we were talking about earlier today." He pressed the number for the Internal Medicine floor.

"Don't tell me. You want to know if you'll still get napping privileges." She gave a gapped-tooth grin.

He responded with a forced laugh. "Noooo. I actually wanted to know how many people stay on, after the program. Is there like a percentage, an estimate you could give me?"

"That's easy. I thought you were going to ask me out on a date."

Again, Clint pushed out a short cough of a laugh.

"I'd say about fifty percent. Doesn't mean they don't leave eventually, though. It's a good place to get your feet wet, so to speak." She stepped off on the fifth floor and gave a small flip of her hand. The elevator door closed together.

It reopened on the sixth floor. He walked straight to the head nurse. "What is that foul odor?"

"We have to spray for caccarroaches." Amelia's thick Spanish accent mixed in with a little Bronx landed hard and fresh in his ears.

"Is it toxic? Somebody's going to get sick from that shh . . . somebody is going to get sicker than they already are up in here." Clint had already turned to walk away.

She raised both hands. "I'm not the one that authorized it. It's not my job. All I know is that there are little brown monsters running around here terrorizing everybody. One day of stinks not gonna kill nobody."

"All right, Amelia. If you say so." He pulled the collar of his coat across his face and headed down the hall.

"It's not that bad, Dr. Clint. Quit being a sissy," she quipped.

"Yeah, we'll see who makes it back to work tomorrow," Clint called back out to her. He went to the stockroom and grabbed a face mask. He snapped it on and went about his business of seeing patients.

Thinking about Venus's accusations made it hard to concentrate. He had enough on his mind without her adding grief. It was true Kandi had a little edge about her, he'd seen it firsthand. But stalking, no way. In fact, she seemed more like the type who would be well about her business by now. Hanging on to something that didn't pan out didn't seem her style. She called him once and left a message after the hospital incident with the little boy. Clint hadn't gotten back to her. With the news of his job offer, and being at the hospital almost twelve hours a day, there was no time.

Kandi. He shook his head. She wasn't capable of doing what Venus had insinuated.

"Dr. Fairchild, call holding on extension 7411." The loudspeaker blasted through the hall. He let it hold and took the elevator to the third floor, where he picked up the line. He didn't see any need in letting the toxic fumes build up in his system.

He picked up the phone at the Pediatric nurses' station.

"Cora, this is Fairchild, who's holding for me?"

"Clint, it sounded like your sister again. I asked who it was and she said it was personal."

"That's cool. I'll take it. Thanks."

"Clint Fairchild." He picked up the line.

"Hello, Dr. Fairchild." The sultry voice belonged to Kandi.

"How ya doing, Kandi?"

"I'm well, thank you."

"To what do I owe this honor?" His smile was showing through the telephone.

Kandi had a way of bringing out the gentleman in him, as well as a few other things. He felt the space in his crotch area tighten. He turned to face the wall, just in case someone walked by and noticed the bulge. He couldn't contain being pleased to hear her on the other end of the phone. He'd actually missed her.

"Well, I was hoping you'd be a nice friend and help me hook up the new computer I bought today."

"Oh yeah? What makes you think I know anything about computers?"

"I just need your muscles over here to put everything in place. I can't even get the stuff out of the car," she confessed.

He stared at his roster to see how many more patients he had before wrapping up to leave. "Six. I can be there by six. You going to feed me for my labor, woman?"

"You know I will make sure you're well fed."

"All right, check you later." He tapped the pen on the clipboard. Why not? Venus Johnston was becoming a distant memory. He was holding on for her recovery from Nutsville, but it wasn't happening quick enough.

He'd been getting play thrown at him from every direction. Cora, the floor receptionist, could spread a word faster than the Associated Press. All the nurses and staff were congratulating him for making it to full doctor status with big smiles and low lashes. He couldn't even get from his car to the entrance without somebody giving him the eye, letting him know he had free rein to make a move, or start a conversation. But what was the point if all he could do was think about Venus?

He threw the pen across the desk. She'd taken enough of his time and energy. Too much.

Kandi must've been watching for him. As soon as Clint pushed the button, the flashing green light went on to let him enter. The building was lit up with the huge dome lighting that filled the hall and lobby. The air was clear. After fighting with those pesticide fumes all day, the place was literally a breath of fresh air. He stepped on the elevator and pushed the eleventh-floor button. A tall fresh-looking brother slid in before the doors closed.

"What's up?"

"How ya doin'?" They acknowledged each other. The man went to push eleven, before he took note it had already been pressed. He was sizing up Clint, probably hoping he wasn't a new neighbor to contend with, especially if he was insecure about his woman. They both stepped off in the same direction. The man's tension eased when Clint stopped in front of Kandi's door. She opened it before Clint had a chance to knock.

"Long time no see." She reached out, giving him a firm hug.

"It's nice to see you, too. You look good, as usual." His eyes swam over her.

"Thank you. You ready? Let me get my keys." She slipped on those little Swiss Alps shoes that he hated on most women. The ones that made their feet look thick, and larger than they were. But of course on Kandi, it all flowed well with her baggy jeans and cutoff sweater. They walked the empty corridor silently.

She didn't speak until they entered the garage. "I'm glad you came. I really appreciate it," she said while unlocking her trunk.

"No problem." He lifted the largest box out first and set it on the ground. "I can't believe none of these men running around here wouldn't give you a hand with this stuff."

"Just can't trust anyone these days, putting their grubby little hands on my stuff."

"Right about that." He looked her over standing next to the car with her arms crossed over her chest, giving them an extra lift. She moved to reach in the trunk, exposing her slim waist. She pulled out a second box.

"Here, put that one on top of here. I can carry them together."

"There's two more." She pointed.

"We'll come back and get 'em."

She slammed the trunk shut and moved quickly in front of him to clear passageways.

"So what made you want a computer?" He put the boxes down gently in the entryway of her apartment. They made a return trip to get the rest.

"Promise you won't laugh."

"Laugh? Hey, there is nothing funny about spending all this money. What's your plan?"

"I want to write a book." She had her head down shyly.

"A book? Well, go 'head now!" He gave her a small pat. "What's it going to be about? Oh, let me guess, another man-hater Waiting to Choke book."

She giggled. "No, I'm not sure what it's going to be. I've been keeping a journal for years, starting back in college. I just have so much going on in this brain, I've got to start filing it away. I just figured a computer was the best way instead of writing in notebooks with my chicken scratch handwriting. I'm not sure what kind of book it's going to end up, I just know it's a goal I've had as far back as high school."

They slowed down near the garage entrance. "I'm proud of you, Kandi." He swung the door open for her.

"Thank you, Clint. Don't be proud of me yet, though. I've got a lot of work ahead."

"Ain't nothing to it, but to do it. Kandi Treboe, the great novelist."

The floor was littered with all the pamphlets and packaging from the computer. Kandi went a tad overboard. Clint guessed she must've run into a salesperson who needed to make his car payment this week and saw Kandi coming. A simple system with a printer would've been sufficient. But instead, she must've had over five thousand dollars worth of equipment. Clint didn't see the need for the scanner, or the eight-color printer with digital enhancement. He didn't question her, though; he wasn't there to steal her joy.

Clint was trying to manage her small space, but with all the components, one of those L-shaped office systems with lots of shelves would've been a wise choice. He feared if he mentioned it, she'd be out the next day spending hundreds on that as well.

"If we put this under here, all the other stuff can probably fit on top."

"Okay, whatever you think will work." She was still leafing through stacks of instructional pamphlets and disks.

He was on his hands and knees scooting the computer minitower under the desk when he saw it. The small crumpled note. He smoothed it out with one hand. *Bitch*, then flipped it over, nothing. He slid out from underneath the desk. "Kandi."

She glanced up. "That's fine, right there." She put her head back into the instructional pamphlet she was reading.

"Kandi." He called her name again and moved in front of her. "What's up with this?" He lifted the paper so she could see it. "It was under there."

She took the wrinkled notepaper out of his hand and scanned it lackadaisically. "Oh that. It's nothing." She balled it back up and tossed it into the trash. When she saw that he wasn't moving, she looked up.

"It's nothing, really. Somebody left it on my windshield a couple of weeks back. I don't know why I kept it. But I forgot it was even here." She grabbed his hands while looking up at his expansive chest. "You worried about me? That's so sweet," she purred.

"If someone's calling you names like this, leaving notes on your car, you got to watch your back. You don't have a clue? No enemies?"

"I just assumed it was somebody who didn't like the way I parked." She stood up. "But thank you for caring."

"No problem." He stepped back. "Let me finish this. I don't want nothing holding up your great works." He only let Venus's accusation dance for a moment before pushing it aside. What Venus had said earlier had nothing to do with the note he'd just found. It was a coincidence.

Kandi slid halfway under the desk where Clint continued plugging in cables. "So did you ever take care of all the things that were keeping you so preoccupied?"

"Kinda."

"So . . . are you kinda ready to talk about it?" Her warmth was filling up the space under the desk.

"Babygirl, I'm not going to be able to do this with you flaming me."

She gave a pout and backed out from underneath. "I'll go ahead and start dinner."

"Thank you," he whispered to himself. He couldn't think straight with her sexy breath all over him.

It stayed quiet for a while. The only sound was her small rumblings in the cabinets, gathering up her chef tools and ingredients. He couldn't help but get a little excited watching her in the kitchen. Every time he looked up she was swishing around in there, like it was a mad science project. A few strands of her wild curls fell in her face. She swirled the hair back behind her ear. She caught Clint staring.

"What?" She smiled.

"You don't get in the kitchen much, do you?" he asked, coming up for a break.

She let out a small laugh, covering her mouth. "You can tell, huh? It's usually only me, and I eat Lean Cuisine most nights."

"If Leen-a-queen is good enough for you, it'll be good enough for me." He got up and stretched his long body. He walked in the kitchen to see what she was throwing together. "You don't have to go through all this trouble." He went to peek in the pot that was chortling and spitting out steam.

"I'm sorry," she said while pushing the lid back closed. "Don't look in there."

"Wait a minute now. I'm not eatin' no bat wings and frog legs. What's in there?"

She wedged her body between Clint and the stove. "Stop tryin' to see." She blocked his view of the boiling contents. "It'll be okay now, go back to doing what you were doing," she ordered.

"No, I want to see." He pulled her to the side and she locked one of her small but powerful arms around his waist. They swung gently together, landing against the refrigerator. He kissed her loosely. It didn't take long for them to engage fully, caressing one another. He kissed her harder, letting all the feelings go he had been trying all evening to hold in check. Lifting her up, he heard her shoes hit the ground. She entwined him, wrapping her long legs around his waist.

They kissed hard and long while he caressed her thighs and moved his hands slowly up her sweater. He didn't want to let go, yet he didn't want things to go too far. He didn't want to play her. She deserved better.

She sensed him thinking too much and slid down off the counter and began pulling him to follow her into the bedroom.

"It's okay," she whispered.

"I missed you, Kandi," he breathed into her ear while he held her tightly against his body.

"I missed you, too." She moved her hands up his back, pushing up his shirt as she went along. Clint didn't protest when she lifted the shirt over his head, exposing his hard chest. He was in no position to start analyzing his feelings. All he knew was at this moment, she had his heart skipping beats and every part of his body screaming for her touch.

Instant gratification.

I dipped the almost melted vanilla pecan ice cream into two large bowls sitting on the kitchen countertop. Wendy was tucking in her off-spring and telling bedtime stories so we could have an uninterrupted and much needed girlfriend parlay. Sidney was conveniently working through the night. As one of DC's finest, he kept strange and long hours, making Wendy feel more and more like a single parent.

"It wouldn't be so bad if he really was gone, out of my life, you know, then I could start dating." She stirred her ice cream, making it turn into thick creamy-colored sludge.

"Believe me, you do not want to have to start over. It's rough out here in the single world. Excuse me, the free world." I nudged her with my foot as we sat facing each other from the opposite sides of the couch. "That's the new term; single is played out."

"Freedom. I miss it. I don't care what you say, I had a good time when I was single. And if I, heaven forbid, ever did become single again I sure wouldn't be sitting here on a Friday night eating ice cream with your pitiful ass."

"Oh yeah, hot thang. What would you do? Tell me. Go club hopping, or join some kind of singles club, or no . . . better yet, meet some serial killer on the Internet?" I sucked on the cold spoon. "It's hard meeting someone new."

"See . . . that's why I don't understand why you just kicked Clint to the curb. What was your plan? You got no prospects. You don't quit a job unless you got another. And you certainly don't turn in the best thing you ever had for nothing."

"I guess I never intended for it to go this far. One thing just led to another and now. . . ." I stared into my bowl with only pasty remnants left. "Now I just feel like it's too late to go back. It's like when you take a stand on something and go on strike; if you give in before your demands are met, you're screwed. When you go back, things are going to be worse than before, because they know you don't mean business."

"Kind of like when I tell Tia I'm going to beat her ass if she plays with the cord of my curling iron, then after she plays with it once and gets away with it, she can't stop herself. No damn consequences."

"There you go. We got ourselves an analogy." We clinked spoons. "No consequences. If I go back now, Clint's going to be like these bad-ass kids of yours, just running around taking advantage."

"Shut up." She flipped a few drops of her melted cream on me. It landed on my arm.

"I believe this is yours." I crawled up and rubbed the wet drops on her face. She squealed and we started play wrestling on the couch.

"Get off me. Take your aggressions out on some innocent man. Not me."

I was knocked to the floor on my butt, landing in between the couch and the coffee table. She fell down next to me laughing. We both started bellowing out healthy tension-relieving cries of laughter. My laughter was deep with hysteria. I swam with thoughts of Ray's kiss, the office crisis, the insulting notes, Clint, my self-induced loneliness. The laughter quickly became tears. Wendy stopped short to watch me. The confusion in her face was my only indication something was wrong. I reached up and felt the tears streaming uncontrollably. Wendy ran off and brought back a box of tissue. I pulled two, three sheets and poured more grief into them.

"Don't cry. Please don't cry, Venus." She hugged me and rocked me gently. "It's going to be all right, Venus. You know. You'll get through this."

I managed to garble a few words through the sadness I was fighting. "But what is this, what kind of *this* are we talking about here? What exactly is *this*?" I blew into the tissue some more.

She rubbed my smooth head. "This is just you making changes. Deciding what's best for Venus." She spoke softly. "This is you starting over." She consoled while I released.

It felt good letting go. No matter how much time and energy was spent putting up the defense, the gate that held the waters could not be contained. It was ready to break, like a dam bursting past its capacity.

Crying is the release of all the negative toxins in your body. I was told that once by a healer, a person I'd paid two hundred dollars to for her serendipitous advice. It was six years ago when I was almost as bad as I am right now. I'd just gone though a difficult breakup with Garet Holson. He had all the makings of a good husband, professional, mildly good looking. I actually believed I had finally found my prince. He had the looks, and intelligence, but when it came down to intimacy, he shut down like a mechanic's garage on a cold day. No sign, just gone home for the day. Luckily it didn't take me four years to find out there was no future as it did with Clint. I pretty much got the hint after listening to Garet carry out all of his telephone conversations with his mother in the bathroom with the water running. Kissing or touching in public was a narcissistic trait that he found appalling. His status as the first black professor tenured in the School of Economics at UCLA gave him the right to tell me Victoria's Secret purchases were going to be the downfall of my monetary independence. It would have really shocked him to know the bill I was tallying up on the physical properties he perceived as natural beauty. Men like Garet actually couldn't even conceive of the concept of nappy hair. New growth was something that happened only on a man's chin after a day's shave.

After listening to Garet lecture a friend on the necessity to communicate and show your feminine side, I approached him about his own lack of communication. I asked him how he could know so much about managing others' relationships when he couldn't even share the same toilet seat with me. After splitting the CD collection and the videos, we went our separate ways. A couple of days after our official breakup I saw him spoon-feeding a young blond, most likely a student of his, cherry vanilla yogurt. Ask me how I knew the flavor. I walked straight up to them while they were sitting outside of the small shop "exchanging germs," as he used to put it; "tasting or sampling each other's food was unacceptable." How many times had he reminded me of the germ count in the human mouth?

I slapped the cup out of his hand making yogurt land all over her embossed happy-face T-shirt. Some landed on Garet and myself. I licked as much from around my mouth area as I could reach. "Nice flavor," I told him. "Thanks for sharing." For two straight days I cried. When I realized I wasn't crying over him, but for the simple fact that I'd lost again, I just stopped. No more tears. A climactic calm washed through me and I became free, pardoned of the misery.

This time it didn't feel like it would be so simple. Closure was farther from my reach. Wendy watched me cautiously from the couch as I stood up and walked to the pine armoire in the center of the room. Pictures sat in frames on each shelf, some of her children, individual shots of each one as they progressed through the stages of their lives. Her husband, Sidney, in his cadet uniform, graduating from the police academy. Wendy in her high school cap and gown, the only person I'd ever known proud enough to display a picture from their high school days, pimples and all. I swiped at my puffy eyes. I wiped and dabbed again.

"I guess I'm thinking I might have to live without all this." I picked up the baby picture of Tia. The baby picture was taken by me. I had it framed and gave it to Wendy as a birthday present last year. Tia's big honey-colored eyes like her mommy's pierced through me. "I want a family of my own, so badly that it hurts, and it's never going to happen. I know it."

186 / T r i s h a   R .   T h o m a s

"How can you think that way, Venus? Why are you so sure you've got nothing good coming your way? Where did all this come from?" She'd always admired my strength to go after whatever I wanted. She had always thought of me as the smart one, going after a long-term career, holding out for nothing but the best. She was staring at me, puzzled by my defeated attitude.

It was true. I had lost all belief in the happy-ever-after.

"You know what I think. I think you're having a thirty-something midlife crisis." She snapped her finger like she'd figured it out. "You're having a midlife crisis."

"You think so?" I focused on her through tear-stained eyes. "You think that's all it is?"

"It's elementary, my dear." She came up and gave me good solid hug. I let the last stream of tears get pressed out of me. I inhaled her baby powder scent and exhaled a scattered breath. She whispered again, "We got it all figured out and it's going to be okay."

"When?" I asked her as if she could pull the answer out of the air, predict the future. I sincerely wanted to know *when* everything was going to be okay. As it stood, I was plain out of hope and ideas.

"I don't know when." She faced me directly and pushed my chin up with her mother hands. "What I do know is you're an intelligent, loving, and creative person. You're special, Venus. You're beautiful and strong, a combination that's unbeatable. I wish I had an ounce of your spirit." She whispered in my ear as she pulled me close for a good strong hug, "What I do know is that when you do come out of this, you're going to be better than ever. You're going to look back on this moment in your life and be grateful for the lesson." I still cried. I couldn't stop even though I knew she was right. I needed this cleansing. I needed to wash myself of the doubts and fears.

I cried all the way home, straining to see the lights turn green. Slowing to make sure I stayed on my side of the yellow bands in the road.

Everything in front of me was a blur. I turned onto the Lee Highway, not aware of the large gasoline tanker that had already laid claim to the entire road and had to slam hard on my brakes. The truck sped by, making my Hyundai shake from its velocity and weight. I sat in the car on the road slightly twisted from skidding to a stop, holding on to the steering wheel as my life flashed before me. But it wasn't the past. It was the future. In that moment I'm someone to be reckoned with: shoulders straight, head held high, briefcase in hand, suit crisp and tailored, taking long confident strides. I'm headed somewhere feeling good and looking good. When and how it was all going to take place wasn't in this picture. *When* wasn't important. As grateful as I was to God for not letting that truck turn me into a crinkled soda can, I was more grateful for the knowledge that good things were in store. Just like Wendy said, better than ever.

Going Home

THE AIRPORT TERMINAL WAS
packed with people moving around
like ants. Everyone was traveling for
the holidays. I had packed light to avoid the check-in lines. It wasn't like
I had any elegant evenings planned. I'd sleep in, spend the day cooking
with my aunts and mother in the kitchen. Have dinner, find a quiet
place to read, and then spend the next couple of days eating leftovers.
Two pairs of jeans and a couple of sweaters were appropriate.

"Anyone sitting here?" the long wiry man asked.

"No, go ahead." I picked up my jacket without looking his way and
flung it over my lap.

"Thanks." He sat down and made himself comfortable.

I prayed he didn't start a conversation. I was too tired for small talk. Too tired to give him a fake smile and pleasant disposition.

"Are you waiting for the 10:30 flight to Dallas?" he inquired.

I nodded yes.

"I hope it's on time. I've been flying nonstop for six days and not one plane has taken off or landed on time."

"Umh."

"Gum? It's sugar-free." He extended his pale hand, reminding me of the inside of a coconut.

"No, thank you." I kept my face in my book.

"How is that book? I've seen it in every bookstore window."

I smiled. Not giving him an answer purposefully. I looked at my watch and said a miniature prayer.

It wasn't answered. Not in the least. Airic, with an "A," Coleman took advantage of the uncharted seating and followed me to the back section of the plane. He talked for the whole three hours to Dallas. I learned about his new software business, his two children whom he hasn't seen in over a year, claiming that his ex-wife's new husband forbids visitation, his Labrador named Kenan, and his promise to himself to never marry again. At least not in this lifetime. The only thing that kept me sane was that by the time I really got a good look at him, he could be classified as decent looking. His pinched straight nose that blossomed slightly at the nostrils must've been passed down by an old white grandmother; the rest was clearly contributed by African descendants. Other than that, his strong chin and open-hearted smile made up for it. That is, when he finally did smile.

After he cleared the plate of all his drama, he opened up with some laughter and high spirits. We drank Bloody Marys and ate pretzels while we talked loud over the plane engine's roar.

"Would you be interested in going out when you get back to DC?" His question took me by surprise. I had felt a little something while we were talking, but I thought it was the buzz of the vodka.

"I don't see why not," I slurred.

"So I'll take that as a yes." He pulled out a business card and flipped it over. "Put your number here."

I reached over the arm of the seat and scribbled my name and number as legibly as I could. "You promise you won't forget whose face belongs with that number." I was giddy. "I don't want you acting surprised when you see me for the second time, claiming it was the alcohol."

"I won't forget you. This has been the best flight I've had in a long while. You're very refreshing, Venus."

"Refreshing, now I haven't heard that one before."

"Tell me what you've heard. Enlighten me." He leaned close for me to do tell.

"Bossy, mean, unmerciful, and unbending." I smiled proudly. What could he do to me? I was already a castaway. This stranger couldn't punish me for being honest, for not being perfect.

"I don't believe it. There isn't a chance you could be all those things with a smile like that."

"Thank you." He declawed my defense. I toned down just a bit.

I stared out the window at the rows of land sectioned off like ticktacktoe. It was a clear sunny day in Dallas, Texas. Too bad this wasn't my stop. Thank goodness this wasn't my stop, or Airic would have a golden-brown kitty following him in search of more strokes.

He tucked the card with my number written on it back in his generic black wallet. His long slender fingers could be those of a pianist.

When we touched down, I extended my hand for a good-bye. "It was nice meeting you. And seriously, don't feel obligated to use that number." I began walking in the direction of the connecting flight.

"Would you mind if I wait here with you? Your connection flight doesn't leave for what . . . another hour or so?" He stood tall and erect. His business suit was reasonably wrinkled from the wear and tear of the flight.

"I'd like that. Sure." We walked, taking our time, being bumped occasionally by the hurried passengers.

"Has anyone ever told you that besides a night club, an airport is the worst place to meet someone new?"

"No," I answered.

"Good. Glad no one's ever told you."

I leaned into him, pushing his lean body out of balance a little. "You're silly."

We sat down facing the picturesque window, where my plane was already parked.

"Would it be possible to get your number . . . where you're staying in Los Angeles?"

I took my time answering, but I was thinking . . . fast. Why not?

"I'm staying at my mom's, and if you call one minute past the time I'm no longer there she's going to treat you like a cold-calling salesman. I'm just warning you. Got another business card?" I asked, holding out my palm. I wrote my parents' number down with the dates of my stay. He really did have a nice smile.

      ⑨   ⑥   ⑨

Everything Changes but Stays the Same

THE TIME WARP OF TRAVELING FROM the East Coast to the West Coast always left me dazed. I stepped off the plane after a total of seven traveling hours. The Bloody Marys from the earlier flight were slept off, but I still felt the weight of exhaustion.

"Venus. Over here, honey!" My mother was waving, trying to make her way past the wall of people searching for their companions.

"Mom." I reached out, pulling her in for a firm hug. "I'm here. I finally made it."

"Sweetpea, what did you do to yourself? You cut off all that long pretty hair." She was affectionately rubbing my head in public. Like a pregnant woman's belly, my head had become open game.

"I guess I forgot to mention that."

"It's cute. It really is adorable on you. I guess Clint didn't like that too much, though?"

I let out a long sigh. "Not now, Mom. Please."

We moved through the crowd and made our way out to the car. It was a hot afternoon. The sun was focused directly on top of my head and burning like a laser as we walked through the parking lot.

"Your father is working on the floors. I told him I couldn't let you come home to dirty carpet. He spills everything. I told him, if he's going to continue eating in front of that TV, I'm going to sell the dining room furniture and turn it into a workout room. Gotta keep my figure." She swanked, patting her round bottom. "Timothy will be here tomorrow. Did I tell you he was bringing somebody with him? I hope they're not going to be trying to sleep together in my house. I can't stand that."

She made the long stretch to Pasadena seem like we were walking, instead of riding in a car.

"Mom, why don't you take I-5 up from here. We can go around all this traffic."

"No, no, that's even worse. Traffic's just gotten so bad these days. I remember when you could be in LA city within fifteen minutes after you left the house. Nowadays, it takes a good hour. No way around it, baby. Just got to stick it out. How's your girlfriend? What's her name, the one with those pretty eyes?"

"Wendy. She's good."

"I'm so glad you have somebody out there. So far away from home. I just knew you and Clint would make it. I just don't understand what went wrong. Was it your hair?" She lowered her voice and turned down the squelching of Patti Labelle. "You can tell me, he doesn't like it that short, does he? Most men don't."

She quieted for a moment to hear my response. "It had nothing to do with my hair. I did this after the fact."

She pushed the volume back up. "Well, then, I just can't figure it out. If you guys weren't having any problems, what made everything just blow up?"

"I told you, Mom, I just didn't want to wait anymore. I really don't think it was meant to be. I'm almost afraid to say it, but sometimes I think he was just using me to get through school. He never had any intention of marrying me."

"Oh no, no. I don't believe that. Clint was a nice fellow. Are we talking about the same fellow? He was a good boy. I can tell these things. So well mannered, and honest. You can see honesty in the eyes. I don't believe that, Venus. Not at all."

"Mom, you're not the one who lived with him. I am. He is a man, pure and simple. That's half the problem right there."

"Oh Venus, you're going to learn. One day it's going to be clear as a bell to you. Men and woman are puzzle pieces. No two pieces are alike, they've got all those different sides and shapes, jagged and smooth, but when there's a fit, when that piece goes with the other, the search is over, it's done. You don't have to pull it back apart and try it again to make sure it works. It either does or it doesn't, there's no guessing. Now if another piece comes along, it'll fit the other side, maybe if it's a corner piece, or a center piece, it may have three or four different pieces it goes with to make the picture come to life. Each piece is vital to the next. Do you understand what I'm saying? Other pieces may fit, but none can take the place of the other. Do you understand what I'm trying to tell you, honey?"

I watched the couple in the red sports car next to us. They were staring straight ahead, not talking to one another. I wished for that kind of ride. Forty more minutes I was in for; at this pace, I would surely die of agony.

The white asters and fuschia star gazers were still growing in the front yard, banked up against the faded pink stucco. The grass was green and manicured neatly, a vast contrast to the staid winter season I'd left on the East Coast. Trees still had their green leaves here. Dad was standing inside the screen door when we pulled up, grinning ear to ear.

"There's my girl," he called out, pushing through the doorway. "Uoooh. Look what she did. You cut off all 'em locks. Still pretty as can be. Come here, precious." He squeezed me tight. His large mass encompassed me like a blanket, blocking all the sunlight.

"Dad. I missed you, Daddy." The stale smell of cigar smoke was familiar and comforting.

"Go on in. I'll get your bags."

"This is all I brought."

"Well, there ain't nothing in them little bags. Give 'em here." He toted them inside, dropping them as soon as we stepped through the door.

"I want you to see what I did with that caboose you sent me. Uoooh, that was a real find, precious." He led me by the hand to what used to be Timothy's room in the back of the house. He used the whole room to set up his miniature city and trains, under the vigilant protests of my mother. There was barely enough room for one extra person in the room.

I had found a Lionel Train on one of my many scavenger hunts in the Virginia suburbs where people threw out things you only read about, eighteenth-century settees, porcelain dolls, patchwork quilts. When I sent the train to my father over six months ago I didn't know what its value was. It just looked like an old toy that a grandmother held onto for too long, sentimental value. It turned out to be one of the first miniatures Lionel Trains ever made, and he hadn't stopped thanking me yet.

"Look at that. Cleaned up like new."

The lime-green original paint was dry and cakey; the wording was cracked, but you could still make out what it said.

"That's nice, Dad. It fits in real well." I walked around examining all the detail. Each piece was delicate. Everything was so small and distinct, the tiny trees and landscaping surrounding houses and general stores. Miniature stop signs were placed at the corners, replicating a small town. "You've done a lot of work since I saw it last."

"Oh, yeah. All that time I used to be at work, I spend it right in here."

I grabbed his arm and gave it a tug. "I'll come back and look at it some more after I get a little rest. That trip beat me pretty bad."

"Oh sure, precious. Sure."

I could tell he was disappointed. He wanted to show off all his hard work, but I wasn't sure how long I could keep standing. My knees were buckling, partly from the seven-hour trip and partly because of the drinks I'd had on the way.

I crawled my way to the top of the stairs and slipped into my old bedroom, closing the door quietly behind me. The same yellow floral bedspread was draped over the twin-sized canopy bed. I still remembered being the first person on my block with the contemporary whitewashed pine furniture set. The stuffed animals still held their place at the end of the bed. My mother came in systematically and dusted and vacuumed, but never changed anything. The academic achievement awards were still framed and positioned on the walls. Photographs of me were still hung in chronological order. The one where my hair was in two fluffy balls that erupted on the sides of my head brought back the most memories. I remembered getting into trouble when I got home in the second grade for letting my hair get into disarray before picture time.

I had seen an advertisement of a little girl wearing the Afro-puff styles a week before and thought it looked cute. So I had purposely unsnapped the little red-bird-shaped barrettes on the ends of my twisted ponytails so they would come undone. Later of course, I would claim it was no fault of my own. My mother didn't believe me, though. For the rest of the school year I was sent to school with double barrettes on each end. Pauletta Johnston's daughter would not be running around with unruly hair.

I pulled back the somewhat faded spread and climbed between the cool sheets. If I could sleep for a week with no interruptions, I would. I dozed slowly. Too many thoughts of uncertainty flapping through my mind. Would I have a job when I returned? Would Clint suddenly realize I was the best thing he ever had? I rolled over, pulling the spread close, covering my nose. I inhaled home, the familiar smell of simpler times. I felt my senses leaving my body as I fell into a deep calm.

Would You Marry Me?

KANDI WAS SHAMEFULLY HAPPY, not just content, but truly euphoric. It's embarrassing that her happiness has come to be through a man, the opposite species, the male inhabitants of the earth who are put here to make our lives complicated, and functional all at the same time. It's so un-nineties to be dependent on one of these . . . these men, she thought, while running the comb through her hair. Yet that was all she'd ever really hoped for. It was her secret.

Clint and Kandi had spent a beautiful night together. Maybe it could be classified as perfect. She didn't know, she'd never known perfect before. Truly incomparable would be a better description. She hummed and bounced to the Janet Jackson CD playing in her bedroom, remembering the details of the night before.

After she and Clint made love, they stayed up talking, eating grapes, cheese, and drinking Chardonnay. In one flash, that fast, they were on another level.

It was a big leap, him trusting her with his childhood memories. It didn't seem like he really could be the person he is today with all the strife, growing up without his parents, having no one but his brother and sister to depend on, who were merely children themselves. For the first time, Kandi didn't mind hearing Venus's name. Knowing what happened between them gave her an inside look, a road map so to speak, of where not to go.

With all he had been going through in medical school, Clint had enough problems without the pressure Venus had put on him, wanting to get married and start a family. It was so simple and obvious how afraid he was of the whole idea. And who could blame him? He had nothing to go on but the memories of a mother who walked out on her children and a father who had slowly killed himself from the regret. Kandi prided herself on being a good listener. She knew by listening and listening well you could learn from others' mistakes. Last night she had learned from Venus.

"I feel like marriage is not the point." Clint turned up his glass to finish the last of his wine. "The point is being with someone you trust and love unconditionally. All the other stuff just falls into place." He leaned on one elbow. "I just wasn't feeling that. I felt like I was given a list of rules, and conditions, and, here, sign here on the dotted line." He pressed his finger into the mattress. "Is that how you'd want someone to ask you to marry him?" He looked up at Kandi, like he remembered she was there.

She shook her head no.

"Of course not, you'd want someone to show you that more than anything you meant the world to him. That he would be there unconditionally giving you everything he had, no rules or regulations. That who you were inside was all that mattered. Then after all that proof, all that love, you come to him with your heart and you say, here. I'm trusting you with this. Now if you jack it up, I'm taking it back." He ran his words together, the result of the first bottle of wine. And they were well on their way through the second.

Kandi stayed quiet, listening to him, watching his dark silhouette move in different positions.

"Has the question ever been popped to you, babygirl?"

"Can't say that it has." Kandi was too smart to fall into that conversation. Then she'd have to tell him about Tyson. He asked her quite often to marry him. But it's illegal to have more than one wife in the United States.

"Well, how would you want someone to ask you, if he did?"

"I don't know. I never really thought about it. I've dreamed of the actual wedding day. You know, what'd I'd wear, who would be there looking on, but that's all after the fact. Huh." Kandi thought for a minute. "I don't know."

"Men dream, too. They may not want to admit it. Especially when he finds that special woman, the one that blows him away. Damn, I want to pop the question and have her melt like butter on a roll. Just all over me." He snapped his finger and let out a swift laugh. "Damn, I want to be the knight. I want to be the prince that rides in on the horse and sweeps her off her feet. Makes a brother feel like a man, you know what I'm saying, Kandi?"

He propped himself up. Kandi was sitting cross-legged, Indian style, resting against the headboard with the sheet crumpled through her legs, holding what was left in her wineglass.

"I'd say to her, *I've always wanted a woman like you to be in my life. I've prayed for someone as beautiful as you my entire life.*" He moved in closer, picking up her free hand. "*You are the answer to all my wishes and desires. You're funny, you're wise, you give my heart a place to feel safe.*" He kissed her hand and placed it on his smooth dark chest. She could feel the vibration in her hand. It was his heart, beating at a lightning speed.

"Then, I'd take that special person in my arms and whisper," he pulled her closer into him, "*will you marry me . . .*"

Kandi's eyes welled up, ready to spill at any moment. The heat that was circling her face was partly from embarrassment, from the thought that for a moment she actually believed he was really talking to her.

"Would you marry me?" he finished.

The tear broke through, but stayed suspended in time, dropping slowly, and finally landing in her crystal wineglass. The sound of the drop so infinitesimal, at that instant, could have shattered her eardrums.

She could feel and hear everything so clearly. He leaned over to her and kissed her gently. The tears streamed out of her in uncontrollable bursts, moistening and meshing their faces together.

She felt the urgency in him, through his body, his kiss. "Will you, Kandi? Will you marry me?"

She stopped short of collapsing. She couldn't breathe for an instant. She fell forward on him and they began passionately making love. She'd never know if he was crying, too. She'd always remember knowing that at that moment they were saving each other's lives, giving the other a purpose and strength to keep going.

When she woke up the next morning, she figured it would all end, the fantasy. He'd come to his senses once the wine wore off and apologize for the histrionics. That would be that. But he didn't. He was staring at her from across the room where he sat in a wicker chair by the window, wearing nothing but a towel wrapped around his waist, his chest and shoulders still moist from the shower, his dark skin glistening. She rose up and stared back at him. Go ahead, she was thinking, *tell me it was just the mood, the wine, and the endless lovemaking.*

He breached a smile. "Do I have to say it all over again, or do you remember?"

"I remember." Kandi bit her lip to keep it from shaking.

He stood and moved in close, sitting on the edge of the bed. His scent barely allowing her to breathe, she nodded up and down, inhaling deeply.

"You sure? When I do this thing, it's for keeps. No games."

Kandi reached around his neck and hung on for dear life.

So call me a fool, she thought as she pressed on the finishing powder on her cheeks as she prepared for work the next day. She smiled to herself in the mirror. She knew he was wounded, on the rebound, but what was she supposed to do, tell him he'd better think about it, *give it some time just in case you have a realization that Venus is the one you really want, and not me?*

"No way," she said out loud, as she snapped the foundation compact closed.

Welcome Committee

THE SOUND OF MUFFLED VOICES was rising through the floor. The screen door slammed itself shut while footsteps shuffled up the stairs. For a minute I had to orient myself to where I was. I opened my eyes to a dark room, with only the faint glimmer of the street lamps coming through a small opening in the curtain. I dragged my arm out from underneath the cover to press the light on my watch. I must've really been tired. It was close to eleven.

"Guess who?" I heard a voice pressing through the closed door.

"She's asleep, boy. Get away from there." I could hear my mother shooing someone away. My brother, Timothy, must've arrived early.

I popped out of the bed and flung open the door.

He screamed. "You scared me, Venus. Oh my God, your hair." He put his arms around my neck and I buried my face into his narrow chest. "Long time no see, shorty."

"Same to you." I lifted my face to give him a kiss. The prickly hair budding through his chin scratched my forehead. I squeezed him tighter as a way of thanking him. He hadn't rubbed my head. He didn't even ask "why." Timothy and I were balanced for a pair of siblings. We never fought over anything when we were growing up. When I wanted to watch TV, he wanted to play outside, when he wanted to use the family room to have his nerd meetings, I graciously stayed in my room having three-way telephone conversations with my girlfriends. He wasn't like most of the boys I'd grown up with. My brother wasn't looking for a battle to win or a world to conquer. His slim boyish face and lazy brown eyes always seemed prepared for a smile.

We walked arm in arm down the stairs to the kitchen. This was where our usual meetings were held, the two of us. I kept my eye out for the mysterious new person.

"So where is she?"

"Oh, she couldn't make it."

"Broke up, huh?"

We both broke out in a rowdy laugh. "Sounds familiar."

"Damn. We're just two unloved people. I've got to investigate this." He pulled out some plastic containers from the refrigerator. "What is it about us? Doesn't this happen *too* often?"

"So I guess that's your next theme, the Dysfunctionality of the Middle-Class Offspring of the Black Family in the Hood."

He threw an olive at me. "Now you know that didn't make no kind of sense. I'll have to work on it, though. Needs a little work."

The morning brought in a few family members who didn't want to wait until Christmas day to see Timothy and me. My uncles Edward and

Gordon were sitting in the kitchen drinking coffee. My father was doing the cooking, wearing my mom's tattered apron.

"Naw, man. I told you if Tyson hadn't bit that boy on the ear, he woulda been beat fair and square in front of the whole world."

"Hell, nah. Tyson was winning before he bit that Holyfield. He was. Ask anybody." Uncle Ed was talking too loud.

I walked in with my robe wrapped tight around my waist. It was thick and wooly, perfect for DC right about now. Here in California, I was feeling like a polar bear stranded in the desert.

"Hi, Unc. Hi, Uncle Gordon." I leaned in between them and kissed them on their cheeks.

"What you think about that fight, lil miss?"

"I think fighting is a disgusting sport. Reminds me of chickens pecking each other to death."

"Jonesy, your girl has always been a firecracker. Always telling it like it is."

I poured myself a cup of coffee. "Daddy, what has the world come to, you cooking?" I reached over and pulled off a piece of the bacon draining in the plate.

"Pauletta claims she had errands to run before the holiday crowds. So she must be in the mall right about now. She won that Sunday night bingo, and that money was burning a hole in her pocket."

"That's right, women can't keep no money. Got an extra dime and they gotta spend it on some little pretties, getting their hair all fixed up or buying new clothes. Always something."

I gurgled on my coffee, causing Uncle Ed, Unc as we called him since childhood, to look my way.

"Speaking of hair, what the hell happened to yours? You haven't gone crooked on us, have you, lil miss?" Both of them were chuckling, slapping their thighs. I didn't share in their humor.

"You know that Belinda Kelroy been dipping on both sides. Remember her in school, Gordon?" Unc kept talking. He was the youngest of the six brothers on my father's side. He was known for not having the good sense that God was supposed to have given to all men, creating them equal. He'd been married at least four times, as far as I could recall. He was oddly handsome with his berry-colored skin and pointy nose and chin. The earring he wore in his left ear seemed to get bigger from one holiday visit to the next. I wondered what expired players did when they reached sixty or beyond. Were they still planning to run around looking like pirates with their gold hoops in each ear?

These days, Unc was living with an older white woman, as my mother tells it, supporting him and all his child support payments. Even good looks couldn't make me support a man, at least I thought they couldn't. I guess I had supported Clint for almost four years, mentally as well as physically, all with hopes that someday we'd be married. Maybe that was where I had made my first mistake.

"Yes, indeed. I saw her sitting up with some woman at the VFW, nice and close. I'm surprised they let that kind of thing go on in the club." Unc's eyes widened for exaggeration.

My father kept cooking, not looking up or bothering to participate in the conversation. I could tell it made him a little uncomfortable. The thought of his daughter possibly switching to the other side or walking a little crooked, or *crookt* as my Unc would have said, left my father wondering.

"Hey Unc. What's up, Uncle Gordon?" Timothy walked in, breaking up the tenseness, greeting both my uncles with the secret manhood handshake including knuckle butting and open-hand slapping.

"Boy, when you gonna get some meat on your bones. Still walking around here like you in puberty."

Timothy grabbed a cup of coffee, ignoring Unc's comments. "I'll visit with you later, Unc. I want to finish watching that interview on channel six." He sprinted back up the stairs without spilling a drop of his coffee.

"Now that's the one you need to be worried about, Jonesy. Sitting up in that room watching the public broadcasting channel. Real men don't watch that kind of stuff." Unc elbowed my father and gave him a half snarl. "That boy is definitely teetering on the crookt side. You know what I'm saying?"

My father gave me an apologetic glance over his shoulder. I rolled my eyes as far back as I possibly could without letting them get stuck.

"I have to get dressed." I packed up my dried toast and greasy bacon in my napkin and headed up stairs. I shuffled off in my slippers. They all stayed quiet until I was halfway up; then their voices fell back into their heavy rumbling.

I picked up the phone and dialed out using my company calling card. It was the least they could do. If I didn't keep checking in with Sherri, I would feel completely alienated from my life. First Clint, now my job. Sherri answered on the first ring.

"Donnely Kramer; how may I direct your call?"

"It's me, Sherri. How's everything?"

"Oh girl, how'er you doing? You enjoying your vacation any?"

"No. Not at all. I can't relax. Have you seen anything else? Did that woman come back?"

Sherri started whispering. "As a matter of fact, John just came up and asked me if any more notes came. I told him no. But Venus, one did. I really tried to get here early enough to catch the person who left it, but it could've been delivered the night before."

"Did you open it?"

"I did. Please don't ask me to repeat what it said. I'm not proud of being nosey. I opened it and I was just sickened. You know there are some sick people in the world. Just sick."

"What did it say Sherri?"

"Venus, I can't. I still have it, though. I have it hidden so you can see it when you get back. I just didn't want another one to get away, and you not have any proof. You know just in case we catch the person doing it."

"Thanks, Sherri. I really mean it. You've truly gone out of your way . . . even when I wasn't the most pleasant person."

"Oh girl, I don't pay that kind of stuff no mind, 'cause when the mess hits the fan, you little *upwardly mobile types*," she enunciated the words heavily, "always come back down home. And people like me, we'll always be there to catch you." She took profound joy in her statement, feeling noble, and in that way, better than the rest of us.

I gave a quiet laugh. "Thanks for covering my back."

"Anytime, sweetie."

"I think it's time I apologized to Ray Chambers. What a fool I was; they must all think I'm a lunatic." Sherri patched me through to his voice mail.

I hung up feeling somewhat at ease. There really was no resolution to this thing. It helped having eyes and ears on the case, making me feel I hadn't completely run away from the situation.

I punched in the calling card numbers again, this time to listen to my voice mail messages.

"I hope I haven't missed you this morning, just wanted to wish you a good trip, and I'm thinking of you." Wendy was probably still worried about the state I was in when I left her house the other night. I'd call and tell her I made it safely.

The next message played. "Hello, Venus, this is Tyson Edwards. Call me, nothing pressing. Just wanted to kick a few ideas with you."

I replayed it three times, trying to decode the message. *Kick. With. You. Nothing pressing.* It was probably just what it was. Nothing.

"Venus, you know our African American Ski Weekend is planned for the first week of January. Don't forget to send in your money. Call me.

Bye." Sarah's thick sultry voice came in louder than the other calls, making me pull the phone away from my ear.

Nothing from Clint. I really hadn't expected to hear from him anyway. Just something about the holidays makes you long for the comfort of old times.

The afternoon came quickly. My uncles had dispersed as soon as my mother had returned home from shopping, leaving the house with an empty abandoned feeling. My mother and father were in their own environments, he tinkering with his trains, and she perusing through the classifieds to see how much used dining room sets were going for. The house was quiet. Not in a peaceful way. The silence was disturbing. I could feel our individual thoughts flying across the room like ghosts bumping into each other. We were all here, but not together as a family. Timothy was holed up in the guest room writing in his journal. I knew we were his subjects for his next pyschobabble thesis.

"Mom, you want to go to a movie or something?" I plopped down on the couch with my legs hanging over the arm of the sofa and my head pressed close to her spreading thighs.

"See what?" She doesn't quite look up, but I know she sees me.

"I've been wanting to see that one with Harrison Ford."

"Oh, not that. I'm not really in the mood for a movie anyway. We can ride to the reservation and play some slots. I'm feeling lucky."

"No, that's all right. Maybe I'll just go do some sight-seeing. Go to Wilshire, or Westwood. Can I take your car?"

She peeked over the newspaper. "Be careful, sweetie. It's not as safe as it used to be in those areas."

I swung my legs from over the couch. "Yeah, I know. I'll be careful." I pressed a kiss into her plush cheeks. Her skin still glowed without the assistance of color in a bottle or pressed powder. "See you later. I'll be back before it gets dark."

"Oh, please do."

I didn't check to see if Timothy or my father wanted to come. I knew even before I asked that my mother would politely turn me down. I started my mother's car and slowly backed my way out of the driveway, content to be alone. Solitude was something I was used to by now. Listening to my own thoughts, caring about only my feelings, had become an easy way of life. I drove silently, without the radio, only my thoughts coming in loud and clear.

The birds had decorated my favorite park with their droppings, almost to the density of black and white paint speckles. The cool shaded areas were the worst hit, especially the benches, and along the sidewalk. There was no place for me to sit and enjoy the full trees and green grass. Going back home is never the same, but always the same. It's a cruel dichotomy.

I got back in the car and headed west to the Santa Monica beach. It wouldn't be a disappointment if there were changes, if a building was missing, or a street name had been changed. I would see it all through noncritical eyes.

The graphic images painted in inexplicable language marred each side of the highway of the 10 freeway. Sometimes, without warning, out of nowhere, on a freeway sign, on a building, the alien scripture screaming in black or red paint would take your eyes off the road. The assault on the eyes would disrupt your view like an egg splattering on the windshield. It was one of the signatures of Los Angeles I did not miss.

After several miles, the villagers' language started to dissipate. Palm trees and clear air began to replace the mire of smog and defacement. The smell of the salty ocean let me know I was getting closer to the beach. The little shops and boutiques that depended on some unknowing tourist to walk in and drop a week's worth of income on something authentically Californian were snuggled close to one another. From the outside they looked like square stucco blocks painted in neon pinks and greens, but once you entered, each store had its own wild theme, clothes from Africa, India, Mexican tie dye, there was something for everyone.

I turned down Santa Monica Avenue. It seemed to be a civil group, mostly college kids walking the streets, going in and out of coffee shops and small boutiques. I fit in nicely with my boy-cut jeans, square-toe boots, and leather waist coat. I had always looked much younger than my age, as most people of color do, but even more so because of my size. I had always attracted the attention of the younger men, boys to be exact. Always ready to try their high-school-style rap, they would approach me with their latest come-ons. It fascinated me to hear the new euphemism for *lady;* it had gone from Tenderoni, Babe, Honey, and Cutie Pie to Boo. I considered myself to be none of the above, but hearing it occasionally did wonders for the self-esteem. But of late, there really hadn't been much of that either. I was beginning to believe, more and more, I'd be back sitting in Tina's chair, on the long road toward growing my hair back. It didn't necessarily have to be relaxed. I could let it sprout out of my head like a rebel from the seventies. My career path would probably be sprinkled with a few obstacles. The principals of the corporate establishments didn't look kindly on ethnic-friendly styles, like Afros and braids. They assumed you were a radical with your fists balled up. If I had to start all over, look for a new job, it would be difficult. Where would Oprah be today if she'd kept her little Afro? Where indeed?

I walked into a small contemporary art museum. Nothing like being culturally enlightened for free. The museum was featuring a new artist, and some of the better-known locals. I strolled down the hall until I caught up with a tour group, guided by an elongated woman with glowing yellow hair. She stood taller than everyone in the group, men and women, giving her a natural ability to lead.

I wound my way into their small group. The museum guide led the tourists to the last painting on the wall. She pointed her long arm to the massive canvas that spewed loud splashes of pink, dark red, and burgundy, with faint black accents.

"This painting gives life and offers abstruse symbolism. Ladies and gentlemen, if you'll close your eyes for about ten seconds . . . and think about your happiest moment in life. Something that brought you an immense feeling of goodness, strength." There were low murmurs in the restless crowd. "Go on, please just a few seconds more. Keep them closed. Think happy thoughts. One, two, three, . . . okay, open your eyes."

The painting suddenly exuded lightness and joy. I was impressed. It reminded me of the rose garden in my grandmother's backyard. Roses bigger than grapefruit bloomed like children's smiling faces. My grandmother and I would spend all afternoon tending to her rose family, taking the fresh cuts and putting them in clear water vases. In her presence, I was flawless. Mama El always made me feel bright and special. Any crazy wish or dream I confided to her would get her stamp of approval. "Nothing can stop you from doing or being anything you want. You know why?" she'd ask. "Why?" I would respond, as if it was a knock-knock joke, always knowing the answer. "Because you've got wings like a beautiful butterfly, and those wings will take you anywhere you want to go." She'd trace the wings with her long finger on my back, as if she really could see them. And while I was with her, I'd feel as graceful as one of those colorful butterflies that flittered around in her garden, my feet didn't feel too big, my nose wasn't too wide, and my teeth brandished with braces seemed to blend in with my smile and disappear.

"Okay, great. Now we're going to close our eyes again. This time think of a sad time, a hurtful experience. Close your eyes." She counted again. "Open them."

I opened my eyes and was horrified by the same painting that only moments ago brought me such joy.

It screamed out at me. Memories of my first period. Getting it away from home at seventh-grade summer camp. Waking up in the blood-soaked sleeping bag. The other girls unsympathetic, the stares, the teasing. I wrapped my arms around my shoulders to fight off the inexplicable chill. How simple it all was. Just your state of mind. The way you feel, perceive, and think can change an image, can turn good into bad. Or exactly the opposite, bad into good. Had I been doing that in my daily life, walking around with subjective glasses? Seeing only the negative? Had I been treating Clint the way I had for the past few months because of my own perceptions? Maybe none of it was real. Had he truly loved me all along and I'd been trying to force him to prove it?

I scurried out of there like I'd just found the secret to this life. It was something I couldn't wait to share. If I changed, if I put on different lenses, everything would appear different, better. *The rose-colored glasses.* I'd always wondered where such a simplistic saying came from. I needed a pair. I wanted to see things differently. I walked with a fierce determination. My feet led me across the street, down the pier stairs, into the sand. I stopped briefly to take off my boots and began walking again. I didn't have any idea where I was going. I couldn't have stopped if I wanted to. My legs just kept moving. The sound of the crashing and rolling of the waves engulfed me. The seagulls overhead, children laughing, calling out for their mother, a young couple running and splashing in the ocean water. I walked past it all, seeing and hearing everything, yet feeling like I was in another space and time. I walked until I realized I didn't know where I was or how far I'd strayed, and didn't care. Out of breath, I was knee high in a foamy wave. Again, I didn't care. I stared out into the depth of the sea and for a brief moment felt as light and careless as the ocean. In that moment my senses were heightened. I stood quiet, swaying with each rise and fall of the tide. The gentle waves held me each time for a minute, then ran away to start again.

With my eyes closed I took in a long deep breath. The blue sky, the soft wind, and the expansive sea were all a part of me. I was in love. This was what love was suppose to feel like. No worries, no fears. This was sincere and true love.

The realization of the fact that I didn't need Clint to feel this happiness made me laugh. At first it came out in a soft giggle, followed by an honest deep belt of laughter. I would be okay. Simple as that, everything would be fine. Like the natural order of the elements, in their perfection and imperfections, like this sea in its ability to provide beauty and warmth and just as quickly create a natural disaster. Storms pass, winds die down, and rain stops falling eventually. I would be *all right*. Proud that I didn't need to be the account manager at Donnely Kramer, proud that I didn't need hair flowing down my back. All I needed was what I had, me. I was grateful for me. I had no right to depend on Clint to make me feel this way. Something so powerful weighing on one man's shoulders.

As I watched the sun set, I wanted to emulate the waves in the beach, flowing, rolling, too powerful to be tamed, but still able to calm and soothe. I would be the ocean.

By the time I'd returned, my mother and father had gone to bed. Timothy's door was shut. Light crept up from the bottom edge. I tiptoed past to escape conversation to my old bedroom and threw myself onto the bed and dialed Clint's number straight through.

There was no answer. I was brimming, overflowing. I couldn't wait to tell him it wasn't his fault. I had heaped my dreams on his shoulders. I had given him the responsibility of making me happy, of fulfilling my life. I could see all of that now. And yet, having given him all that responsibility I hadn't allowed myself to trust him. Always waiting for the end of the ride, waiting for the ax to fall, the shoe to drop. Assuming the worst of the worst. So what, I put in four arduous years, so what? I was ready for four more, without expectations or fear. Not because I was going to get something out of it. This was different. I wanted to do something for once without expecting a prize at the end of the ride. I wanted to live, laugh, and love without purpose.

I tried Cedric's place, assuming that was where Clint would be for Christmas.

"Cedric, how are you? It's Venus."

He paused as if to let it register. "Venus, good, good. How are you?"

My phone call must have woken him. I didn't take into account the three-hour difference when I'd dialed.

"I'm fine. I was wondering if Clint made it out that way yet. He is going to be there for Christmas, isn't he?" Where else could he spend it? It was a holiday, for God's sake.

"I'm really not sure, to be honest with you, Venus. If I hear from him, I'll tell him you called."

"Yeah, please do. Let him know I'm at my mom and dad's in California. He has the number here."

"Will do," he answered, unconvincingly.

It appeared I had become the bad guy.

In Too Deep

THE HOSPITAL STAFFERS HAD A potluck in the dining room. He hadn't been able to eat all day. His stomach was in knots. He had taken the leap off the deep end asking Kandi to marry him. With the snap of a finger, his whole life had changed. He'd been pushing himself through this day, trying not to think too hard about it, but it kept popping up in his mind. *Am I doing the right thing?* He hadn't spent a whole lot of time around Kandi. Not like he'd spent with Venus.

"What's up, partner? I hear we're going to be working together."

Clint felt a hand land on his back. He turned around to see Eddie standing close behind. They hadn't seen each other since the boys' night out, the night Clint had met Kandi.

"E-man. What's up?"

"You accepted the offer from Greater Washington Health?" Eddie asked.

"Yep. Time to get paid, man." They slapped hands.

"So what's in line for celebration?" Eddie was staring eagerly up at Clint. He depended on Clint and Kurt to attract the women while he stood idly by waiting for one of them to fall off and land on him by accident.

"Not much. Me and my lady'll probably go out, do something." Clint responded.

"You and Venus back together, man?" Eddie assumed the answer was yes. "That's cool." He reached down to stop his pager from singing. "Aay, check you later man, got to go. If you change your mind, give me a call."

Clint continued filling in charts. He didn't really know how to answer Eddie, anyway. That's not the kind of thing you brag about, being engaged to someone you've only known for two minutes of your life. He didn't want to explain who his lady was, that they'd met a solid month ago, four weeks if anyone was counting. How after two bottles of domestic wine, he believed he had found true love, the kind that doesn't run or hide from problems, the kind that holds you tight and lets you fail without judgment. He'd seen all of that staring into Kandi's eyes that night. Or maybe he'd just seen Venus, the way she used to be. The way she was before she'd decided Clint was nothing more than a T-bond waiting for maturity.

He and Venus had stopped talking so long ago. The conversations were always progress updates. Pep talks for striving harder, strategies for competing stronger. For all of which he was appreciative. He'd achieved the final goal. Dr. Clint Fairchild. But whose goals were they, really? His brother's? Venus's? All the work, sweat, and tears, and never once did he feel like he was doing it for himself, more so to make Cedric proud and to keep Venus happy. She wanted to marry a doctor. She'd said that to him, those very words. "I want to marry a doctor, not a pharmacist," she'd responded when he'd confided to her that he didn't think he could pass the medical board exams. Pharmaceutical school was his alternative, an option. But that wouldn't do. It wasn't enough.

Venus was definitely a believer in standing by her man, behind him, pushing, shoving, and whatever else had to be done to achieve the necessary goals. Her goals. Clint finally put the pen down when he realized the smudge marks were the result of his own tears.

He was tired. He attempted to wipe his eyes dry with one finger, but only more tears followed, leaking onto the paper in front of him, making it more illegible as the blue ink trailed over the page. He laid his head down on his white sleeve and heaved deeply. He let the pain wash through him and didn't try to suppress the coarse sobbing. He was all out of ideas on how to fix things. He'd always had the answer when someone else couldn't find their way. He'd always had a solution for his friends when they were having woman trouble. So simple, why couldn't I think of that? But here, sitting in his own mess, his life, he had not a single answer. He just wanted to be home, wherever that may be. He wanted to go home and lay his head down, transfer his burdens in love's arms, stay a while. Where did he have to go? Who loved him?

Clint lifted his head up and pressed the salty tears away, this time for good. The time had come when he had to take control and make decisions. His life depended on it.

         ⓢ   ⓢ   ⓢ

Dreaming of a Pink Christmas

I ROSE WITH THE SUN. I WAS STILL reeling from the discovery at the museum. The high of starting my new life with the positive outlook was still in full throttle. Today would be a good test. Being around most of my family, the good, the bad, and some downright ugly ways were sure to reveal their heads. Holidays served up the mandatory confinement of individuals with little more in common than shared ancestry. The other 360 days or so of the year were spent living their lives on their own terms.

"Wake up, sleepyhead." Timothy was tapping lightly on my door.

I pulled the door open and gave him a full model's turn. "I've been awake."

"You think that skirt is short enough?" He was staring down at my brown suede skirt that covered a legal amount of thigh in addition to a small slit up the right side.

"I bought this yesterday."

"Getting risqué in your old age."

I followed Timothy downstairs. My mother and father were sitting at the table, silent. It was torturous for my dad, I could tell. The small-seated wood chairs were not his favorite place, since his sixty-year-old body had flattened and softened. But Pauletta had laid down the law, no more eating or drinking in that living room, or else. We Johnston women were good at ultimatums, we just had problems with the *or else* part.

"Nice legs," my mother spoke in her cup.

"Why, thank you."

My father gave me a knowing look. He knew this new little purchase was probably an attempt to keep my uncles from accusing me of moving to the other side of the tracks. The more feminine I looked, the easier it would be to spend the day around them.

"Everybody ready to go?" My father stood up, putting his hands in the small of his back for a stretch.

I leaned in my mother's direction. "Maybe you should just buy a new dining set, Mom, or replace the chairs so Dad can sit there."

She gave me the mind-your-own-business eye.

We filed into her car and headed to my Auntie Katha's place in central Los Angeles.

The kitchen was already packed with way too many bodies. I skimmed the living room for a quiet distant place to sit. One of Unc's daughters was sitting in the middle of the couch flipping the channels with lightning speed. I watched her eyes glaze over, not really responding to anything.

"How you doing, Angie?"

"Fine."

"How's school? You're in the eighth grade now?"

"Ahuh."

"So do you like junior high?"

"Ahuh." She squirmed a little from being talked to. I was sure she'd rather be listening to some music with a headset on, but there was no space to hide in my auntie's home. It was the size of a shoebox, exactly like the playhouses I used to make when was a child. I'd take a shoebox and section it off with cut pieces from the box top and quarter off each one of my children's rooms. Then I'd draw the furniture with crayons, cut out the door, draw on windows. *Voilà*, a house.

I watched her contently for a few moments, wondering if I should be grateful for her silence, contemplating whether I should give up on the pleasantries.

"Do you have a boyfriend at school? It's about that time, isn't it?" I hadn't seen Angie since she was five or six years old. The talkative, happy child had transformed into a quiet private teenager.

She released a grin. "Maybe."

"You can tell me. Is he cute?" I joked.

A wider smile. "Yeah."

"How old is he?" I was making headway. "Is he in any of your classes at school?"

"We don't go to the same school."

"Really, then how do you guys see each other? No holding hands, walking down the locker halls?" I teased.

She started rocking a little back and forth, riding the couch like a racetrack jockey. She was anxious to tell me.

"He's outta school. He already graduated. He's nineteen." She smiled with confidence. She flipped her ponytailed hair from one side to the other. That's when I noticed the full breasts, bigger than mine would be in two lifetimes, and the womanly hips hidden underneath her

Puma sweatshirt and baggy jeans. Sweet mother of Jesus. Nineteen? Where were my rose-colored glasses now? Thirteen.

"What's wrong with you? Have you lost your mind!" I screamed. "You're not grown. Does your mamma know? "

She cut her eyes over at me, dropped the remote on the couch, and tore out the front door.

"Who was that? I heard the door." Aunt Lacy, my mother's youngest sister, came in to see if there were new attendees at the party.

"That was just Angie going outside." I gave her the best congenial smile I had to give. Four younger cousins continued imitating the adults they'd seen playing cards, slamming them down in no particular fashion, yelling, "Bouya! How ya like me now?"

"What you doing sitting out here with these kids? Come on in the kitchen and help out." An invitation to a ritual that probably was meant to make me feel welcome and appreciated, but I couldn't see it.

I followed her into the kitchen.

"Here you go." My cousin Sheila tossed me an apron.

"Thanks."

"You can help me cut up these onions."

She had already chopped enough onions for every dish being prepared in this kitchen, even the ones that didn't call for them. I moved by her side and picked up a knife.

"So how's the East Coast treating you?" she asked, not taking her eyes off her project. She wielded the knife better than the Jr. Osterizer I had at home.

"Good. It's definitely different from here."

"I heard there weren't no men out there."

"There's men. You just have to know where to look. If you're looking." I quickly surveyed her left hand. She was ringless. She was probably thinking we were in the same boat. Manless. Inadequate for not showing up with our own brood among our cherub cousins overflowing with fertility.

Growing up, Sheila and I'd had many things in common, the dance lessons, gymnastics, a love for lemons dipped in salt, even the same boys on occasion, and definitely big plans for our futures. I remember her dream to be a singer. She'd throw a towel over her head and make her big entrance out of the bathroom as I started "Good Morning Heartache" on the record player. On a more realistic note, all we really wanted to do was marry well and drive a car that didn't require the gears to be shifted.

Sheila's bout with college ended after the first year at Pomona Polytech. She'd worked a succession of entry-level jobs, never getting past the first tier. With reasonable good looks and a bodacious body, I expected Sheila to have fared a lot better than she had in the man department. She was still living with her mother and working as a receptionist for a law office in downtown Los Angeles.

"I guess you don't have to worry about that, huh? You're through looking for men." Sheila let out an irritating laugh and tossed one of her long braids out of the way of her knife.

It was obvious Unc or somebody had passed the assumption of me not liking men anymore. *Crookt.* I sliced through the thick white ball, letting the acrid fumes rise too close to my face. My eyes began to water.

"Why would you say that?" I asked, staring at the six gold rings placed in order of size up her small brown ear lobe.

"'Cause you're still dating that doctor. Right?"

I blinked the stinging tear out of my eye. "Oh . . . yeah." I was rueful. "You mean Clint. Yeah. We're still seeing each other."

As hard as I tried, I couldn't seem to keep those rose-colored glasses on. I couldn't give the benefit of the doubt to any words spoken, any gestures made. I was constantly searching for the ulterior motive. It wasn't by design. I just couldn't get this positive thinking thing right. It had worked in the museum. Just like magic. Think happy thoughts, think happy be happy. As I pictured the ocean, calm and strong, I was interrupted by the sound of an onslaught of more relatives who had settled in the living room, sitting on chairs, couches, and floors. This was so ridiculous. People sitting on top of each other. Did this really have to happen? This reunion, this holiday.

I slipped my way out the back door carrying the lump that had formed in the back of my throat and found a dilapidated bench to sit on. The reddish-colored paint was chipped off, leaving rotted wood exposed. I felt the rough edges going through my opaque hose. I didn't care. The peach tree sprawled in my auntie's backyard was still in season, abundant with fruit. They'd rot and go to waste, no doubt, even with all this family around to help out. My auntie hadn't been getting around too well lately. Everyone meeting here was probably supposed to make her feel needed and appreciated. If I was eighty years old, I think I'd just rather be left alone.

"What you doing out here, precious?"

My father sat down close to me. I could smell the extinguished cigar on his clothing and breath.

"Just getting some air."

"Kind of tight in there, I know."

"Where do all these people come from? Every year it seems like this family multiplies."

"People got families. Babies grow up and have babies of their own, next thing you know you got three or four generations in there."

I blinked and squinted under the pressure of the sun's rays.

"You don't seem too happy these days, precious. Your mother told me about Clint. I wouldn't worry about nothing like that if I were you. You got plenty of time to find yourself a good man."

I looked down at my skirt, concentrating on the shortness, now feeling absurd.

The weight of it all. The expectations.

"But what if I don't? What if I'm never like these people inside, with the children, and the grandchildren? What if it stops right here with me?"

"Is that what you worried about? You don't need to worry about that, Venus. You are a beautiful girl. Plenty of men out there would be proud to have someone like you on their arm."

"Daddy, you're not listening." I repeated the words clearly. *"What if I don't?* What if I never get married, never have children? It is possible you know. I may actually be alone for the rest of my life. There's no guarantee."

He laid his cigar down in front of him on the matching shirred table. "What are you trying to tell me? Have you decided you don't want all these things? I can live with that. But I'll tell you what, Venus, you were our last hope for grandchildren. I don't think we're getting *any* out of Timboy." He tried to make light.

I rested my head on his shoulder. "It's not that I don't want it. I do. I'm just saying there's a chance that it might not come to be. Will I still be your *precious*?"

"You'll always be my precious. You don't have nothing to prove to me. Long as you're happy. That's what matters. Look a here." He turned my face toward his. "You've got to be content with Venus. A husband and a couple of kids aren't going to change what's inside there." He pressed his finger gently on my forehead.

"Make Venus happy and all the rest will follow. You hear me?"

"Ahuh" is all I could manage to squeeze out.

"What you crying for? Uoooh, babygirl, you just got too much on your mind."

He wrapped his big softened arms around me and swayed us with ease side to side. I relished in his smell. The safety of his arms.

"You don't have to worry, precious. Everything is going to be all right. You'll see."

I wanted to tell my father that I already knew everything was going to be all right. I didn't need to hear it one more time. There could have been a marching band and sky sign in jet smoke that read, *Venus, you're going to be all right*, but it didn't prevent the pain I knew I had to go through.

Too Dark
Too Wild

Since the proposal, Clint seemed distant. He didn't want to really talk about details, the date and such. Kandi guessed it was just like he had told her, the men don't care about the theatrics. He did his part by asking. By making the first call, telling someone, that would make it real, Kandi thought as she dialed her mother's number. The phone rang four times before Jolene picked up.

"Hello?"

"Hi, Mamma. How are you?'

"Fine, Kandi. I have been worried sick over here. I thought you were coming to Tennessee for Christmas. You didn't call. I left two messages. I know your sister left at least two herself, I was standing right there when she called."

"I'm sorry. I told you I'd let you know if I was coming."

"That means you let us know either way. I can't believe you. Is everything okay?"

Kandi pictured her mother's deep-set eyes wide and questioning, her hair pulled neatly in a bun on the top of her head with fine baby hairs smoothed into a line around her face. It wasn't hard picturing her mother with the same frown she'd worn for the last twenty years as well.

"Never better. Guess what?"

"Oh God. Just tell me. You know how I hate anticipation. Just say it."

"I'm getting married."

"Married? To who? I haven't met any fiancé. Kandi, who are you marrying?"

"You ready?"

"What do you mean am I ready? Just tell me."

"A doctor, Clinton Fairchild, M.D.," Kandi professed proudly.

No response. "Mamma, did you hear me?"

"Well . . . I'm happy for you. When did all this take place? Is this why you can't ever be found? Never home when anybody calls you. A doctor now. I have got to see this."

"And you will. I need help planning this, Mamma. I really want it to be nice."

"Well, how nice? You know your father isn't going to help with anything. I just retired. I don't have hardly nothing that I'm not going to need myself. How nice are we talking?"

"Not that kind of help, Mamma. I just need your planning expertise. You know how you can run a tight ship. I've got enough in my savings to pay for it."

"Well, what about this doctor? He doesn't have any money, his family, nothing?"

"He's just getting started, Mamma. I mean, he's been in school up to now."

"That's just beautiful, Kandace Lillian Treboe. That's just great, a broke doctor. I didn't know they could exist, but if they could, you'd be the one to find him." Jolene let out a disappointing sigh. "You know, you never stop surprising me. I raised you to be something. Not to be nobody's fool, and it just seems on every turn you're showing me that college and education just numbs your senses. I have to go. Jezzy's waiting. We're going shopping. You know, Alex just became a junior partner with his firm. Jezzy says they're looking at those new houses over in the Warrington district. You know how much those cost!"

"That's nice. Tell Jezzy I said hello. I'll talk to you later." Kandi hung up frustrated. She needed to release the aggression and resentment, which meant writing in her journal. She pushed the power button on her computer and drifted to the past.

Jolene Treboe. What else was her mother going to say? Nothing she had ever done was good enough compared to her sister, Jezzine, who'd married a lawyer straight out of law school. His parents were rich, not nouveau riche either. The kind of rich that was handed down from generations of well-educated black doctors, bankers, and lawyers.

Kandi's mother hadn't thought too highly of Alex the first time she'd met him until he dropped his last name. Everyone in Tennessee knew about the Lancasters. They owned the Lancaster Bank. Kandi watched her disposition change from "what you doin' in my house?" to "so pleased to make your acquaintance." Kandi was fifteen then, and it had never been clearer to her what was expected, what was acceptable. Her own father had been sent packing because he couldn't keep a steady paycheck rolling in. But Kandi didn't remember that part, until that day, listening to her mother's voice turn soft and palatable with the smell of money.

Kandi's mother hadn't done too bad as a single parent. She was an elementary school teacher. Including the sporadic child support payments her father sent, she assumed they had everything. What they didn't have, Kandi never missed. Every once in a while, her daddy would come around with a big wad of money, flashing it at Jolene, hoping she'd soften up enough to let him come back home. But Jolene had her eye on a bigger prize, Mr. Honely, who owned a brewery outside of town. He'd come through once a week and take her mother out for a Saturday or Sunday evening.

When Mr. Honely was around, Jolene was witty and full of laughter and girlish giggles. Around Kandi's father, by contrast, Jolene used language Kandi hadn't even heard in the movie theaters. The scowl Jolene wore on her face while Kandi's father was in her presence was so callous, Kandi thought it might hurt, with her brow squeezed tight and her teeth grinding on each other. Kandi went to bed many nights crying and praying her daddy could be rich so Jolene could love him, then they could be a whole family. Wishing one day he'd walk through the door with more than his same old red-and-black flannel jacket and twill pants, maybe even driving something shiny, without all the rust and sanded spots on the door. But it never happened.

Mr. Honely was seen as the way to the promised land. He smelled of black licorice and always had his chemically curled hair full of squeamish gel. Kandi aptly became her mother, laughing charmingly when Mr. Honely gave her a pack of Big Red gum, or two dollars to go to the matinee. She ignored his hand that sometimes slipped onto her doorknob breasts. If he smiled, she smiled, hoping for a bigger prize. Hoping all the smiles and good manners would win her mother the husband she wanted.

When Jolene became aware that after six years of weekly visits, he was not going to trade in the wife and kids he already had in Mottsville, the scowl showed up, permanently.

Vicariously, through her daughters, Jezz and Kandi, she hoped to make up for Mr. Honely and their father. The girls had inherited their mother's Dorthy Dandridge beauty, but the determination and skill would have to be taught. Jezz fulfilled her part of the bargain. Kandi, on the other hand, fell through the cracks of Jolene's educational system on how to snag a rich man and keep the bums away.

Jolene had kept her daughters' appearances to the quality of the only real references there were to go on back then, the society pages of *Ebony*, which featured the junior misses and debutantes with their manicured smiles and silkened hair. Jolene tutored children on the weekends for extra money just to keep up their bimonthly visits to Emma's House of Beauty.

"Don't no man want a nappy-headed woman," she'd retort every time Kandi and Jezz whined about spending a whole Saturday being sequestered in the broken-down shack that was propped up with two bricks on each side. House of Beauty, more like house of horrors. A whole day wasted listening to whose wife had taken a knife to who for sleeping with someone else's. And the screams of yet one more scalp burned and scalded. "Let me put some butter on it," Emma would whisper in her customer's ear. Grease on a burn was like petroleum oil to a fire, but who knew. The forty-five-minute drive back to their side of town was spent with Jolene's rearview mirror tilted just so, for a perfect view of her little girls in the back seat, with their perfect ringlets and freshly cut bangs. If they dared to doze off, Jolene would squeal in shock, reaching back to pinch them as hard as she could. "I didn't drive all this way and pay all this money for you to smash those pretty curls. You'd think you girls would appreciate all I do for you."

"We appreciate it, Mamma," they'd say in unison, wishing just once they could spend a Saturday playing and jumping in the lawn sprinklers like the Eldridge brothers. Those boys had not a care in the world, their dark half-naked bodies doing flips through the water until it flooded their lawn and ran down the street. Needless to say, Kandi and Jezz were prohibited from playing with the Eldridge boys, in the sprinkler or anywhere else. "Too dark and too wild," Jolene would say as they pulled up in their driveway. The Eldridge boys would be out front with their long narrow bodies soaked with water, seeing who could slide the farthest in their makeshift water slide.

"Not going to amount to much at all. You'll see," Jolene would repeat as she escorted the girls into the house.

That's what she would say about Clint when she saw him, Kandi thought, as she logged off her computer. For sure he wouldn't be passing any brown paper bag tests. And no, he wasn't rolling in trust funds and inheritance, but he was caring, sincere, and honest, and most importantly, in love with Kandi. For the first time she actually felt she had accomplished a huge part of her dream. Someone loved her, truly loved her.

Kandi heard the intercom buzz and pushed herself away from staring at the now-blank screen. It was another flower delivery. She signed the delivery man's log sheet and carried the ceramic pot to the sofa table. The flower arrangement had a fall theme, full of bright yellow sunflowers, daisies, and rich eucalyptus. She tore the card open, hoping it was from the right person.

"Puhleeze." She tossed the shredded card from Tyson in the trash. He couldn't seem to understand she was serious this time. It was over between them.

The intercom buzzed again.

"Yes"

"It's me, Kandi. I'm double-parked, babygirl. You're going to have to come on down."

"On my way."

She flicked off all the lights and blew out the candles she had burning. She made one last stop in the mirror and held up her two crossed fingers to her elephants. She had one more milestone to accomplish, and that was winning over Clint's sister. They were invited for Christmas dinner, and it was her chance to make a lasting impression. Kandi knew how much Clint's family meant to him.

She walked quickly from the elevator and made her way through the slush of rain into Clint's waiting car. She laid a fresh wet kiss on his lips.

"Don't you look handsome."

"Thank you. Had to kick those tight-ass Dockers to the curb. Those pants were not made with a brother in mind."

"Oh, been shopping I see."

"A little." Clint adjusted himself, smoothing a large hand down his chest.

"You're already out trying to spend your big doctor bucks." Kandi leaned over and put more lipstick on his face, this time on his cheek. She dabbed it off with her thumb. He grabbed the offending hand and kissed it.

"I haven't told my brother, you know, about us, so . . ."

"I won't spill the beans."

"I just want to be the one to tell him. I don't want it being like, oh by the way, me and Kandi are getting married. You know. He's like my father. More like my father than a brother."

"I know. I understand."

Cedric's boys, Daryl and Rodney, were out shooting hoops in the front driveway when Kandi and Clint pulled up. They were jumping around in their little hard-sole shoes. Their mother, Shelly, must've forced them into the buttoned-up shirts and ties. They looked so cute, Kandi thought to herself.

"Uncle Clint's here." Rodney ran up to the car. "Uncle Clint, did you bring me anything?"

"Yeah. Me."

Clint got out and tipped the little boy over his shoulder, rounded him down his side landing him on his feet. Clint kissed him and sent him on his way.

"Hi there, Rodney. Hi, Daryl. I have something for you guys." Kandi pulled out sticks of gum from her purse.

"Thank you." The boys ran ahead, inside.

"We were getting worried." Shelly came to the front door.

"Traffic was a mother . . ."

She put her finger to Clint's lips. "Don't make me pop you."

"I wasn't going to say it. Daaang."

"How you doing, Kandi? Nice to see you again." Shelly sped off back toward the kitchen.

"Is there a doctor in *tiz-house*." Alison came in and gave Clint a long hug. "Congratulations. I hear you're in the big time now."

Clint blushed a little. "Not quite the big time, but I'm on my way." He moved from in front of her, "Alison, this is Kandi."

Alison's face was bright with enthusiasm. It was strange, seeing a female Clint. They had the same features, the dark-toned skin, only she was softer, more polished. Her hair was pulled back, showing off her deep dimples and slanted eyes.

"Nice to meet you." Kandi stuck out her hand, only to be pulled in and embraced by Alison.

"No handshakes around here, girl, we're all family."

"Hey man, you made it." Cedric walked in with beer in tow. "Kandi, sweet Kandi. Good to see you." He squeezed her, leaving her a little off balance. "Come on in, y'all. Don't just stand in the doorway."

"What you want to drink, Clint?" Alison was right behind them as they all made their way down the hall.

"Beer's cool."

"Kandi, what about you? Can I get you something?"

"Oh, I'll come with you. Maybe I can decide then." Kandi followed Alison to the kitchen, where Shelly was moving around like she'd had too much premium lead coffee.

"I'd be glad to help out," Kandi offered.

"We've got it covered, pretty much." Shelly whisked past Kandi. "Go ahead and have a seat." A small stool appeared out of nowhere.

Alison, moving at a much slower pace, put a wineglass in front of Kandi and began pouring. "You look like a Zinfandel kind of girl."

"Thank you. I didn't want to ask for it in front of the guys." She smiled as if they had a secret.

"Believe me, they know we're not in here because of our health. Right, Shelly? Girls got to have their fun, too."

"Got that right." Shelly slid her glass next to Kandi's. "Fill me up." After the first glass, Shelly's rushed gait was replaced with one movement at a time. Their giggles were ringing through the other room.

Cedric pushed his way through the saloon-style shutter doors.

"Hey, what's all this noise coming out of here. A little less hee-hawing and get that food on the table, woman." Cedric slapped Shelly on the derriere. She giggled wildly. "Uh oh, you guys been hitting the sauce. Hey, Clint," he called out, "we might have to put on the aprons. These women are in here getting lit."

Clint walked in and let a warm breath rest on Kandi's face. "In that case we need to be getting home. I need to take advantage of someone before it wears off," he chided in her ear.

The music from the radio was on and went unnoticed until Marvin Gaye's soulful voice blasted, "*. . . betcha wondering how I knew . . . You could've told me yourself, instead I heard from someone else. . . .*" Cedric turned it up and captured Shelly's hands and spun her around. "*Don't you know that I heard it through the grapevine.*" They were dancing and singing with the music. Alison pulled Rodney and Daryl, who had been watching the bizarre behavior of adults silently, to the middle of the kitchen floor. They were shaking their little butts. Clint pulled Kandi up to her feet and started clapping and swaying in his suave style, reminiscent of the first time they'd met. Kandi started snapping her fingers, moving her hands above her head, feeling the beat that was rising through her. The wine on top of an empty stomach left Kandi uninhibited. Together all at once, in unison, they started singing at the top of their lungs. It couldn't have been better if they'd planned it.

Don'tcha knooow that I heard it through the grapevine and I'm justabout to lose my mind. . . . You could've tooold me yourself, but I heard it from someone else, don'tcha know that I heard it through the grapevine. . . . How much longer would you be mine . . .

They sang a few more bars of chorus before Alison belted out a solo. She could really sing, and they all clapped and cheered for her.

"Thank you." She bowed and blew kisses. "Thank you. No applause. No applause needed."

Instead of the traditional turkey and stuffing, Shelly served up cooking from her hometown of Baton Rouge, shrimp creole and gumbo. The delicacy of each bite left Kandi wanting more. She ate unabashed. This was no time to be cute. Her lipstick was gone, and she didn't care. It was by far one of the best holiday meals she'd ever eaten. One of the best holidays period. This family was pure love.

Kandi caught Clint watching her a couple of times. He did that a lot, watching, studying her. The heat he sent through his eyes surrounded her. Left with a rush in unspeakable parts of her body, she'd quickly turn away. She didn't want to be that transparent, not in front of his family, anyway.

After dinner Kandi stayed in the kitchen with Shelly and Alison. They loaded the dishwasher and put away food. Alison updated Shelly on her long-distance love affair with the Jordanian man she'd met while he was an exchange student at Georgetown, where she worked as a financial aid counselor. Alison did not want to hear Shelly's warnings of all his possible motives for choosing *her* to fall in love with. "Those men like their women wrapped tight, subservient, and anxious to please. What's he doing interested in you?" Shelly had asked Alison when they'd first started writing each other back and forth. "I'd say sistahs fall as far away from that description as possible, wouldn't you?"

"What do you think, Kandi? Doesn't that seem a little odd to you? Keeping this longer than long-distance relationship going, when this guy knows he has no chance of returning to the States unless he can tie the knot with somebody who lives here." Shelly scraped the last of the gumbo into the large plastic container and tapped the wooden spoon excessively on the side.

Alison stepped up and answered for her. "Okay, Shelly I get your point, and you know what, I agree with you. But who cares? If that's the only reason he sends me five letters a week and calls every Sunday like clockwork, I'll take it. Because guaranteed, everybody's got an agenda. Fahja's no different from the guy who chooses a woman because she's got big tits or a big heart. He has a need for me, and if I can fulfill it, regardless of what it is, I'll do it, because that's what it's all about."

Kandi was relieved when Alison spoke. Kandi didn't add anything, but only let out soft sighs where appropriate. She herself was guilty of ulterior motives. At first, she'd seen Clint as a conquest to be had for only one reason, his good looks and doctor status, but that was all in the past. Since then she'd found a thousand and one reasons to be in love with Clint Fairchild. Did it matter what motivation started the process, as long as what happens after is the hard work that helps the relationship survive?

"But what's going to happen when he stops needing you, when you've served your purpose? That's all I'm saying. There has to be so much more there for a relationship to last."

"And how do you know there isn't, Shelly? He might actually be in love with me. It's not impossible." Alison was brimming with animosity.

Kandi swallowed her fear and stepped in as a buffer. "You know what, you're both right. There's always that first motivation for choosing the person you fall in love with. Always. But I know for a fact that when that person makes you feel good about yourself, and takes you to another level, one you thought you'd never reach, how you got there doesn't matter."

Kandi turned directly to Alison. "Fahja's not going to remember what was going through his mind the day he laid eyes on you." She grabbed Alison's hands. "Maybe he *was* thinking, hey, if I marry this one, I can come back to America. So what? We all have an agenda. We've all got a spec sheet and qualifications before we allow ourselves to love, otherwise we'd never get what we wanted. This ain't high school, we're in the real world. Remember what our mothers told us, or at least what my mother told me, 'it's just as easy to fall in love with a rich man, as it is to fall in love with a poor one.' Well, we've all got standards, right? And then, at some point, all that stuff doesn't matter. If he really has fallen in love with you, 'why' or 'how' doesn't matter. It won't hurt to give it your best shot if he's got what it takes to make you happy. Right? Who cares why he loves you, as long as he does?"

Shelly broke through, half laughing. "Oh, that is just sad and pathetic. Don't you stand there and listen to that horse, cow, manure, whatever mess. A man has got to take the good, the bad, and the ugly. We all do. You can't be running around with some little list, talking about what you want. You get what you get. Love is truly blind."

Alison turned toward Shelly, "Oh, so I guess you didn't notice my brother's debonair good looks and solid abs when you met him, huh? You just saw a great personality from a mile a way and honed in. And he didn't see all that Jayne Kennedy hair hanging on your head? Huh, is that what you're saying?"

Shelly couldn't keep in the laugh. She remembered her instant attraction to Cedric when she'd met him at a friend's birthday party ten years ago. They'd slept together that first night. "You got a point there," she admitted shamefully.

"I'm with Kandi." Alison spoke heroically. She was on a roll now. "When a person chooses you or you choose them, it's got some kind of reason behind it, and who's to say which is the noble one. We've all got our needs. I might have started loving Fahja because he's got a big dick, but that's my business." She let Shelly's eyes pop back into her head before continuing. "And what keeps our relationship going is not going to be that big dick, well maybe a little, but what keeps it alive is truly going to be the sincerity of my love for him; then, and only then, can I accept the good, the bad, and the ugly."

"Lord, help these wayward souls." Shelly was raising her hands and looking up while she was talking. "These poor children know not what they say, Lord."

Alison nodded and turned her body toward Shelly, giving her a full body embrace. "Keep praying for me sister, 'cause I'm getting mine."

They all fell out in fits of boisterous laughter.

Clint and Cedric looked at each other as they sat on the couch watching the Holiday Bowl football game and shook their heads as the sound of the women's laughter wafted through the den.

The drive home was dark and peaceful. The gearshift and armrest didn't prevent Kandi from getting as close to him as she could. The fullness, the contentment, was still swelled up inside of her. She meshed her face in his sleeve to get a good fill of his scent.

"I love your family. They are so sweet."

"They love you, too." He massaged her through the fabric of her dress.

"Do *you* love me?" Kandi asked out of the blue.

"Do I love you?" He paused for a second. "You know I do."

Kandi closed her eyes, abandoning any more skepticism. Feelings don't lie. It really didn't matter that he'd never said the words *I love you*.

How many times had she heard it? Since the days of platforms and polyester, she'd been hearing "I love you," and it meant nothing. She didn't care that he was unable to say it. Actually mouthing the words held little value when you could feel it. Like something gripping your heart, tight, making breathing difficult at times, but when you finally took a deep breath, it's only because the other person is there. Kandi saw Clint for a moment as she was dozing, his smile, holding her, whispering, "You know I do." She fell off into a deep sleep *of course I do*.

Friends?

I WAS GLAD TO BE BACK IN DC. THE voice mail messages sailed through the room on the speakerphone. I turned it to the highest volume and listened intently while I opened windows to let fresh air and light on my plants. It was odd that Clint hadn't called me back.

I picked up the receiver and dialed his place.

"Talk to me," he answered.

"Clint. Hi. How was your holiday?"

"V, what's up? It was cool. Very nice. How was yours? You went to LA, right?"

"Yeah, it was all right. I survived. I wanted to talk to you while I was there. Cedric didn't know if you were coming to his place or not. What was that all about? You two not communicating these days?"

"Nah, nothing like that. Me and Cedric are always cool. I just had a lot to do, working and finding a place to live. I can't stay here once I'm out of the residency program."

I held the phone tight. "Can you come over . . . later? Right now I'm on my way out to pick up Sandy. But later?"

"Okay, I'll come around, five?" He seemed anxious. "V, did you have a Merry Christmas?"

"Not really. What about you?"

"It was good. I mean, you know as good as those things go. Merry Christmas, V."

"Merry Christmas to you, too, Clint."

I shook off the foreboding fear that was trying to creep through my throat as I lay on the couch staring up at the ceiling. I'd have to swallow a lot of crow, but it would be worth it. I wanted him to know that I felt bad about the way I'd handled things. He needed to know I was a different person, ready to take responsibility for my own happiness, a whole person.

Her round little bottom switched over to me, waddling like a fat woman unable to control where it landed. Sandy ran across the floor to jump up on me. I kneeled down to let her sniff my face.

"Did you miss your mommy?" I tussled her ears, rubbing and patting her.

Wendy was standing over us with a less-enthused look.

"That dog has chewed up every pair of tennis shoes in this house." Her slim hands rested on her hip. "Jamal thought it was funny and was feeding them to her, literally. Shaking the shoes at her." She nudged the little coffee-dipped boy in the back of his head. "She'd rip right into one carrying it off under the bed or someplace, where nobody but her could find it. Then she'd go back and chew on it some more when nobody was looking." She switched hips. "Never again. Never."

"Were you a bad girl. Were you?" The baby talk was causing her tail to whip in full lashes around, fanning me with the motion. I stood up and gave Wendy a hug. "Thank you."

"Anytime," Wendy mocked.

I picked up the leash and attached it to Sandy's collar. She tried to paw my hand away. The leash wasn't her favorite accessory.

Wendy called out to me while I was getting in the car. "I see you finally got a pair of those hoochie pants. Got the heels, too." She whooped a hearty laugh while she waved. "Looks good on you." She reiterated more seriously, "You're looking good. See you later, girl."

It made me feel good that Wendy had noticed the change. While in Los Angeles I'd spent a small fortune at Bloomingdale's and a trip to a European Day Spa with a mud bath, a full-body massage, facial, pedicure, and manicure, all worth every liberating dollar. But it wasn't the work I'd done on the outside that I was most proud of, it was what happened on the inside. I'd spent every available moment working out the inner me. Rigorous, hard, no-pain-no-gain kind of sessions. Sitting in the middle of my old bedroom on the shag carpet my mother refused to replace, I would meditate. At first I didn't quite know what I was doing. It became natural after a while, listening to my breathing, turning myself inside out so that all I could hear was myself, deep inside. Not the myself that wanted a fresh cup of coffee, or wondered what to wear for the day. It was a deeper self, the one that wanted to be heard, stroked, and understood. For hours, I'd just sit, running energy, feeling like I was floating, and that life was only a series of dreams, none more important than the other. During those quiet periods nothing was important except for the rebuilding, toning, and reshaping of my mind. I couldn't remember ever being in better shape.

I drove slowly, savoring the ride down the Little River Turnpike, admiring the dated buildings made out of brick and wood. Clean. Dull and worn, but clean. The trees were leafless, but that's how it was supposed to be, four seasons. I rode with the back windows down. Sandy's small body was straining, sticking her face out to be voluntarily whipped by the freezing air. I played my radio loud. I blasted my Roy Ayers oldie but goodie "Searching." This was the perfect setting. "Home is where the heart is," I thought out loud. This place with its stubborn and obtuse traffic lights on every corner, narrow pathways, and old buildings was home. I pulled into Whisper Creek, noticing the white Jetta parked in front of my house. I was thankful. This was my life. This was my home. It could only get better.

Clint got out before I was stopped completely. He walked up to my car door and opened it.

"How ya doing, V? You're looking good." He reached in over me, picking up the little brownish, blond mop of fur. "Hey, pretty girl. Hey." Sandy wagged her tail.

I felt the same way, seeing Clint. I wanted to jump into his arms and pant and lick his face. Tell him I missed him madly. That would have to wait, though. First, I had some explaining to do.

Sundays were usually used for writing in her journal and thinking about the week's lesson plans for her third-graders. Most of the time Kandi used it for solitude and a healthy dose of relaxation. But today she was jittery, nervous about Clint going to see Venus. What if he fell right back into her arms? There wasn't anything she could do about it.

She accepted his judgment. He wanted to tell Venus in person about them, make sure things were *square*, as he put it. Kandi poured the hot water from the teakettle, letting the steam rise up into her face. She dipped the tea bag while envisioning their reunion. She could see Clint holding Venus in his strong muscular arms, rubbing his hands across her hairless skull.

Imagining the two of them together made the sparse blond hairs on her almond skin stand up. She hated this feeling of insecurity.

She pictured Clint picking up the phone at Venus's instruction, calling to tell her it was over between them, he and Venus were back together, and of course he was sorry, he'd never meant to hurt her.

Kandi jumped, startled from the intercom sounding. She ran over and pressed the entrance button without hesitation, anxious to hear the news, good or bad. In the few minutes it took for him to get from the lobby to her front door, she sat down, she stood up, she walked to the door, took a deep breath, and swung it open.

"You must really be happy to see me." He stepped in from out of the corridor, picking her up, spinning her around. "Missed me?" Tyson put Kandi down and moved past her into the living room.

She was still orbiting. "Tyson. What are you doing? I told you . . ."

"You've told me lots of times, Kandi. I'm just checking to see which one we're on today." He stretched out on the plush sofa and rested his hardly worn Timberlands on the whitewashed pine coffee table.

"Well, I'm telling you now." She kept the door opened, wide. "You have to leave. Please." The desperation in her voice was hard to mask.

"You're expecting company," Tyson guessed. "How sweet. I'd like to meet him. He's got to be one smooth brother to have you coming and going—the way you've been acting." He let out a disbelieving grunt. "What did he promise you?" He stayed reclined with his hands relaxed behind his head.

"Not now, Tyson. Really. Not now," Kandi pleaded.

"Sounds to me like he may be on his way. Is that it?"

"That's right. He's on his way and if I were you, I'd vacate the premises."

"Is that supposed to scare me? I'd actually like to meet him. Compare notes, that kind of thing."

"You son of a bitch. You have no right!" Kandi was sick of his games, his lies, his assumption that she had nothing to do but wait.

"Easy, baby. Take it easy. No need in being loud." Tyson stood up and touched Kandi's cheek with the back of his hand. "You want me gone, just ask me nicely."

She swallowed the huge lump that was sitting on the back of her throat. She felt prickly beads of perspiration making their way down her shirt. "Tyson, will you please leave?"

"No problem, baby, I just have one request and then I'll be on my merry way." He leaned into her body, pushing her against the door, making it close. He flipped the deadbolt. For one instant, through her terror she wished Clint were on his way and would bust through the door and save her the way it happens in the movies. But in the next second she realized, the last thing she wanted was for Clint to walk in. How would she explain this man with his hands wrapped around her neck, demanding what he felt was his due? *Were you still seeing him? Why did you lie?*

"Noooo!" she screamed as she began to fight.

"You're early. Got a hot date you're trying to get me out of the way for?" It was a nervous, silly laugh I let out.

Clint responded with the same.

"Not really." He kept his sunglasses on, but showed a half-sincere grin.

"C'mon in." I washed my hands and went straight into the kitchen. "You want something to drink?"

He played with Sandy on the couch, tossing her face back and forth between his hands. She snapped at him once or twice, intensifying their reunion. "Whatever you have is fine," he called out.

I stared into my bare refrigerator. "I haven't had a chance to do any grocery shopping since I got back from LA." I carried a glass of faucet water to him. "I'm sorry."

"That's all right." He sipped the chromium-tasting fluid to be polite.

"So you go first. What did you want to talk to me about?" I sat down on the barstool, letting my left foot remain on the ground for stability.

"No, you called me, remember?" Changing his mind, he put the glass down and leaned into himself. "Actually, I wanted to make sure the air was clear between us. I've been straight up baffled by all this bullsh . . ." He corrected himself. "I've been trying to figure out what happened. You know. It's like a damn dream, a nightmare. And it's just been pissing me off that I can't understand it." His voice moved in different highs, then low. "And it's not like I'm never going to get over it. I mean, I'm through, you know. I'm not going to be hassling you anymore. I threw in the towel, but it's still eating the shit out of me. What the hell happened?" Clint removed his sunglasses. His eyes were slightly bloodshot, dull, and tired. He probably hadn't had a good night's sleep since he'd moved into that roach motel.

I gulped in large amounts of air involuntarily. I didn't know how to explain what had happened. I felt like a child who'd been asked to confess her mischief, make a parent understand the workings of a mind that isn't yours.

"I'll do my best to explain. I was feeling a lot at the time. I felt like I had given all that I had to give and felt pretty hopeless, about me, us, as a couple." His eyes glazed over. Men generally didn't understand abstract; they needed concrete interpretations, what, when, how, and exactly what was he watching on television at the time.

"Not that you were making me a bad person," I continued. "I wasn't being true to myself. I thought that's how you make someone love you, by being perfect, hiding your flaws. I wanted to be perfect for you, what

I thought perfection was. You know, the endless workout sessions, keeping my hair up-tight."

He chuckled a little bit, probably remembering the many times I had to choose between the lights, gas bill, and my hair salon visits.

"It was a lot of work. Don't laugh." After being chastised, he quickly returned to the serious expression he'd started out with. "It was a strain, to be honest. And I started to blame you for the burden. I thought if I kept up the pace, I'd win in the end. I'd get the man, the kids, the deal packaged tight. But you weren't giving me enough to go on, and I was getting tired of keeping up the pace for nothing. I wanted you to respond by putting me out of my misery. I thought if we just got married, I could stop working so hard. Relax."

He shook his head in confusion. "By working so hard, you mean, physically? I don't understand."

"Yeah, I mean exactly that. I was in a state of constant motion. Always. Even when I was relaxing I was concentrating on how I was going to look the next day. How my hair was going to be styled, what kind of clothes I was going to wear."

"And you're saying you did all that for me. Or, you thought you were doing it all for me? You're saying you threw away four years of my life, our life together, because you were tired of looking good for me? All this shit, is about your . . . your hair, your appearance? Is that what you're telling me, V? 'Cause if it is, that's pretty fucked up."

"It's not that simple. It is, but then it isn't. It wasn't just about my hair and appearance." I was getting nervous. He shook his head in confusion. No matter how I tried to explain, it really did appear to be so small and petty, when in my head and my heart, I knew it was bigger than this entire room. It was large and dangerous, hanging ominously over every exterior part of my life, like a scab that would not heal, or rain that would never stop falling. Every day, in every way, my life had been affected by the stages of my hair, the hair that was an extension of my every thought. It was only natural that it defined my relationship as well.

"It was the whole attitude, 'the give 'em all you've got' mantra. I'm trying to explain how I interpreted this. I thought if I could be all that I could be and giving all I had to give, you would want me, forever, for keeps. Still things weren't going in the direction I wanted. It just seemed like you really didn't want me, even in perfection, so I thought, 'why bother?' Why should I keep up this pace, playing this false game, keeping myself up to what I thought were your standards, when you really didn't want me anyway, when you showed up for my birthday without the ring . . . I thought, to hell with this. He doesn't love me. He's never going to marry me, so why keep waiting. I was tired of waiting for the day you when would say, 'hey, she's everything I could ever want, what am I waiting for?' By cutting off my hair, I was cutting you out of my life. I'd given up on us."

"Why didn't you just talk to me? We were together for four years, V. All that time just thrown down the drain 'cause you were tired. I was tired, too, but I held on. Do you know how hard it was living here day to day, knowing I wasn't giving you everything, hell giving anything, for that matter? I couldn't even pay my share of the house note. Do you know how that made me feel? No man wants to feel less than a man. I fought with myself every day living here, under *your* roof, and to see you become so unhappy, all I could do was blame myself. Then you started in about how much I owed you. It seemed like every conversation we had turned into a tally sheet. I couldn't stand up to that shit, but I also couldn't be wheedled down by it either. I knew you wanted to get married, bad. There was no way I could bring myself to ask you to marry me when it felt like I had a gun in my back. Couldn't you see that? The timing was just all wrong."

"I didn't see it then, but I do now." He had always accused me of pushing too hard, being aggressive, but those were my good traits, at least I thought they were. Those were the things that were going to get me where I wanted to be in this world.

"I never meant to make you feel small or inadequate, Clint. I just went after what I wanted and that was you. Isn't that what we're all taught? To go full steam ahead, take what you want out of life, because no one is going to give it to you."

He shook his head, "No, I was taught the exact opposite. Not to take, but to give everything I've got, and eventually the good things will follow. I gave, what little of me was left, to you, V. Why couldn't you see that?"

"I realize now how wrong I was. It all backfired. It seems like everything in my life lately has backfired—my determination has knocked down the wrong walls and I don't like any of what I see." I stared down at the rug, which was now bent on the corners from me nervously pushing it back and forth with my foot.

"I wish we could have talked about all this, V."

"I didn't know. I had some growing to do, but now I know I can't force things to happen, especially when I'm constantly in fear of the worst. Even when I've been hopeful, it seems I allowed some cloud to creep into my thoughts and make me second-guess myself. It wasn't clear before."

"And now it is? I still don't understand how you could just throw up your hands." Clint stopped talking abruptly. Staring out the window, caught in some kind of epiphany, he spoke slowly. "Did you ever love me, V? Was it all about the payoff, did you ever just love *me*?" When he blinked, I watched a small tear trace the curve of his face.

"I'm so, so, sorry for hurting you. I never stopped loving and caring about you. I wish we could start over." This was his cue. He was supposed to walk over to me, slide his hands around my face, kiss me softly, tell me he was glad this roller-coaster ride was over, and that he loved me, too, for who I was inside, always had, and the hair didn't matter, the *look*, none of it mattered. I could have naps the size of robin's eggs and he'd still love me. That's what this was all about; I never believed he could love me unconditionally due to the simple fact that *I* had not loved *myself* unconditionally.

He rose up and reached out for my hand. "I'll always care about you, too. I wish things would have worked out differently. I may not have showed it, but I did love you. I'm not going to lie and say looks aren't important to me, or to any man or woman. It matters. It does. But it was never the *only* thing I cared about. I'm sorry I gave you that impression." He smoothed his hand over my round head. "I told you this was cool with me. Just shows off your pretty face. I guess it's sort of the same way I thought you felt about me, that all you truly cared about was my becoming a doctor. We were both so afraid of being found out, seen without the props, simply being a man and a woman able to love each other for what we were."

I sniffed back the trickle that was trying to make its way out to ruin what was a poetic and loving moment. I'd never heard Clint speak so eloquently. I pressed his hand into my cheek and closed my eyes as a sign of relief, until I heard his final words.

"I'm glad it's over . . . I'm glad we don't have to keep beating each other up with blame. I always want us to be friends."

I swallowed hard. The words were tap-dancing on my forehead.

Always, friends?

That was meant for people who were well on their way to the next lifetime. I panicked. Should I fight? Would I be doing it all over again, standing up for what I wanted? I took a step off the barstool, landing on both feet miraculously, and took a deep breath and funneled words out of the logical side of my brain.

"What are you talking about, friends? I thought we could . . . are you seeing someone else? I mean, for keeps?" I touched his face, but he turned away. I knew who the "someone else" was without a doubt. Women like her worked fast and hard.

I drew in a breath. "Okay . . . well, then, I guess that's that." I kissed him on the cheek. "I'm glad you came. I really do wish you the best." The words tumbled out slowly and reverberated back through my eardrum like I was underwater.

"Take care," he whispered, dropping my hand to suffice on its own. He walked out the door. I heard the click of the knob fall back into place and I let it out, the wail, the sob that made Sandy skitter to my side, sniffing all around me for the cause of pain, seeking out where it must hurt to make me cry so loud.

He'd never understand. Not fully. It was too late to worry about it now, after all, there was a new situation on his plate. He wanted things to work out right for a change. He didn't know why it had taken so long for him to let go. But sitting there, listening to Venus made him realize she wasn't the only guilty party. He was equally to blame. Four years, in all that time he couldn't see it. That he'd loved only an image of Venus, the beautiful woman, strong, and intelligent, everything he'd thought would make the perfect partner. He never stopped to listen to the small voice in his head telling him that he had only scratched the surface. Either he hadn't looked deep enough, or she'd kept it all under guard where he could not get to it. He needed more. It had been so easy to let her lead the way, to make the rules and decisions. It was a pattern he was determined to break. It was all right. Better late than never. He was on his way to a woman that would give him everything he needed. Faith in him, love, trust, it wasn't any more complicated than that. She believed in him and he believed in her. And most importantly, he believed in himself. He didn't need anyone to tell him what or who to be anymore.

The Jetta felt like a rocket ship when he moved it into fifth gear and headed up the 95 Interstate.

The more Kandi resisted, the harder he pushed down, until she was stationed on her knees in front of his crotch.

"Tyson. No!" She felt the pressure of his hands pushing on her shoulders. He quickly began pulling his zipper down.

There was no way Kandi would give in to his power play. She would die fighting. She kept struggling, even with the sound of her hair being ripped from the pores in her scalp as she tried to pull away. She scratched at his exposed skin. She knew she had hurt him as soon as she felt the numbing thickness of too much flesh under her nails.

She braced herself for his wrath. He pushed her away hard, knocking her over backwards and sending her crashing into the corner of the wall. She should have felt pain, but instead she was in shock, burning with anger. With all her strength she got up and lunged at him. Tyson blocked her wild swinging arms, twisting her around and sealing her in his grip as she kept struggling.

"I'll let whatever you think is better than me die down," he breathed into her ear. "I'll hold on to these for when you come to your senses." He jingled the set of keys to Kandi's apartment hanging on his index finger in front of her face. The little silver elephant swung around like a hostage on the nickel ring of the keys.

"Get out!" She screamed louder than she knew was possible. But the piercing scream came once again, and she knew it was coming from her body, it wasn't her imagination. "Get the fuck out of here! Get out!"

When Kandi finally opened her eyes to focus, all she could see was his tan suede boot clearing the door before it closed. He had shoved her back to the floor. He mumbled something about her getting over it, and he would be waiting when she did. She couldn't believe she was lying on the floor, and Tyson Edwards had put her there. Had she really been taken for someone with little or no self-worth? All this time she half believed he cared, maybe not on a grand scale, but a little. She had believed he wanted the best for her, and that somewhere in his misshapen logic, she mattered, only to come to the realization that she was nothing to him. Probably at the end of a long string of nothings.

The excruciating pain was loud, thundering through her temple. There was a life-size lump forming on the left side of her head, too tender to touch. The ice she managed to catch from falling to the floor, and wrap in a kitchen towel, seemed to make the pain scream louder. She stood against the refrigerator, preparing herself for the inevitable flood of tears. She steadied herself for the rush of sorrow that was ready to peak, when she remembered she had no time for it now. All her pain would have to wait in a neatly tied ball until she could get to it.

Clint would be there at any moment. She would never be able to explain this other man's right to touch her, in violence or in pleasure.

She ran to the window out of instinct and spotted the Jetta parked on the street. But where was Clint?

Kandi gasped as she watched the two of them, Clint and Tyson, accidentally bump into one another, shoulder to shoulder. Tyson turned around, still heated, watching as Clint passed. Clint walked up to the double-paned doors of the building, completely unaware of the daggers aimed at his back. Tyson took a hesitant step in Clint's direction.

Kandi's lips started moving in an incoherent chant. Her mind was thinking, *Please keep going. Please don't come back, Tyson. Please.* But the words coming out of her mouth made no sense. She pressed her palms against the window and closed her eyes. It was the first prayer she'd said in quite a while. Not actually a prayer, more like an exchange, a promise like the one she'd made when she'd heard Basil had tested positive for HIV. They'd only slept together once, and once was too many. Basil,

Basil, what was his last name. She couldn't even remember his face. But she remembered running down to the county health department to have herself tested, instead of the medical center on the university's campus, so no one would know her. She'd prayed for the entire two-week waiting period, every day, all day, that if she got through this, she'd never sleep with another man out of wedlock again. Fornication was the word she'd found in the Bible.

It was a sin.

Two weeks of praying and private salvation seeking had granted her a negative test. She stayed celibate for three glorious months after that.

Where was that Bible? She couldn't recall. The gold lettering embossed on white leather came to her mind. The inside flap had her name and birth date written in her father's handwriting. *Kandace Lillian Treboe, October 15, 1969.*

Daddy.

This time the exchange would be simpler. Justifiable. Accountable. Reasonable. "I will love him, and take care of him with all of my heart, dear God. I will be true to him in my mind, my heart, my body, and my soul. He will never have to want or need for anything in this lifetime that I can provide. Oh please, dear God."

Kandi opened her eyes to see Tyson turn around and face his car. He stepped off the curb, tweaked his car alarm and unlocked the door with one push of a button. He slipped into the driver's side of his shiny Jaguar and drove away.

Her heart was surging, pulsating, making her head hurt worse with each beat. She ran to the bathroom, throwing water on her face, and tousling her hair, doing her best to cover what she knew were bare spots in her scalp. She threw the torn shirt in the closet and slipped another one over her head. By the time she'd finished, Clint had already been ringing the buzzer for some time. She pushed the security release without saying anything over the intercom. She waited behind the door, this time waiting until she could see who it was in full view through the peephole.

Kandi pulled Clint inside for the air she needed to breathe. His black leather jacket was cool, chilling, against her exposed middle. She slid the coat off his arms, letting it fall to the ground. She didn't ask any questions about his visit with Venus. She just kept kissing him, feeling around his wide back, around to his chest, undoing the buttons of his shirt, using only the sight of her fingers. He squeezed her back, causing her to wince. She ignored the pain until it faded away. He backed her into the couch, one slow step at a time.

She sent herself away. She wasn't in this room, this place anymore. She was lying in the moist Bermuda sand. She could feel his hands moving all over her oil-tanned body, warmed from the sun. We're making love on the beach, she thought. No one there but the two of them, their bodies stuck together. She was immersed in the fantasy, the contrast of his dark skin engulfed in the tangy brown nakedness of hers. She threw her head back. He pushed his face into hers.

"I love you," he whispered.

Kandi opened her eyes to take note of her surroundings. She wasn't imagining his words. It wasn't part of the fantasy. It was real. She focused on the stark white walls, the contemporary finished furniture, the collection of crystal, ivory, and wood, all in the shape of elephants placed on the glass shelf.

Kandi pulled his head up to meet her face. "I love you, too."

The click of the number rolling over to display a prominent *three* on the clock radio was the loudest sound in the room. Somehow they had ended up in Kandi's bed. Their mutual crescendo had left them in a deep slumber. She stirred first and started running her fingers around the outline of his mouth. She pulled herself up close to his face and kissed him gently on his lips. His eyes opened.

"So what should we do today?" he asked, as if he'd never actually fallen asleep, and it wasn't three o'clock in the morning.

"Well, when the sun comes up, we're going to look for a new place to live." She traced his eyebrow, kissed him there.

"What's wrong with here? You don't think there's enough room for both of us? I guess I can't fit in here with all your state-of-the-art computer equipment, huh?" He still had a groggy tone.

"Too crowded. That's for sure." Kandi traced his dark areola, and shaped her mouth around it, skimming it before bringing her lips to a close.

"Hey, hey, these aren't made like yours, they're not meant for sucking."

"How about something else, then." Kandi reached down, taking a handful. "Is this meant for sucking?"

He let his head fall back, sinking deeper in the pillow. They were submerged once more in each other.

When morning officially arrived and the room was brightened by daylight, Kandi found Clint leaning over her. At first she smiled, realizing this was the first day of the rest of their lives together. The smile quickly disappeared when she saw Clint's horrified expression.

"What happened to your neck and arms?" He leaned in closer like a doctor examining a patient. "How did you get those bruises? What happened?"

Kandi felt her throat and mouth go dry. Her hand drifted to the places that hurt, only imagining what he must've seen on her soft brown skin. The colors, black and blue, raised with swelling. She traced over the areas. When she tried to sit up, a dull ache caused her to lie back down. She hadn't felt her body trying to heal itself during the night. Tissue gorging itself with blood so that it could rebuild. Muscles broken down from strain, mending slowly layer after layer. The natural process of healing took time. Then, everything would be fine.

"Tell me what happened," he said, then went into the bathroom and came out holding two moist towels. He laid one in the crevice of her neck and shoulder, and the other across the top of her chest. "Kandi?"

His eyes were afraid, she didn't want him to be afraid. They would move into a new place, start a new life, together. No one would be able to hurt them again. She lifted her hand and smoothed it over his cheek. It would be all right. They would heal together.

"Kandi! Tell me what happened to you!"

She rolled over slowly, unable to face him when she had crushed his heart. He'd given it to her for safekeeping and all he'd asked was for her to take care. If she didn't, he'd sworn he would take it back.

◎   ◎   ◎

Stop or I'll Shoot

THIS DREAM WAS DIFFERENT FROM the others. This time I could see the person spreading the cream on my body, from head to toe. I could see her eyes, and her face. It was me, Venus Johnston, standing over *me* holding the flat spatula, basting *me* like a turkey with the white ooze. It was the old Venus, the one with the long shiny dark hair straight and thick, eyes hard and irritated. She seemed angry, mad at the world. I reached out my hand, grabbing the arm that belonged to me, that was working overtime to get the cream slathered.

"We don't have to work so hard. It's over."

The old Venus dropped the spatula, relieved. I hugged her, me, Venus, tight, stroking the hair that was once mine. It was a new freedom, better than the day I'd sat in Tina's chair for the last time. Now we were both free, on the inside as well as the outside. I hugged her, and she hugged me back.

I woke up feeling Sandy's soft warmth lying next to me. I stroked her gently. I smiled from knowing it was over. I knew it before Clint ever said the words. As hard as I tried to fix things, to make them right, there was a stronger power crying out for this freedom. All the days I'd sat transfixed, meditating, looking for answers. I'd found them, they were there all along waiting for permission to rise up and be heard. I had loved Clint, but the *me* that loved him was long gone. Somewhere in the past. I wasn't that person anymore. I realized that what I was trying to be, a wife of a doctor, a mother with a big pretty house and a picket fence, and all the perks that came along with the ride, were all an illusion. I never let Clint love me, the real me. I was too busy hiding under dreams and fantasies and false expectations. The *Venus* Clint knew was long gone. I was better than ever inside and out. The truth of the matter was that the new me needed more than a fairy-tale happy ending. The prize was no longer winning Dr. Clint Fairchild. The prize was getting me all shiny and new like a freshly picked red juicy apple. Organically grown with nothing but the good stuff, trials, tribulations, love, sunshine, and plenty of water. With that thought, I hurried out of bed to start a sumptuous tub full of lavender and bubbles. The future looked bright and I couldn't wait to get started.

I parked my shiny new car right in front of Manuel's concrete station, enabling him to keep a close eye on it. It wasn't the BMW that I wanted, but it was definitely an upgrade. I checked my face in the sunshade mirror. Confident, intelligent, deserving of all good things. That's the pep talk I'd given myself all morning and was hoping it would carry me through my first day back at Donnely Kramer. I arrived before the sun, but I figured I needed the extra time to get reacquainted with my office and the surroundings. Hopefully it wouldn't be for long. I had already received two calls for interviews with companies that did think I was qualified to be an executive account manager. It was just a matter of time.

The face that came toward me as I was stepping on the elevator looked vaguely familiar. It was hard to tell in the tam and heavy scarf wrapped around her neck almost covering half her face. But the look she gave me was, undeniably, a look of disgust, or loathing. I turned around, letting the door catch me slightly on the heel before it shut.

"Excuse me," I said.

She kept walking, a little faster.

I followed her out to the street. "Excuse me," I called out louder. She stepped off the curb and disappeared into the sheet of falling snow. The misty drizzle left me fighting for sight, but I could still hear the clicking of her heels. A sudden fear stopped me in my tracks. I didn't know who this woman was. I didn't know what she was capable of. I gave up and turned to go back inside the building. The elevator was still open and waiting. I moved to the corner out of habit, overcome by the largeness of the steel box, even larger when no one was in it but me.

The lobby entrance of Donnely Kramer was still dark. I pulled out my pass key and stuck it in the slot. I pushed my way through, stepping on the hand-scribbled envelope. I picked it up from underneath my foot, and without a moment's thought I knew who had left it. The note written this time in a full sentence took on a whole new meaning.

Dear Bitch,
Find your own man and stay away from mine.

I put the note down, stunned. I used the personal voice mail number I was given and tried not to sound too frantic.

"Tyson, this is Venus Johnston. I have something I need to share with you. It's important. Please call me as soon as you get this message."

I hung up the phone and pulled out the Idiot's file. I placed the envelope and note all in its original form and slammed the steel cabinet door shut. It was time to put an end to this mess.

The huge all-glass building sat alone, like an ominous force on the corner of Fifteenth and G Street. The sun was making an appearance every now and then, but it wouldn't stay out. The clouds and varying colors of the sky were mimicked in the reflection of the mirrored building.

I walked to the receptionist, whom I knew on sight was the same one I had spoken to on more than one occasion. Her cocoa skin and ceramic hair were just as I pictured her. Too much of everything, the nails, the hair separated into varying directions looking like fingers spread out, curls on one end, smooth swirls on the front, waves in the back. I was preoccupied with observing all this activity when she spoke.

"Can I help you?"

"I'm here to see Mr. Edwards."

"Your name?" She was looking in a large calendar.

"I'm probably not in there. In fact, could you just let Mr. Edwards know Venus Johnston is here?"

"Sure. Have a seat." She punched in numbers with the three-inch-long nails painted in a sheer French manicure, before returning to her business of assessing me. Her eyes ran over me as mine had run over her only a few minutes before, first my hair, then my suit, and down as far as vision permitted. "Ms. Johnston. It'll be a few minutes."

"Thank you." We both had exhausted all the possible allusions. I could possibly be one of Tyson's new acquisitions. She could be one of the old. I couldn't possibly be his type, but anything can happen once. I took a seat in the expansive lobby with enough furniture to have a sale.

I played with the file in my hand. Slapping it on my knee. Bending and unbending until I heard the voices coming from down the hall. A neatly dressed woman with legs longer than my whole body was strolling in front of Tyson. They stopped and shook hands, for appearance's sake. She did a pivot turn and walked to the exit like she was on a runway. Tyson didn't stop watching until she was completely out of sight. He then turned his attention to me sitting only a few feet away. He'd known I was there the whole time, watching him flirt shamelessly; but the inconsiderateness of being too obvious had evaded him.

"Ms. Johnston." He stood before me dressed in a light brown suit, impeccable as always. "C'mon back."

I smiled at the receptionist as I followed Tyson to his office. She responded with a presumptuous grin.

It was indeed a pleasure just to walk behind him. He glided when he walked. There was no bounce or dip, just one long stride in front of the other.

"What's so hush-hush you couldn't tell me over the phone?" He spoke while he was pulling up his big leather chair to the equally large mahogany desk. "I know you're not pregnant, because we never got that far." He let a large smile creep to his face as he plopped down in the seat. "No, seriously, tell me what's going on."

I opened the file and took the scribbled pieces of paper out. "Do you recognize the handwriting?"

He sat straight up in his chair, picked each note up, and examined them slowly. He tossed them back in the file.

"What's this all about? I'm supposed to know something about this?"

"Tyson, I think your wife's been leaving these notes at my office."

"Are you serious?" He asked incredulously.

"Let me see a recent picture of her."

He turned a silver onyx frame around that was facing him. "There you go."

I fell back into the chair I was sitting in. It was her, round faced, flat-line smile.

"She's been leaving the notes, Tyson. I saw her, myself." I couldn't believe it still, staring at the picture with her standing there, looking completely sane and innocent. Almost naïve and shy in a way, but it was definitely her.

"Why would she have left you notes? She doesn't know anything about you, there's nothing to know."

"Are you sure? She may have seen us together and assumed I was one of your conquests."

He barked out a short laugh. "One of my conquests? You sound like I've got them all over town. I assure you that's not the case. I can also assure you that if she was having us followed, two brief lunch dates do not a passionate affair make."

"Well, if she's sending notes to me for eating with you as an associate, imagine what your other women are getting."

He considered the thought for a moment. "What other women? Why are you so adamant to believe I've got all these *women*?"

"Look, Tyson, that's not the point. My point is simply this, if she's leaving notes with me, based on the meetings we've had, with her suspicions and fears, she's potentially dangerous. She needs help. And I don't want her to get it after the fact, after I've been attacked with her crazy ass jumping out of the bushes somewhere."

"I really don't think that's going to happen."

"This has happened before, hasn't it?" Surely, I wasn't the first. He stayed quiet too long. "You either stop her, or I will. I can go to the police and tell them she's stalking me."

He perked up, dropping the play act. "That's not necessary, Venus. I'll talk to her. Find out what's going on."

I softened a bit. "Tyson, if she's hurting this much . . . if she's driven to these kinds of things, the notes, and no telling what else, you may want to reconsider what you're doing to her, how you're treating her.

Women only do these kinds of things when they've been hurt." I had a brief recollection of me knocking the yogurt all over the young blond imp Garet was feeding. She was innocent. "We do stupid things when we're hurt, Tyson."

I rose up to leave. He stood up and walked congruently to meet me at his office door. He smelled good. He was standing too close. "I'm sorry for the trouble, Miss Johnston."

"You don't even know how much. I was pointing the finger at people in my office, turning things upside down. I definitely know how it feels to have egg on your face."

He kissed me on the forehead. "Believe me, there is no egg on your face."

I hissed when I felt the bolts of seduction moving down my body and landing in the most likely place. Just as I was about to respond, loud voices could be heard just outside the door. The receptionist and a male voice, doors opening and slamming shut, the sounds were moving closer in our direction. Tyson moved me out of the way and opened his office door. I stood directly behind him when I heard the male's voice more clearly this time.

It was Clint.

Before I could get completely out of the way, Clint had shoved Tyson back through the open office door and sent his fist hard into Tyson's jaw. I screamed out for Clint to stop. He repeated the same drawn fist, this time landing in Tyson's nose. They fell into the large glass table, with Clint landing on top of Tyson. I kept screaming for Clint to stop, as if he could hear me through his fury. Two security officers broke through the crowd of onlookers and pulled Clint off of his victim. I'd never seen him so angry. I was confused. Had he seen Tyson and me together and assumed what Tyson's wife had, that we were more than business associates? Or perhaps she had spread the rumor to ruin my life, as she thought I was ruining hers and somehow information had gotten back to Clint. I reached past the security guards to touch Clint's sleeve where blood was trailing down his arm from a glass cut. He flinched.

"It's me, Clint."

He was out of breath, adrenaline pumping. I backed up afraid he might swing at me, too.

Tyson stood up straight, blood dripping from his lip, nose, and down around his forehead. "Get him out of here."

"Should we call for police assistance, sir?" the larger of the two security men asked.

Clint shouted over their shoulders, "Yeah, call the police so you can go to jail for slapping a woman around. Go ahead, call them."

"No, just get him the hell out of here."

"How does it feel? Don't feel too good, does it? Hitting on a woman. You ain't shit!" Clint yelled out as the two security guards escorted him down the hall. He walked calmly, but they retained a firm hold on his arms. The heroic display hadn't been about me at all. Who, then? I had a million questions. I followed them as they released Clint outside.

"Clint, wait." He kept walking. His chest was visibly rising and falling. The anger, the rage, it was bizarre seeing him this way. "Please wait."

He stopped and faced me. There was a small cut bleeding on his forehead. His eyes found every possible way to avoid looking into mine.

"What happened back there? What was all that about?"

"Kandi," he said without hesitation, still not looking me directly in the eye. "Your boy up there put his hands on her."

"Why would he do that?"

"Don't be stupid, V. Idiots like that don't need a reason."

"No, I mean, were they involved, Tyson and Kandi?" He turned away and started walking again. I caught up and stepped in front of him, cutting him off. "I know you don't want to talk about this right now, but when you do, I'll be there."

He nodded and got into his car. I didn't know what else to say. I didn't want to push. The Jetta pulled into traffic, leaving me behind.

I didn't see how these women could do it, partake in the dishonesty. Married men should have to wear dog collars, the kind that send off electric shock signals if anyone comes too close. Since these *other women* obviously don't care, and the men don't want to be responsible, somebody's got to do something.

As I sat at my desk, I let my face fall into my hands. It had been a long day. After the trauma of the morning, I spent the first hour back in Ray's office. I made him understand the reasons for him being the target of my accusations. After I apologized, he still seemed hurt that I'd even considered him as the person behind something so malicious. I took full responsibility for the course of events, even though he lied on the stand. He said he regretted denying the attempt to kiss me in the parking garage, but his *ass was on the line*. I told him so was mine, but I guess he thought his was worth more.

Today was one of those cleanup days, tying up all the loose ends. I leaned back in my chair, reaching up for the needed stretch with my arms, letting my hands come down and rest on my head. I massaged gently. It felt wonderful, maintenance free, undemanding. That was really the life I'd wanted. I was searching for the package deal because I'd heard it was such a good thing. I let out a short laugh, remembering the words of a motivational speaker I'd heard on the radio, ". . . she who wishes for her prince must also remember that she'll have to clean up after his horse." Couldn't be truer.

I started out for home.

"Good night, Sherri."

"Good night, sweetie. You have a good one." She didn't bother to look up, just kept typing.

The elevator held only me. The ride was smooth going down, but it stopped abruptly on the third floor. An average, but strangely comfortable-looking man stepped on the elevator. From the expression on his face, his sales pitch didn't go too well with whomever he'd just met.

He stood next to me.

"Excuse me," he spoke. "Has anyone ever told you, besides airports, elevators are the worst place you could meet someone new?"

"You're not new." I turned around and punched him softly with a languid fist. Airic, with an A, smiled and bumped me back with his bony hip. His smile was genuine, but weary.

"I didn't think you were ever going to return my phone calls."

"A girl can't be too easy. Gotta keep 'em guessing."

"Uh huh, well, I guessed you were off your rocker not to be interested in a catch like me."

I laughed too loud, but it wasn't meant to be insulting. "I'm sorry. It's just that, I've had such a crazy day today with things not being what they seem, and it's just . . . well, I hadn't considered you the type who would be blowing his own horn. You seem more like the shy quiet type."

"Shy quiet types don't make fools of themselves by calling a woman seven days straight with no response. You could've at least called me back to say you weren't interested."

I giggled with my hand over my mouth. "I'm sorry I left you hanging. I've just had a lot on my mind. A lot of soul searching, you could say. Can we start all over?" I reached up around his neck and pulled him to my level. "Like this." I let my lips brush across his before moving in with full force. I kissed him, checking for sparks and the intense bolts.

Airic didn't cause fireworks. Instead it was almost surreal, like sitting on the edge of the ocean listening to jazz on a lazy beach. I let him go. His face was covered with shock.

"Talk about things not being as they seem." He straightened his collar and tie. "Do you kiss like that all the time?"

"Only when I'm hungry."

"Well, I don't know if I want to feed you if that's the case. Are we talking about food, here?" he asked, anticipating the right answer.

I was too tired to keep up the flirtation. "Yes, food and *only* food."

"So what are you in the mood for?"

"Anything, I'm starving."

He looped his long arm through mine and we marched off like Dorothy and the Scarecrow, but unlike the characters in the *Wizard of Oz*, I wasn't planning on following any Yellow Brick Road. I wanted to take each day as it came, without expectations and without fear.

THE PROCESSIONAL BEGAN WITH THE THUNDEROUS CHORDS OF THE ORGAN. The guests all turned toward the entrance of the red-carpeted aisle. The first appearance was from a small child carrying an alabaster basket with magenta rose petals overflowing. He took one look at all the faces staring, and his large brown eyes moistened. The crowd lapsed into a melody of "aaah, isn't he cute." The second appearance was from his older brother, dressed in old-fashioned English Boy pedal pushers and suspenders. The crowd gave an equally blushing sigh. His hands shook but held on tightly to the raw silk pillow he was carrying with the matching gold bands tied on with ivory ribbon. His mother gave him a reassuring wink before taking a picture of him with her camera. She then rushed off to take her own place in the wedding processional.

If there could have been a perfectly defining moment, it had to be when the bride took her first step down the aisle. She stopped as if to gather her strength. She scanned the entire audience, the faces enchanted by her simple Amsale designer gown, without beads or shiny appliqués, illuminated only from the weightlessness of her flowing train. The chords of the organ seized for only a moment, then resumed, not missing a note. She stepped out with the confidence and joy that one only knows when she's come full circle with all the wanting and praying.

She held onto the rail-thin man tightly as if they were holding each other up. He seemed too frail for the job. But as her father, the only one she'd ever known, it was his place and his honor to give her over to the man who would shower her with all that he had not.

When she reached the end of the aisle, she leaned over and kissed him on the cheek. "Thank you, Daddy."

A tear was budding in her father's eye. He squeezed Kandi's hand before taking his seat.

If Clint had any doubts about the decision he was about to make, they'd all been erased the moment she arrived by his side. Clint took the hand her father had just handed over to him, and placed it over his. He stared at her like she was the most beautiful thing he'd ever seen and nothing could be more right than having her by his side. In his heart, where it mattered, he believed he would never regret his choice.

Seeing Clint look so regal sent a chill through me. Each word he was asked to repeat swiped at my heart, "To love and honor for all the days of your life, to cherish, to take care of, in sickness and in health." They exchanged rings nervously. I blinked a cleansing tear out of my eye and joined in the prayer the audience was asked to say for the newly wedded couple: ". . . And for all of their days keep them blessed in your name, oh Lord. Amen."

After the ceremony I waited patiently in the receiving line. The happy couple stood side by side with their bridal party lined up neatly stacked beside them, in order of height. The bridesmaids dressed in their long form-fitting gowns stood glowing with the small round bouquets held in one hand, leaving the other free to shake hands or extend hugs. I immediately recognized one who had to be Kandi's sister. They shared a continuous look of boredom in their eyes that some would interpret as sexy.

Alison stood next to her, shimmering as the maid of honor, holding onto the elbow of an extremely handsome man with smoldering dark eyes that were a startling deep blue when he looked up. I swept my eyes past him and over to Clint. As I got closer, I could see the creases in his cheeks, the dimples, the smile, oh that smile. I wanted to tell him to his face, and look him in the eye, no phone call would do. I'd agonized over showing up, not knowing what his true motivation was for inviting me in the first place. Maybe he wanted to rub it in my face, look what you had, then lost. No, threw away would be more appropriate.

I could see his bride, smiling, proud and beautiful. I could also see how happy Clint was, relaxed and at ease. I couldn't quite remember if I'd ever seen him this way before.

I pushed up closer, one more hug away from it being my turn. My stomach was doing backward somersaults, fluttering with each step as I inched my way closer. Alison hugged me tight when she finally recognized me.

"Venus, girl, I thought you fell off the face of the earth. Where have you been? And look at you, just cut it all off, didn't you? I hear you, girl. We all wish we had the guts to do it. It looks good on you, too."

I reached up and stroked my nearly bald head. Lately I had to remind myself. My hair, or lack of it, had become so irrelevant, so inconsequential, that I'd become unaware of how I looked. At the new company, Strather Mass Marketing, where I'd been hired as a brand consultant, I'd been nicknamed *Ms. Chic* by a few of the office staff. Something I didn't mind at all. They could call me anything they liked as long as the name on the door to the office with the huge window, view of the Potomac River, and a desk the size of a double bed still read *Venus Johnston*.

"Thank you, Alison. But, the question is, where have you been?" I raised an eyebrow to the gorgeous man standing next to her.

"Fahja, this is Venus, a very good friend. Someone I miss a whole lot." She gave me a squinted stare, to make sure I understood its deeper meaning.

"A pleasure." He smiled, and nodded slightly.

"You, too." I turned my attention back toward Alison. "You're next, I can feel it."

"In no hurry, girl. No hurry." She waved me past, and I landed directly in front of Kandi. She extended her delicate hand automatically, before realizing who she had extended it to. Her smile quieted, but remained animated as if she couldn't completely erase it even if she'd tried.

"Congratulations, Kandi." I smiled weakly, but with sincerity.

"Thank you." She spoke, immediately turning me over to Clint, her eyes asking for an explanation. Before Clint could respond, she was swallowed up by the next well-wisher, inundating her with hugs and air kisses. Her glossy smile stayed painted in place.

"I'm glad you came," Clint spoke in my ear, while we hugged.

"Wouldn't have missed it. This has got to be something for the Guinness Book, Clint Fairchild at the altar." I spoke more seriously. "I have to tell you something, Clint." His interest piqued, his strong arms kept a tight grip on my shoulders. I knew he was afraid of what I might say, that I still loved him, and always would. But what I needed to say was much more important for both of us.

"I wish you the very best." I looked deeply into his eyes. "I mean it." I hugged him again, "The very best. Okay. We both got what we needed.

I want you to know that I'm sincerely happy for you. I'm happy for me, too." I did feel the moisture in my eyes, but I fought back. He'd never understand that they were tears of relief, validating the sense of myself, the growth and clarity I'd achieved in the past year. Without the experience, the loss of Clint, I would have drifted around in my bubble of make-believe, never knowing all that I was missing.

"Thank you," he whispered back. "Take care."

I moved out of the line. I knew his eyes were still watching. I knew if I'd turned around right then, I could've willed him into my arms. But I didn't want that. What I wanted was what I had, no bad memories, no hard feelings, and a fresh new start. I walked away and didn't look back.

"So, how are you? How you holding up?" Airic held out his hands to grab mine.

"I'm doing quite nicely, thank you very much."

He pulled my hands up to his lips and kissed them one at a time, lingering a little longer near the solitaire he had placed on my left hand only two weeks before, voluntarily, I might add.

"Has anyone ever told you, the absolute worst place to meet someone new is at a wedding?"

I smiled a big smile, letting his eyes wash over me. "You're not new," I said, waiting for his punch line.

"No, I'm not, but you are. You look so radiant, so happy. That's all new. You, my pretty, are what we in the software business call an upgrade." He kissed me lightly on my forehead. "And I don't want *Doctor Lover Lover* over there getting any ideas about trying out the newly revised version." We both looked toward Clint, just in time to see him looking away.

"You are so silly." I kissed him, long and hard, letting the familiar waves take over. When I let Airic go, the waters were still. There were no afterthoughts of self-doubt, no crisis of insecurity; I was calm in this ocean. I looked up into his intense brown eyes. "Thank you for being a good sport. You didn't have to come here with me."

"And let you come alone, looking this good. No no no, I don't think so." He let the frown lines form on the top of his head, the ones that reminded me that older is wiser. He cupped my face in his pale hands, letting his eyes pierce through mine.

"I love you. I will always stand by you, no matter how big, or small. You got it?"

"I got it." And I did. I knew this was what I'd always wanted to know by name, personally. I'd never been introduced to it, *true love*. The true love that could only come through the love of oneself. The day I started loving myself, the me inside and the me outside, was the day I'd met *true love, and would live nappily ever after.*

Nappily ever after

TRISHA R. THOMAS

A Reader's Guide

THREE RIVERS PRESS
NEW YORK

A Conversation with Trisha R. Thomas

First of all, the question everyone asks: have you ever "gone natural" like Venus Johnston? What did the man in your life say? Would you do it again?

Going natural is a very liberating experience. The first time I cut off all of my relaxed hair was for financial reasons. My first year in college, I couldn't afford to maintain my straightened hair so out of frustration I went in the bathroom one day and buzzed it all off. Everyone was shocked because long hair was my trademark look. There was no particular man in my life at that very moment, but a whole new crop of men popped up and took notice. Mostly it was men from different cultures who liked my short look... not African-Americans. The black men seemed to find me completely unattractive.

I think we all have friends like Venus and Kandi. Are you more Venus or more Kandi?

I identify with both characters. I am both characters. I had to be to write the story, but I'd say Venus is the one that I pulled more personal experiences from. She was easiest to write in the first person because her opinions were my opinions.

In the end Venus and Kandi both get what they want, but do you see one as a better friend-role model-girlfriend than the other?

Venus and Kandi are both good people, friends you'd want in your corner. I wanted everyone to see that they both had faults. No one is perfect in Nappily Ever After, *just like real life. Venus had issues that were just as petty as Kandi, but one's perception is always to side with the underdog.*

When you wrote the opening scene—Clint's wedding— did you always know who would be coming down the aisle, or was that something you only decided when you wrote the end of the book?

I kept changing the ending because I couldn't decide who I wanted to end up with Clint. It was mostly about growth. The more I wrote and rewrote, it looked like Venus was coming out more satisfied with herself and didn't need the false beliefs that she'd held on to before. Kandi still needed to be married. I think all the characters got what they needed in the end.

This is a fun, entertaining novel, but it tackles some heavy issues: negative self-image, sexual harrassment, broken

relationships, stalking, and so on. Why was it important to you to include these things?

The negative self-image that a lot of women deal with was the basis of Nappily Ever After. *That's what ignited my writing in the first place. I was teaching junior high school and watching the students' behavior and remembered my own young adulthood, how hard it was growing up with the images of the Breck girl riding on her horse, her blonde hair bouncing in the wind, as well as the beautiful blonde Barbie that every girl owned, whether she was black or white, Asian or Indian. So I thought that if I my hair didn't bounce in the wind too, no one would want me. The girls in my middle school were heavily into their appearance and worked so hard to fit in with "the look." When I realized nothing had changed in twenty years, I started thinking about why. We have black Barbies, there are black women in commercials, and beautiful black women on the covers of magazines, but they were still a perpetuation of the images I grew up with: long straight hair, big breasts, slim waists, only their skin and hair were darker. (In 2001 Mattel made a Barbie with kinky hair, but who knows how long that will last.)*

The word "nappy" can draw some strong negative reactions from black people. But you intentionally rhyme it with "happy." Do you see it as a positive word, a negative word, or a neutral one?

Nappy is not a bad word. People still try to correct me by saying, "oh you mean natural." No, I mean nappy. When my hair is completely nappy and kinky, hard to comb through without hearing snap, crackle, crunch, so what? The straight hair police aren't going to come and get me. It should be our prerogative to wear our hair any way we feel like wearing it. Sadly though, the judgment usually comes from our inner voice more so from someone else. We're the ones looking in the mirror disapproving of ourselves. I find people accept you if you accept yourself, whatever style you choose.

What was the most surprising reaction or feedback readers gave you about this book?

First of all, I was shocked that people actually thought this was a hair-care book, how to go natural and cut off your relaxer in sixty days or less. It's not about that at all. It's about self-esteem, self-discovery, being true to oneself, whatever that truth is and acknowledging it. A lot of readers have communicated to me that this story has helped them deal with the aftermath of a relationship that they couldn't let go of before. Venus has to walk away from a relationship that she was involved with for over four years with the hopes of marriage. Most women hold on to the notion that since they invested so much time, they deserve the prize at the end. Venus shows that sometimes you just have to walk away and save yourself for the bigger prize, which is self-worth. When you have self-worth then better things will come in the future.

Most surprising was the different cultures that identified with Nappily Ever After. *The self-esteem issue is universal for women. Black, white, yellow, or brown, women have told me that this is their story, the issue of pressure to look a certain way, to fit in, to be accepted. The pressure to be married by a certain time. We're all living by the same insurmountable standards.*

This is your first novel and it's been very successful. What were your expectations when you first wrote it? Do you have any advice for the first-time unpublished authors out there?

I simply wanted to be published. I wanted this story to be told and heard. I knew there would be a great outcry of women who associated with Venus, and even with Kandi. At one time I thought I would have to self-publish because I didn't want the excitement to pass. A lot of women who knew what my project was about couldn't wait to get their hands on it to pass along to friends, daughters, and mothers. Inevitably, I'm glad I didn't have to self-publish, especially after seeing the amount of work that goes into a finished book. Editing is very crucial. The objectivity isn't there when you're paying someone to do it and they're working for you. It's crucial to have a professional editor who understands the message and the author. Distribution and marketing are very expensive undertakings that are also necessary. I can say it now, patience is a virtue, waiting for the right editor and publisher who want to support your work is the best way to go. But I didn't feel that way at the time. I thought if they don't get it, fine, I'll do it myself. The best advice I can give is to be patient and keep writing and reading. Perseverance always wins.

What do you most want readers to take away from this book?

The biggest joy is to know that readers are still talking about Nappily Ever After *long after they've finished the book. They're still thinking…still filtering Venus's words and actions through their brains, trying to decide if she was really happy in the end. Once that happens, I know the reader is incorporating the message into their own lives; trying to find out if they're truly fulfilled or living by perception. Venus does a lot of questioning of herself…we all need to do it at some point.*

Reading Group Questions
and Topics for Discussion

1. Why does the narration start with Clint's point of view, moments before his wedding? What do we learn about Clint's personality and about growing up Black and male, in these first few pages of the novel? What's your first impression of Venus?

2. Why do none of the hairstylists share Venus's excitement and sense of impending liberation when she decides to "just cut it all off"? To what extent is the difficult and time-consuming process of hairstyling a group-bonding experience that she is now betraying by opting out? Do women of other ethnic groups have similarly intense shared experiences in the pursuit of "beauty"?

3. Does knowing Clint's heartbreaking background—raised by his brother and his brother's cruel, abusive girlfriend from

an early age—change your opinion of Clint's current weak-nesses? Is Venus being too hard on him?

4. When Kandi thinks to herself, "there is so much work to be done," she's talking about man-hunting. What is Venus's primary, inner work? Does she know what it is herself? After the first, positive step of cutting off her hair, does she lose her focus?

5. Ray and Venus have a history of conspiratorial chats and lunches before the incident in the parking garage takes place. Although Venus has never indicated an attraction to Ray, she can also understand his misinterpretation of her signals. At what point do personal conversations, casual e-mails, and lunch dates become inappropriate in the workplace? Do you consider Ray's actions a case of sexual harassment or simple miscommunication? Where should the line be drawn?

6. Kandi vacillates between a ruthless energy in pursuing her dreams and a crushing lack of self-esteem. What do you think of Kandi when you read "She knew she couldn't have every-thing, never would"? How about when she saves the child's life on the playground? By the end of the novel, have you settled on a definitive opinion of Kandi? Could she and Venus be friends under different circumstances?

7. Why does Venus allow her employers to handle the issue of the racist note so casually? Does her ambition to meet with Tyson Edwards blind her to the fact that she ought to keep a

copy of the note and possibly contact an advocacy source out-side the office? Is John's solution—forcing Venus to stay home from work until further notice—logical or fair? If not, what would have been a more appropriate decision?

8. How does Kandi's reminiscence about life back home with her perpetually disappointed mother shed some light on Kandi's character? How is the visit to Clint's family healing for her? What do we learn about Venus from her trip home for Christmas? How has her family influenced the woman she has become? And what takes place while she's there that alters her entire perception of herself?

9. Venus finally comes to understand that she never let Clint love her unconditionally because she had never let herself love herself unconditionally. The stress of trying to live up to an unattainable version of herself exhausted her and prevented her from seeing the good in their relationship. Now that she has gained some enlightenment, is it surprising that she wants Clint more than ever? Do you think they could make a new start at this point if Clint were available? Does Clint really understand Venus's very female dilemma?

10. What is the significance of the television episode featuring obese women in sexy lingerie that Venus stumbles upon during a pity party at home?

11. Why doesn't Venus sense that Tyson is a smooth—and unsavory—operator and come up with an avenue for exploring

her marketing ideas other than compromising get-togethers with a creep? What lessons does she still need to learn? How does the author set up the tension in their first meeting?

12. When Clint visits his brother Cedric after the breakup with Venus, he is depressed and tired of being pushed and pulled by the expectations of others. "He felt a big hook in the side of his mouth where he'd been caught like a fish and led around by whoever held the extended pole. It had been passed from Cedric's hands to Venus's with the hook and wire still intact...." Why does Clint immediately become entangled with Kandi, when her desire for a husband (a doctor husband, at that) is so obvious? What makes him think that it will be different this time?

13. Venus describes "losing her footing" as a young girl whenever her hair lost its smooth, artificial texture and hinted at becoming nappy, only to regain her social confidence, "almost like a light being flicked on," after a visit to the beauty parlor. What is at the root of this correlation between appearance and confidence? Would things have been different if there had been no white children in the neighborhood to compare herself to?

14. After a tough journey of self-discovery, Venus arrives at the conclusion that she needs only her true self, and self-respect, to be happy. Yet the end of the novel finds her engaged to a new man, only months later. Is this a disappointing end for Venus, or a satisfying one? Why?

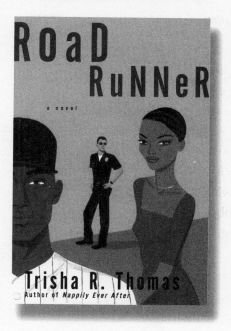